CATRIONA CHILD was born in 198
the brightest prospects among a t
writing talent,' she has a degree i
ty of Aberdeen and an MA with I ⸻ative Writing from Lancaster University. Her ⸻ novel, *Trackman*, was published in 2012 and was described by *The Herald* as 'having all the makings of a cult hit.' Her second novel, *Swim Until You Can't See Land*, was published in 2014. She has been published in *The Sunday Herald*, the 404 Ink *Earth* literary magazine, *Northwords Now* and in the Scottish Book Trust *Family Legends* anthology. She lives just outside Edinburgh with her husband Allan and their two children, Corrie and Alasdair.

Us vs the World

CATRIONA CHILD

Luath Press Limited
EDINBURGH
www.luath.co.uk

First published 2021

ISBN: 978-1-910022-48-1

The author's right to be identified as author of this book under the
Copyright, Designs and Patents Act 1988 has been asserted.

The paper used in this book is recyclable. It is made from low chlorine
pulps produced in a low energy, low emission manner from renewable
forests.

Printed and bound by
Severnprint Ltd., Gloucester

Typeset in 10.5 point Sabon by Lapiz

For Alasdair

Prologue

Winter 2023

I don't know what month it is, but I know it's winter. It's dark and it's cold and it's becoming even harder to survive. Every day it seems like there's less of us and more of them.

The world (or what's left of it) versus them.

Alice and I were always so fixated on using the written word to try and save history. We were kids though and it was all a game back then. We never really believed something like this would happen to us.

They say that history is written by the victors. At the moment it doesn't feel like I'm on the winning side, but if I don't leave some record behind then who will?

Sam

Mum's crying. Why's she crying?

Not just crying, sobbing.

Something bad has happened. Really bad. That's not the way she cries when she talks about Granny, or when she watches *The Notebook*.

My stomach flips, churns inside me.

It's still dark outside, what time is it? I reach over to my bedside table, feel for my watch, press the button on the side that makes it light up.

5:33am.

What's she doing up so early?

She doesn't sound real. More like an animal. Out of breath. Suck, suck, sucking in the air, like her lungs have stopped working. The noise is all around me, as if I'm wearing headphones and she's inside my ears.

I should get up. Go and see her. But I'm stuck, unable to move. My legs frozen. I don't want to get out of bed. I'm terrified of finding out the reason she's making a noise like that. It might get me too.

I close my eyes against the shapes of my bedroom. I wish I could close off the noise as easily. I try to relax, to find the fuzzy images and muddled thoughts of sleep. Force myself down into dreams rather than have to deal with reality. But I can't. The noise, the fear of what's causing that noise won't let me. I'm wide awake.

Something's telling me that when I find out the cause, I'll never be able to sleep again.

Where's Dad? Why isn't he looking after her?

She stops for a moment and blows her nose. I can hear the thickness of the snot. Her breath shudders and I visualise it scraping through her, catching on all the ridges and organs, making her body tremble. She's still crying but it's no longer the full-on belly ache of before. Now she's whimpering like a child. Sucking in, in, in, trying to catch her breath.

My hands shake and I clutch my duvet. It's warm under here. Not just in bed, but in the moment before I find out. Once I get up I'll wish I was back here in my room, in this moment. I know I will. The me in here is different. The me who doesn't know what's happened. Once I go out there, the me of now might change forever.

I hear the kettle start to boil and the rattle of a teaspoon. I picture Dad pouring hot water into Mum's mug. The one with my handprint on it from when I was a baby. Dad said he had to push the pram up and down the street outside the shop until I fell asleep, as that was the only way he could get me to stay still long enough to make the print.

Will he take the new baby to get one when she arrives? Will Mum use that mug instead? Put my one into the cupboard.

Dad'll get the milk now. Open the fridge. Glance at the scan picture stuck to the door with magnets. The black and white blob of my sister.

What if something's happened to her? To the baby? Dad said this time would be okay. The magic scan, he called it when he stuck it to the fridge door.

We're okay. We have the magic scan. We know she's a girl. Nothing can happen to her now she's a girl.

No, it can't be the baby. Dad would have taken Mum straight to hospital. He wouldn't be making her a cup of tea. Decaf now. Everything about the baby, even the teabags.

Maybe it's just hormones? Dad said we have to be patient with Mum. It's harder to have a baby at her age, harder than when she had me. If she shouts at me for no reason, I just have to let her. She doesn't really mean it.

It's quiet now. No voices. No crying. Just the creaks of the house.

Maybe Mum's in labour? I still don't move. I definitely don't want to see any of that. Alice tried to get me to watch an episode of *One Born Every Minute* when I told her Mum was pregnant. I watched about half before I had to turn it off. Still, Mum didn't sound like any of those women. Especially that one the midwives all made faces about as they sat in the staffroom eating biscuits and drinking tea.

Tick, tick, tick, tick. The sound of my watch on the bedside table. It fell under my bed once and I woke in the middle of the night, could hear something ticking underneath me.

Tick, tick, tick, tick.

I started to imagine someone under my bed. Hiding there. Lying beneath me, looking up at the bottom of my mattress. Giving themselves away by the sound of their watch.

Tick, tick, tick, tick.

I convinced myself someone was under there. And even though I imagined hands reaching up, or a knife ready to plunge through the mattress, I still couldn't move. I just lay there and listened to the tick, tick, tick, tick.

If I get up I make the bad thing happen. I set it in motion. If I don't get up, the day won't start. It stays still as long as I do.

Mum's silence is worse than the crying. I have to get up. I can't leave her like that.

Tick, tick, tick, tick.

I count down in my head. Three, two, one. Three, two, one. Three, two, one. I'll get up on one, I'll get up on one. But every time I reach it, I start the countdown again. Three, two, one. Three, two, one. Tick, tick, tick, tick.

I start at ten instead, give myself longer.

Ten, nine, eight, seven, six, five, four...

Three, two, one.

I kick the duvet off and jump out of bed before I have a chance to stop myself. It's not cold but I pull on socks and a hoodie. Anything to delay the moment. I open my bedroom door, stand in the hallway.

The kitchen light's on and I can see Mum sitting at the breakfast bar. Arms out in front of her, hands cradling the mug. I don't think she knows I'm here, even when I start to walk towards her.

'Mum,' I say from the doorway. It comes out a whisper, the phlegmy rasp of morning voice. I try to clear my throat but I can't make my voice go any louder.

'Mum?'

She stands and empties her tea down the sink before she notices me. She opens her mouth but the words get stuck somewhere and it's just a noise that comes out.

I look around for Dad. What's happened?

I want to tell Mum how much she's scaring me, but I can't. She doesn't look like she's really here. Like she's some weird CGI version of herself.

'Sam,' she says.

Her voice is different too. Not Mum's voice.

'Sam,... I think... your dad..., he's..., I think he's died.'

Her voice rises and squeaks on the word died.

What she says isn't complete. I wait for the next part of her sentence.

He's dyed...

Dyed what? Dyed his hair? Dyed blue? Red?

But, no. That's it. She's looking at me for a reaction.

I can hear her voice saying the word over and over in my head. Died. Died. Died. The way she squeaked when she said it. I want to laugh at how funny she sounded. I have to clench my teeth to stop the laughter from blurting out.

'Your dad. He's... I think he's...'

She can't say it again.

That word that made her voice squeak.

Died.

Died.

Dead.

Dad.

Dad. Dead. Dad. Dead.

No. That's not right. That can't be what she said.

The fear inside surges through me. I knew something bad was coming, but not this.

She takes a step towards me, reaches out to take my hand. We've not held hands since I was in primary school. I can tell by her face that she's not joking. There's a pounding in my ears.

Tick, tick, tick, tick.

I need to wake up now. This isn't happening. This is just one of those bad dreams where you wake up and find yourself with your head under the pillow gasping for breath.

I try to force myself to wake up. Wake up. Wake up. Wake up, Sam.

But it doesn't work. I'm already awake.

'Sam? Sam, darling.'

Mum's hands are clammy. She stands in front of me. Her belly touches mine. I can feel the heat of it against me.

Sam, you've always been my little hot water bottle.

'What happened?'

I was sure I heard Dad come home last night. But maybe that was the dream? That was the dream and this is reality. It's all the wrong way round.

Mum shakes her head.

'I don't know, Sam. He said he had the flu or something...'

She can't speak, can't finish what's she's trying to tell me.

I'm embarrassed to cry in front of her.

I feel the pressure build in my throat and mouth, look at the floor. There's a pea lying under the breakfast bar. I bend and pick it up, step away from Mum, pull away from her clammy hands. From the words coming out of her, from the heat of her belly. The pea is hard and shrivelled. I roll it between finger and thumb, finger and thumb, drop it in the food bin.

It takes this movement to process what she's just said.

He had the flu.

You don't die of the flu.

I don't understand. When she said he'd died, my brain leapt to the conclusion that he hadn't come home last night. Had been in an accident.

Nothing makes sense. Words turn to treacle inside my head. How am I supposed to trust what's happening when I can't trust my own brain?

'I don't understand,' I say.

'I gave your dad some paracetamol then I fell asleep on the sofa.'

She sits down again.

The floor tilts.

White noise in my head.

'Why didn't I wake up when the ambulance came? What did they say it was?' I ask.

'What?' Mum replies.

'The paramedics?'

'What paramedics?'

'The ambulance?'

'I didn't phone an ambulance.'

'How do you know he's dead then?' My voice gets louder and higher. Cracks on the word dead. Why can neither of us say that word? I'm shouting. She's not making any sense.

'He might be okay. Why don't you phone an ambulance?'

'I'm going to phone someone now. I just… needed a moment.'

I know it's wrong, but I want to shake her, hit her. Why isn't she behaving the way she should? Why isn't she acting like my mum? I run out of the kitchen into the hall, head for their bedroom.

'Sam, no! Sam, don't!' I hear the scrape of her chair against the floor as she gets up to follow after me. Slow with all the extra weight.

She grabs the hood of my jumper, tugs me back, but then lets go. I stop at their bedroom door.

'Sam, please. I'm not going to stop you but, please, just think if you really want to do this.'

I ignore her. I don't care. Because he's not dead. He had the flu, that's all. I don't know why Mum's decided he's dead, but she's wrong. She's wrong. She isn't making any sense at all. She's not a doctor. An image of her standing over Dad, feeling for a pulse, flickers through my head and I feel myself start to laugh again.

I push open the door.

The bedside light's on. I can make out the shape of him under the duvet. I stop at the bottom of the bed. Hold my breath. Listen for his. Watch to see any rise and fall.

The duvet is still. The thunder of blood is in my ears.

What if she's right? There's a bad smell in here, like BO and farts but worse. Much worse.

Move, please move, Dad. Throw a pillow at me. Shout at me to get out, you're not well. Ask me to bring you a coffee. Anything. Just do something.

Dad? I think I say it aloud, but then I realise I'm saying it in my head. Over and over. Dad. Dad. Dad. Wake up, Dad. Please, wake up.

I take a step forward.

His arm hangs out of bed, fingers brushing the carpet.

I stare at his fingertips, will them to twitch.

I take another step forward.

I can see Dad's head properly now. His eyes are closed. His face doesn't look right. His cheeks are blotchy, like corned beef. Has someone replaced Mum and Dad while I was asleep?

'Dad?' I say it out loud now. I don't care if he's not well. He needs to wake up. Stop scaring us like this.

'Dad?'

My voice comes out all weird again. What's happened to us? I went to bed like normal last night but something shifted while I slept.

'Dad, please. Stop messing about.'

'Dad, please.'

'Sam, darling,' I jump as Mum touches my arm, tries to hug me.

'No! Get off me!' I pull away from her and stumble beside the bed. Dad's hand droops in front of me. I reach out, but stop before I touch it. It's not right, it doesn't look right. I poke it, poke it again, but it just hangs limp. I pinch it, nip it. Harder and harder. I want to hurt him. Why won't he wake up?

I hit out at his hand, slap it over and over and over. I can't stop thinking about that time in primary seven when he tried to hold my hand to walk me to school and I told him not to. My friends would laugh at me if they saw. And the way his face looked as he said no problem and let go. For the rest of the day I couldn't stop seeing the way his face looked when he said no problem and let go.

'Sam, Sam.'

Mum's on the floor next to me now. She pulls me away from his hand and squeezes her arms around me, gripping me against that warm over-sized belly. She strokes my hair and whispers to me and it's only then that I realise I'm crying. The tears blur everything and I can't see her properly. I feel her fingers squeezing my shoulders, her voice soothing, telling me over and over that she loves me and it's going to be alright.

21st October 2014

Hey Sam,

It's 10:53am and I'm in Science. We're meant to be watching this film on the eye, and long and short sight, but I'm writing to you instead. Mr Bennett – the science genius, has just worked out where the volume button is so we can actually hear what the film is saying! He's now trying to get the film back to the start so we can see the bit we missed but I think that technology is beyond his abilities!

Anyway, I was thinking last night we could write an autobiography to each other so we know about each other's lives before we met – what do you think? Well, it doesn't matter what you think really as I'm going to write one for you now anyway. This is what this letter is supposed to be although I've just wasted half of it on other stuff about Science.

So here goes:

Name: Alice Elizabeth Wilson

Born: 10th April 2003 in Edinburgh

Life Story:

Hi, I'm in English now. I had to stop writing in Science because Mr Bennett made us all stop and draw a diagram of the eye. Anyway, I shall continue.

Life Story: Mum was super young when she had me, like a teenager. She told me

Okay, I'm at home now. Louise who I sit beside in English was being totally annoying and kept asking me what I was writing. Then we all got split up into groups to act out scenes from *Twelfth Night*, so I couldn't finish this. So, where was I?

She told me... what? Oh yeah, so she told me that her waters broke in the middle of a History exam but I think she made that up. But yeah, she was super young. My dad was the same age but he left when I was two or something so I don't remember him. I think they met at a Foo Fighters concert or something. Or maybe that was their first date?

Hi, I'm back. I had to stop writing there because we had a power cut. Exciting or what?! Not really, because I couldn't see anything and Mum didn't have any batteries for the torch! Anyway, it's back on now, so I'll continue. Again!!

When I was really little we lived with Gran and Grandad (he was still alive then) next door to you! I don't really remember that though. There's lots of photos of me there as a baby and sometimes I get mixed up between real memories and memories from looking at photos. Then we moved to a flat in Gorgie and I went to Dalry Primary School. When I was in P5 my Grandad died, it was really sad and Mum and Gran both went a bit weird for a while and that's when they decided I was going to Mary Erskine's where I am now. Mum says Gran is conflicted as she's an old socialist at heart but she doesn't want me to get pregnant at 16 and she thinks a private school will prevent that! Whatever?! As if I'm going to do that anyway. It's all a bit *Gilmore Girls* really. Do you watch that? If you don't, you should. I bet you'd like Rory!

My best friends at school are Emily, Rachel C and Rachel M – confusing, I know! I used to have a pet fish called Spektor but not anymore. I used to go to Guides on a Monday night but I stopped going. I play the flute at school and I'm in the school band. I'm learning to crochet right now as Gran is teaching me. I've been to France and Italy with the school but my best holiday ever was when Mum hired a camper van and we drove round Scotland and camped on beaches and stuff.

Anyway, this has taken me all day to write so I'm going to stop now. You have to write me back your life story, okay!

    Alice

    xx

Jude

'Was that you, Sam?'

We're both lying on the floor, like two wrestlers, tangled up in each other. How long have we been like this? Time isn't moving the way it should.

'What?' he replies.

I try to work out how to get myself up off the floor, which limbs belong to me. The bump gets in the way.

'Hang on,' Sam says as I start to move. He pulls himself out from under me, then he's on his feet, helping me up.

I hear it again. A groan.

The heartburn kept burping up into my windpipe, burning as I swallowed it back down. I forced myself out of bed to get a glass of milk. It was freezing and it went for my teeth as I gulped it down, but the indigestion dissipated almost immediately. I patted my belly, imagined the baby bathing in white, like Cleopatra. Adam kept telling me to take proper antacids, Rennies or something.

'It's just chalk, it's not harmful. Like eating coal.'

'Why would I eat coal?'

'Loads of pregnant ladies crave coal, and it doesn't harm the baby.'

'Who do you know that has ever eaten coal?'

'Ask your midwife next time you see her.'

I didn't want to take anything. Not even antacid. Nothing that could harm the baby. Milk works for me and it feels like my bones and her bones strengthen with each glass. Chalk is brittle, full of air pockets, it dissolves in the rain.

Maybe she'd have a full head of hair when she came. An old wives' tale I'd heard. Indigestion in pregnancy equals a hairy baby.

I rinsed out the glass and left it to drain on the counter. My feet were cold against the kitchen lino and I wished I'd put my slippers on. As I headed back to bed, I anticipated the cosiness of snuggling under the duvet.

'His hand moved, I saw it,' Sam says.

I look at Adam's hand. His fingers twitch.

'Thank God. Oh, thank God. Adam, Adam,' I lean over the bed, shake him by the shoulders. 'Adam, you gave us such a fright.'

Sam takes his dad's hand, cradles the arm that hangs out of bed.

'His arm's all cold, Mum.'

'Adam, Adam, wake up, darling. Oh, God. I should have phoned an ambulance.'

I honestly thought he was dead. The shock of that was so great I couldn't think straight. I didn't want to set things in motion. Make the call that would lead to him being taken away.

I glance across at the bedside table. The paracetamol lies untouched, next to the glass of water. Adam's phone is there too. I bring it to life, my finger hovering over the button for emergency calls.

I checked the alarm clock as I got back into bed.

1:38am

I pulled the covers right up to my neck, pushed my feet between Adam's thighs to warm them up. He was roasting, heat radiating from him. His pyjamas were damp, the sheets around him clammy.

'Adam, are you okay?'

I rolled towards him, rested my palm against his forehead. I lifted the duvet, wafted it up and down.

'I think you've got a fever,' I said.

He groaned and turned over. Deep and phlegmy snores rumbled up from his belly.

I went back to the kitchen, filled a glass with cold water and pressed out two paracetamol from a packet lying in the cutlery drawer. When I got back to the bedroom, I switched on his bedside light and shook Adam awake.

'Take these. I think you're coming down with something.'

Adam opened his eyes and looked at me, but he was still half asleep.

'I'm going to lie down on the sofa. I don't want to catch anything with the baby. Shout if you need me.'

He grunted.

I bent over to kiss him but stopped myself. I could feel the heat, the moisture, could taste the salt without my lips touching him. I was scared of catching what he had. I pressed a finger to my lips instead, touched his forehead and left him alone.

'He's hurting me! Get him off me, Mum!'

Adam grips onto Sam with both hands. His fingers press into the skin, leaving white marks. He's trying to pull Sam onto the bed, a strange rasping sound coming from his throat. His eyes are still closed, eyelids fluttering. He must be having some kind of seizure.

'Mum!'

I hear Adam's teeth snap, snap, snap as he tries to bite down. Maybe this is like sleepwalking? He's in a sort of delirium and doesn't know what he's doing?

'Adam. That's Sam. What are you doing? Let go of him.'

I drop the phone, manage to prise Adam's fingers away and pull Sam out of reach. Adam's arms stretch out, grabbing and clawing at the air.

I woke under a blanket on the sofa, the TV flickering in front of me. I fumbled for the remote control, pointed it at the screen and checked the time.

5:02am.

I started to drift off again, but the need to pee stopped me. I kicked off the blanket and rolled off the sofa. While I was up I decided to check on Adam.

I laid my hand on his chest but I couldn't feel him breathing. I couldn't hear it either. I held my fingers over his mouth, under his nose. Waited for his musky morning breath to warm my fingertips, but there was nothing. Only the cold tingle from my washed hands. I pushed my fingers into his neck, dug deep to find a pulse. Pressed harder, trying to gag him awake. If only he would choke, ask me what the hell I was doing.

But he didn't move. I tried his wrist. No pulse. I pulled the duvet aside, lifted Adam's t-shirt and pressed my face against his chest. I wasn't sure where his heart should be, so I moved my ear all over him, his chest hair fetid against my cheek. There was nothing. Nothing but silence. I started to say his name, over and over and over.

'Adam, Adam, Adam, Adam, Adam.'

I shook him. Slapped the sides of his face. Gentle at first, but then harder, harder, not caring if I hurt him.

'Adam, Adam, Adam, Adam, Adam.'

Adam writhes around on the bed, pushing himself up, desperate to get at us. I get flashes of his eyeballs, bloodshot and rolling. He's not there. That's not him in there. He's having a fit or something. I feel like I'm underwater. All I can do is stare at him.

'Mum, Mum!' Sam grabs my face in both hands, pulls my gaze away and I break the surface again. He drags me out of the bedroom. We both stand in the doorway for a moment, stop to look back at Adam.

'What's wrong with him, Mum?' Sam asks.

'I don't know.'

Adam tumbles out of bed and half crawls, half drags himself towards us. Without thinking, we slam the door on him. I'm reminded of the way we would play *We're Going on a Bear Hunt* with Sam when he was younger.

Forgetting to shut the door like the characters in the book, then laughing as we jumped under the covers to hide and vowing we'd never go bear hunting again.

There's no ambiguity here between savage or lonely. Adam is savage and will hurt us if he catches us. His gentle bear hugs replaced by a mauling beast.

Hey Alice,

How are you? It's 7:32pm and I'm meant to be doing Maths home-work but I'm writing to you instead. Thanks for your letter and your life story. I guess I can write one back to you if you want me to? There's not much to tell though.

My name is Sam Redpath. I was born on the 19th February 2003 in Edinburgh. We used to live near the Botanic Gardens but then we moved next door to your gran after what happened to Dad. You know about that so there's no point writing it all down, plus that's Dad's life story not mine.

My friends at school are Nick and Bryan. I used to go to an athlet-ics club after school but I don't anymore. I sometimes

My mum just came in and asked me if I was writing a diary! What is she on?!

I've totally forgotten what I was going to say now, and I can't real-ly think of anything else. I told you my life story wasn't all that interesting. It's now 8:46pm and it has taken me over an hour just to write this! Dad has just come in and told me to get on with my homework. He is so annoying sometimes.

Bye for now,

Sam

X

Sam

He gives us a moments relief before we feel him on the other side of the door. It's like that scene in *Jurassic Park*: relax, and then the handle starts to rattle. The velociraptors have worked out how to open the door.

'There's a key,' Mum says.

I grip the door handle, fight against him on the other side, as she rummages in the cabinet next to the front door. Out of the corner of my eye I can see her pulling out drawers full of paper, envelopes, old phone books, pens, rubber bands, medals.

'Hurry up, Mum.'

'I'm trying. We've not used them since we moved in.'

Finally she pulls out a keyring with a pile of old keys attached to it.

It's almost like Dad knows there's not much time. He's doing his best to make it out here.

Mum tries key after key after key, fumbling with them on the keyring. It feels like forever, but the fifth one finally fits and clicks: the door locked. We both sink to the carpet, out of breath.

'Thank God we never got rid of these old doors like we meant to,' she says.

Dad sounds like a trapped dog. Whining, scratching, bashing himself against the door.

Mum's face is pure white. It's such a cliché. But she is. White as a ghost. Another cliché.

Mum's a ghost and Dad's a zombie.

Wait.

He's what?

Why did that just come into my head?

A zombie? Don't be fucking stupid, Sam.

There's something seriously wrong with him. But a zombie? There's something wrong with me too if I believe that.

'We should phone an ambulance,' I say.

'They'd have to get the police to restrain him.'

'Mum, we need to do something.'

'I know. Let's see if he calms down.'

'But...'

'Sam.'

That voice. The one she's used on me since I was a kid. Don't argue with me, Sam. I'm not changing my mind.

Why is she being so weird, still refusing to phone for help? If she'd just done that in the first place, instead of diagnosing death when she clearly has no fucking idea what's going on.

Zombie.

The word pops into my head again.

Zombie.

I shake it away.

Zombie.

Is that why she's being so strange? Does she think he's one too? No, it's just me being stupid.

There's a crash and we both jump.

'I think that was the wardrobe,' Mum says.

Seven years bad luck.

There's another smash as the other mirrored door goes.

Is that fourteen years now? Does it go up and up and up depending on how many mirrors you break, or can you break as many as you like in one complete incident? Alice's gran would know.

Mum doesn't look right at all. She's usually so calm. The one with the plasters, who doesn't panic at the sight of blood.

'What's wrong with him?' I ask.

'I don't know. Sorry, Sam. I didn't mean to snap.'

I take the key out of the keyhole and try to peer through. The hole's too small though, too dark. I can't see anything. There's a bash that makes the door shudder. He must have heard me move the key.

'Sam, get away from the door.'

Mum takes the keyring and removes the key for the bedroom. Puts it back in the lock. Then she shoves everything back in the cabinet again.

'Come on, Sam. He'll never calm down if we're out here. Get away from there.'

Zombie.

I want to say the word to Mum. Say it out loud, take its power away.

I follow her into the kitchen.

We both stand looking at each other. Listening.

Evidence that he's calmed down doesn't come. Ten minutes later he's still going. Moaning, pacing the bedroom. Trashing the place.

I shut the kitchen door and Mum sits on a stool at the breakfast bar. We can still hear him, but it's muffled now. I put the kettle on to drown him out even more.

Mum's mobile lies in front of her. She picks it up, swipes the screen and enters the passcode. I watch her dial 999 but she doesn't hit call. She looks at the numbers until the power save kicks in and the screen goes blank. She swipes the screen. Dials 999 again. Watches as it goes blank once more.

999. Blank.

999. Blank.

999. Blank.

I want to shake her. Just phone them or put the phone down. Stop messing around. Make a decision. Tell me what we're going to do.

The kettle clicks off.

'Do you want a cup of tea, Mum?'

'Tell me what to do, Sam.'

'Have a cup of tea.'

'No, I mean… who should I call? An ambulance? The police?'

What? She's actually asking me that?

'I don't know.'

She puts her phone down. A picture of me and Dad on holiday last year is her background image. Her shortcuts arranged in such a way that nothing covers either of our faces. Then the screen goes dark again and I just see her reflection.

'Yes, please.'

'What?'

'I'll have a tea, please.'

I flick the kettle back on again, make us both a cup, sit next to her at the breakfast bar.

Zombie.

Zombie.

Zombie. Zombie. Zombie.

I saw someone driving one of those 4x4 cars the other day, the ones that have the spare tyres hanging on the back door. They had a joke tyre cover, at least I think it was a joke. Instead of the usual rhino logo, or picture of a dog, it had the words Zombie Outbreak Response Team.

It made me laugh at the time. I thought it was cool.

Maybe we should call them?

'Are you sure he was...' I ask.

I can't bring myself to say it. The word.

Dead.

I think I might cry again if I say the actual word. And I don't want to. Today was the first time in years that I've let myself cry in front of her. Even during all that shit with Dad, when people at school were giving me a hard time, when Mum and Dad kept fighting, I didn't. I locked myself in the bathroom, did my crying in there.

'I thought he was. I was sure. Not that I'm medically qualified or anything.'

'I thought he was too,' I reply.

I did. I've never seen a dead body before, but when I went into their room and saw him lying on the bed... He didn't look real. He didn't look alive. It wasn't Dad. I don't know how I imagined a dead body would look, but he looked and felt like someone not there anymore.

Zombie. Zombie. Zombie.

I sip my tea. I'm suddenly hungry. Starving. I've been up for ages and I've had nothing to eat yet. Don't people stop eating when someone close to them di...

But he's not de...

Is he?

All I can think about now is food. What can I eat? I just sit there though. What would Mum think of me if she knew what was going through my head?

30

Your dad's a zombie and you're thinking of your stomach!

That's two of us then.

What's wrong with me? Why am I thinking these dreadful things at a time like this?

And he's not. He can't be.

Zombie. Zombie. Zombie.

Neither of us speak.

Sausages.

Bacon rolls.

Zombie.

Cornflakes.

Crisps.

Zombie.

Mars Bar.

Cheese.

I'm being totally heartless. My dad is...

Dead?

Alive?

Both at the same time.

What's that word? The one they always say in *Buffy* to describe a demon. Alice's favourite TV show.

Corporeal.

That's it. Corporeal.

I don't even know what that means.

Fuck sake. That's my dad in there. And I'm sitting here thinking of *Buffy*. And zombies. And ways to initiate breakfast.

Maybe I'm in shock? Mum is. She's being so weird.

'Do you want another cup of tea, darling?' she asks.

The darling makes me feel like an even bigger shit for wanting to eat. I nod. She gets up and flicks the kettle back on. I think about denying myself food now, even if Mum puts it in front of me. Punish myself on purpose.

I'm too hungry though.

Like Dad.

Zombie. Zombie. Zombie.

Maybe I've got it too. I'll become like Dad. Turn into that... whatever that is.

'I should probably eat something,' Mum says as she pours water into our mugs.

She rubs her belly. 'I'm not sure I can face anything.'

I take that as a sign to make toast. The bread's soft when I take it from the bag and it takes all my willpower not to just ram it in my mouth there and then.

Where has this hunger come from?

'Sam! No wonder we never have any butter.'

I stop spreading the toast. Pile it on a plate. I'd made it all for myself but when Mum sees the plate she helps herself, so I place it down as if I'd always intended for us to share.

The first slice disappears before I can even savour the taste. I help myself to another. The butter greasy on my fingers.

There's a blob of butter on the side of Mum's mouth. She doesn't notice it's there. I can't stop staring at it. It's starting to bug me. Why hasn't she noticed it? Why doesn't she wipe it away? I feel like a total shit again for allowing myself to get irritated at something so stupid and which makes her seem so vulnerable. Eventually she takes a drink of tea, wipes her mouth, and it disappears.

'He seems quieter now. What do you think?' Mum asks.

She stands and opens the kitchen door, but it's still the same. The scraping and scratching, the incessant moaning.

Zombie. Zombie. Zombie.

Mum shuts the door and sits down again.

'If we're going to phone an ambulance, we have to do it now.' she says.

'Do you think we should?' I ask.

'I don't know. If we leave him any longer, and he doesn't get better, they'll ask why we didn't phone straight away.'

'Why didn't you phone straight away?'

'I don't know.'

'You should have.'

'Don't tell me what I should have done.'

She stands and clears the mugs and the plate, loads them into the dishwasher.

'Can't you put anything away?'

She puts the lid on the butter and puts the tub back in the fridge.

I'm still hungry, I want more.

Mum leans against the counter.

'Do you remember what Dad was like when he took the drugs?'

'What do you mean?'

Where has this come from?

'Like, his moods. He lost his temper over little things.'

I nod as I remember the incident with my Lego. I used to have a big box of the stuff and I was always making these elaborate constructions out of it, castles, houses, forts. Each one bigger than the last, with different levels and rooms and staircases. I'd tip the Lego out onto the floor and scrabble through it for the right bit. I was doing that one afternoon when Dad came home from training and then I heard him and Mum start to argue in the kitchen. The next thing I remember was him bursting into my bedroom and smashing up my Lego castle.

'Will you just shut up!' He shouted at me.

He didn't touch me but, for a split second, I thought he was going to. Mum went mental at him. Told me we were leaving. That made me even more upset though. In the end we stayed but Mum didn't leave my side. I'd never seen Dad like that before. He apologised later, like really apologised. I think it scared him too, how close he got. That was just a few months before he was caught.

He never put that anecdote into his autobiography.

Mum said to me later that she thought he got careless on purpose. Got so ashamed of himself he wanted to be caught.

That wasn't your dad, Sam, she said. That wasn't your dad.

That's not him now either.

Zombie. Zombie. Zombie.

'Is he on drugs again?' I ask.

'No, no. I don't mean that. I just wonder if it's like those mood swings? If we leave him, it'll pass and we can get in there and see what's going on?'

'We've left him quite a long time already.'

'I know. Listen, if you want me to phone someone, I will. Just tell me that's what you want me to do.'

'Do you want to do that?'

'Part of me does and part of me doesn't.'

It's on the tip of my tongue.

Zombie. Zombie. Zombie.

I don't know what I want her to do. This isn't fair. She's the grown-up. She should decide.

Maybe she's right? About the drugs. The mood swings.

'You go and get ready for school. I'm home today, so I'll keep an eye on him.'

School. School? I'd almost forgotten it's a school day. I can't believe she wants me to just get ready and head to school like nothing's happened.

Zombie. Zombie. Zombie.

The moment's gone now. I can't tell her.

I get up from the breakfast bar.

'I'll go for a shower then.'

'And, Sam. We can't tell anyone until we know for ourselves what we're going to do. Not even Alice, okay?'

'Okay,' I reply.

Fall From Grace by Adam Redpath

I'm not trying to deflect blame but it was my coach, Kennedy Jones, who first suggested that we try something different. In all of our early conversations he never stated explicitly what it was we were about to do, but it was definitely implied. Words such as drugs, illegal, banned substances, cheating, were never said out loud, but we both knew that was what we were discussing. Maybe if we'd been more direct with each other, I might not have gone through with it. I just buried my head in the sand. Kennedy knew exactly how to pitch it to me. He massaged my ego, played to my sense of injustice, my love for my family.

You're such a talented athlete. I wouldn't suggest this to just anyone. You work hard, train hard. You already have the ability, you just need a helping hand.

Everyone else is doing it. This is about making it an even playing field.

You don't take it during competition, it's for training only. To aid recovery, help you train harder. You're getting older now. Your body takes longer to recover.

You'll be able to provide for your family. Give them everything they need.

Jude

I'm due to test someone who lives in Bruntsfield. The testing mission they call it, as if I'm about to embark upon some intensive operation, when the truth is all I'm doing is watching someone pee in a pot.

It's an out-of-competition test which is why it's at the athlete's house. I check over my paperwork again. Scan the photo of her so I know who I'm looking for. I don't think I've tested her before, don't recognise the name or the face.

Yvonne Mercer. A swimmer and a student at Edinburgh Uni. A butterfly specialist. Silver medallist for the 100m Butterfly at the Commonwealth Games in Glasgow.

Her specified sixty minute time slot is 10am to 11am. I can't turn up before that. The instructions she's put into her online Anti-Doping profile say to ring the buzzer, so that's what I'll do. Usually these tests are pretty standard. The athletes know the drill. They must be in their stated location during their designated hour in case someone like me, a Doping Control Officer, turns up to test them.

I put the paperwork back in my bag, alongside all my testing paraphernalia; the forms, the sample collection vessels, the courier bags to send everything off to the lab, bottles of water in case they get stage-fright. I have to be able to give them a choice of at least three different sample kits and make sure they're all sealed, intact, not damaged or dirty in any way. It's a fair bit of kit to lug about and it's getting harder the more pregnant I become.

I sit in the window, sip at my decaf latté, pick at the piece of carrot cake I've bought. It crumbles apart as I pick it up. I press the crumbs together until they form a squashy ball which I can eat. Leave the icing until last. The handle of my coffee cup is sticky and I think about the marks I'm leaving. On this cup.

On this table. On this chair. I've spent the last few days feeling like a carrier. Worried I'm about to be struck down at any moment with the same thing Adam has. Infecting everyone I come into contact with. Every time Sam coughs or sneezes it sends me into a panic.

Coughs and sneezes spread diseases.

I've moved into the spare room, but I barely sleep. I lie awake, listening to Adam. Missing him. Feeling like I'm in a hotel room rather than my own home. The clean white sheets. The strange bed. The room that's not my own. The baby moves and squirm as I try to get comfortable. Sometimes I get up and check Sam's okay.

Adam's not better. He hasn't calmed down and the days have just slipped away. The longer it goes on the harder it becomes to let the outside world know what's going on.

The loneliness of night is completely different to the loneliness of day. The brain works differently. Everything feels much worse, irrational fears take hold. In the first few weeks after Sam was born, I felt so much sorrow and anxiety through those long nights. Adam was in serious competition training and so he slept in the spare bed. I was exhausted and terrified and my body was all over the place. I felt like the only person awake anywhere in the whole world.

I check my watch. Still plenty of time before I have to be at the appointment.

The irony of my job in relation to Adam isn't lost on me.

How did a drugs cheat who was married to a doping control officer get away with it for so long?

The tabloid newspapers had a field day.

I worried I'd lose my job. He was banned from doing his. What an almighty fucking mess it was.

I can genuinely say that I had no idea what he was up to. Not everyone believes that, but it's true. Maybe I was too close? It made me blind to what was happening.

I felt like such a fool when the truth came out. It was all so obvious. I should have recognised the signs. His mood swings. That awful time when I thought Adam was going to hurt Sam.

Changes in his libido. Changes in his appearance, the veins on his arms, in his neck. His appetite. The money going out every month to pay for it all.

Yes, I should have worked out what was going on, but I genuinely never thought he'd do such a thing.

And of course, he had the missed tests too. I knew how serious that was. I knew it was unbelievably careless of an athlete to miss one, let alone two. Yet I believed his stupid excuses. Stuck in traffic, fallen asleep and hadn't heard the doorbell. Excuses that I'd never have believed from anyone else. That should have triggered some sort of internal alarm, but I never imagined he was capable of something I thought we both found so abhorrent.

If I'd known would I have told him to stop? More than one reporter actually asked me that. What a question. Of course I would have told him to stop. I'd have told him not to be such a fucking idiot. To think of the damage he was doing to himself. To Sam and me.

And I would have told him that it was only a matter of time before he got caught. Even though one of the most frustrating parts of my job is that not everyone who cheats get caught.

We were out for a walk when he got the call. He brushed it off at the time, told us it was nothing, but I could tell something was wrong. When we got home, he locked himself in the bathroom. It took me an hour and a half to get him to let me in. I was frantic, I had no idea what was wrong. Then, finally, he unlocked the door. I sat on the closed toilet seat while he leant against the bath and confessed everything through his tears. I love him, but I still don't know if the tears were because he was sorry or because he'd been caught.

I felt completely betrayed.

He gave me the usual excuses.

You can read them all in his autobiography. He and his ghost-writer emphasised them over and over again as part of his quest to find forgiveness. Spinning the negative stories to make people put themselves in his shoes, feel sorry for him. Start to understand the man behind the scandal. Start to forgive.

This is me, Adam, I remember saying. Don't bullshit me, I deserve the truth, not the soundbites. Save those for everyone else.

He couldn't give me anything different though.

I check the time again, debate with myself whether to get another decaf latté. I'd better not. It's the athlete who needs to be peeing, not me. My bladder isn't as strong as it was.

It didn't take long for the story to break. Adam was a big deal. The nation's darling. A super Saturday star. He was talking about retirement at that stage, only kept going after 2012 because the Commonwealth Games were in Scotland. His home nation.

Now he was front page news. We had the press camped outside our house, outside Sam's school, phoning us night and day. They drove us out of our own home.

Adam got hate mail, death threats. We had to get the police and the Royal Mail to check our post before it came to us. A lot of it went straight in the bin without being opened. You could tell how vicious the content was just from the envelope.

He had to hand back his medals. He was dropped by all his sponsors. People would abuse him, swear at him on the street. Everything he'd achieved before the drugs stood for nothing. And he'd achieved so much without them, but it was all tainted forever.

People are weird about celebrities. You see it when someone famous dies, people react like they were best friends. The 'Diana' effect. I mean, I cried my eyes out when Carrie Fisher died. I was affected by the loss of a hero who had meant so much to me when I was growing up, who I felt a strange connection with even though we'd never met.

It's the same kind of thing when a celebrity lets down their fans, except then they become vitriolic and hateful. It was crazy, as if Adam had hurt those strangers out of spite.

Then they all wanted more of him. Wanted him to tell his story. Wanted to see the broken man apologising. Wanted to read about it so they could judge him all over again.

So they could feel superior. Those perfect people who felt they had the right to sentence him.

I've dealt with athletes who've failed drugs tests. I knew it was a horrible position to be in. But I never thought it would be him. I had that superiority too, that smug pride at his talent. That he was doing it all 'clean.' Until everything came crashing down around us, I never realised what a sin it is to be a fallen hero.

The scale of his crime did not reflect the treatment he got. You'd have thought he'd murdered children, or massacred puppies.

The general public.

The masses.

Those who decided they knew him from TV or from interviews. They didn't know him at all, but they behaved as if they were loyal friends who had been betrayed.

And all those people who hated him, who thought he was pure evil, they all then went out and dutifully bought his book. To find out all the juicy, intimate details of his public humiliation. They bought tickets to hear him talk, hear him apologise in person, watch him shed tears of remorse.

Maybe that gave them some sense of justification? Those perfect, vengeful people who pass judgement on others, based on what they choose to believe to be the facts.

It was then that I knew what true love was too.

Stand by your man.

Yes, I was angry. I was hurt, let down, betrayed. But I didn't hate Adam. And the need to protect him was overwhelming.

One of his team mates, Mark Rogers, became obsessed with Adam. He started stalking us. Not just Adam, but me and Sam too. Adam never put that in the autobiography; too nice a guy to attack someone else to get some sympathy. Mark Rogers became the new hero of athletics, all because he spoke out against Adam and told everyone how he'd been affected by Adam's actions. Yes, it was a shame for him, but his behaviour was worse than anything Adam had done. Mark followed me and Sam home from school one day. I kept telling him to leave us alone, but he wouldn't go. He asked me if I thought my husband would kill himself over the shame of his actions. Asked me that, in front of Sam.

And the awful thing was that, while I was telling him to leave us the hell alone, I was really fucking terrified that Adam might. He became a recluse. He didn't leave the house for almost six months, apart from going running in the middle of the night. That obsession with athletics never left him. That compulsion to train, to compete, even if it was just himself that he was racing.

That desire to win.

Even now, I still see Mark Rogers on our street sometimes. Like a ghost, he's there one minute and gone the next. It terrifies me.

I don't think I realised at the time how fragile my own mental health was. Looking back, I think I was clinically depressed. I stopped going out, even with friends. I couldn't face seeing people and having to explain. I don't think I've ever fully recovered and I only held it together for Sam. The line is so thin. It just takes one tragedy and suddenly life is out of control. I could lose myself again and not realise until it was too late.

Adam made a second career out of the book and the interviews. Talking about the dangers of drug taking. Going round schools, athletics clubs, passing on his wisdom.

Do as I say, not as I do.

All his other retirement plans were closed off to him now. The coaching, the commentary.

The hardest part for me, and the part I found hardest to forgive, was the effect it had on Sam. That was almost the tipping point that made me walk away. He was only nine and he went from having a dad that everyone envied and wanted to meet, to being bullied and teased at school for the bad choices his dad had made.

And two years later, along came Glasgow 2014. The spotlight on us again even though Adam was serving his ban by then and had effectively retired from sport. The Scottish athlete who won't be representing his country, who has brought shame upon the nation. The Commonwealth Games that should have been his swansong.

Adam knew he was taking us all down with him and he did it anyway. That part still hurts. That, even if he was tempted, the thought of Sam and I didn't stop it there and then.

A lot of the athletes I deal with know who I am before I know who they are. If it bothers them that the person watching them pee into a cup is married to a high-profile drugs cheat, they don't let on. Even now, there are still whispers. People still point. There's still the occasional piece of mail that goes straight into the bin. The doorbell rings but nobody's there when you open it.

Which is why I can't bear to let anyone know about what's happened to him. God, I can't even imagine how vindicated Mark Rogers would be if he knew. I don't know what's happened to Adam, what's caused this, but I know people will jump to the conclusion that it's a side-effect, a by-product, of all the years of abuse he inflicted on his body, and we've already experienced enough side-effects. Why else did it take so long to get pregnant again? I rub my tummy. This precious little person who was almost prevented from coming into existence. The fact that I've had these thoughts myself, means it won't take much for the papers to print it as fact. Giving him back to those judgemental masses. The Mark Rogers of the world. Allowing them to sentence him all over again. The story that just keeps on fucking giving.

I can't go through it all again. Not now, not while I'm pregnant. I can't put Sam through it.

I look out the window, watch the bustle of Bruntsfield. The retired couples. The students. The mums with buggies and prams, meeting for classes and coffees and cakes. The endless cars and delivery vans.

There's a break in the traffic. That's when I notice it. The sign under the window of Oddbins across the road. White writing painted on a black background.

Bikes, Prams, Dogs, Cats and Zombies: All Welcome

I lose it again as cars, taxis and buses go past. At first I think it's my imagination. But, no, another gap in the traffic and I see it again.

Bikes, Prams, Dogs, Cats and Zombies: All Welcome

I've never noticed that sign before. Someone's idea of being trendy or ironic, but it stops me short.

Zombie. Zombie. Zombie.

Fuck.

It's so close to home that it sucks all the air out of me.

That word. That fucking word.

Zombie.

That's almost a perfect description of what Adam is.

Why haven't I thought of that before?

Because zombies aren't real.

But...

Now that the word's in there, I can't shake it.

44

Zombie.

Bikes, Prams, Dogs, Cats and Zombies: All Welcome

I've always believed that nothing is ever coincidence. I like the concept of synchronicity. Meaningful coincidences. Signs that tell us we're on the right track. The universe giving us a knowing wink.

It happens so often it can't just be nothing.

When I was thirteen and got my period for the first time, I kept hearing that fucking Tampax song everywhere I went.

It's My Life.

It followed me, I swear it did. On the radio, on the TV, at school. And maybe I was just young and hyper-sensitive and embarrassed about periods, or maybe it was the Universe being an asshole.

Bikes, Prams, Dogs, Cats and Zombies: All Welcome

If nothing had happened to Adam, would this zombie reference even exist? And if it did, would I notice it? Has it been put there deliberately to point me in the right direction, to convince me that Adam is a zombie?

Zombie. It's laughable if it wasn't so accurate right now.

Adam.

Zombie.

Jesus, I need to get out of here. I need to get to work.

Bikes, Prams, Dogs, Cats and Zombies: All Welcome

12/08/15

The Story of How We Met

By Sam

Mum and Dad were arguing in their bedroom again. They would always go in there to fight, then act like I had no clue what was going on.

A typical fight would go:

'How could you be so selfish.'

'Selfish. I was thinking of you and Sam the whole time.'

'If you had, you wouldn't have risked your health like that.'

'I was trying to provide for you both.'

Etc, etc, etc...

That day I was hiding in the spare room listening to them through the wall with an empty glass. The sound was all muffled, and I probably would have heard them better without it, but I'd seen it on TV and it seemed like a good thing to do.

I thought they were going to get divorced.

They stopped shouting and there was silence. They did this a lot. Sometimes it was because they were whispering, but most of the time they just sat there not talking. Or one of them started crying. I got bored of listening to nothing and started raking about in the old shoe boxes we kept in there (from Dad's millions of trainers and spikes). They were full of memorabilia and newspaper and magazine cuttings about him.

I took one off the book shelf and opened the lid. There was Dad on the front cover of *Athletics Weekly*. Under that was an invitation to Sports Personality of the Year. Photos of him on the podium somewhere. A folded up Union Jack flag that somebody once handed him for a lap of honour.

46

I got so mad looking through that box. I felt like ripping it all up or throwing it in the bin, but that just didn't seem enough. It had to be something really final. That's when I decided to burn it, so I got some matches and took the box down to the bottom of the garden.

I took out the first newspaper cutting. I can remember exactly what it was, even after all this time. It was an interview with Dad after he won the UK trials with a new British 400m record.

It took me two or three attempts to get the first match to light. Were you watching me the whole time, because I must have looked like a right weirdo? I almost stopped myself, was so close to taking the box back inside. But then the match lit and I held it to the side of the newspaper.

Anyway, you saw what happened next. I took out the next cutting, then the next, then the next. Burnt them all one by one until there was only one match left. That one I dropped into the shoe box. I think it was the flag that caused all the problems, the whole thing just went up.

I totally panicked at that point. I didn't know what to do so I stood back and watched until it died out.

That's when you appeared out of nowhere. All I could see was your face peering through the hedge. I thought I was on my own and you gave me such a fright. I can't remember the exact conversation we had but it went something like this (you were pretty annoying by the way!):

You: What are you doing?

Me: None of your business.

You: What are you burning?

Me: (I didn't say anything at this point, just ignored you).

You: Fine, be like that. I'll work it out myself. I'm psychic you know, like my gran. It always skips a generation.

I didn't believe you, even if your gran can be a bit weird!

47

You: My gran told me about your dad.

Me: So?

You: You'll regret burning that stuff, even if you are mad at him.

Me: Get lost. It's none of your business, or your gran's.

You: It's not like it's a big secret. It's been on the News and everything.

Me: Will you leave me alone.

I know we're friends now but you were totally getting on my nerves!

You: You shouldn't burn all those memories.

Me: Shut up.

You: I'm right though.

Me: No, you're not. None of it was real.

You: It was. It all happened.

Me: I thought you said you'd seen it on the News. Don't you know he cheated?

You: Not all the time. You don't make it that far without talent. Your dad made a mistake. That's what my gran said and I agree with her.

Me: Good for you.

As you no doubt remember, I was on fire with my comebacks that day.

The burning was meant to be this big gesture, but I just ended up feeling like an idiot. Plus, you weren't exactly helping the situation. That's when I noticed the big, black mark on the path. And you were right, I started to regret what I'd done, but only because Mum and Dad would be pissed off and I was scared it might make the divorce happen.

You: Here, take this.

You passed a garden hose through the hedge to me. You had on those homemade friendship bracelets you always used to wear.

Me: You're as weird as your gran.

You: For the path, dumbass.

Me: You're the dumbass.

I tried to wipe the mark away with my feet, but I only smudged it and made it look worse.

You: Just take the hose, okay?

I did take it eventually and then you ran off to turn the outside tap on. Water came pouring out and I pointed it at the charred remains of the shoebox, until it blasted away all the evidence.

You turned the tap off and took the hose from me.

Me: Thanks.

You: That's okay. We're both criminals now. You're an arsonist and I'm an accessory.

Me: If you say so.

You: It's just a shame you've destroyed a chunk of history.

This was when you started going on about destroying history! On our very first meeting!

You: Hardly anyone keeps hard copies of anything anymore. Once the apocalypse comes, and we can't access anything online, we won't have a history. Our generation will just disappear.

Me: If it's the apocalypse, who cares?

You: What about future generations?

Me: We'll all be dead.

You: Some of us will make it.

49

Me: Bit of a pointless apocalypse then. I'm going now.

You: I'm Alice by the way. I know you're Sam. My gran told me.

Me: Well done.

I went back inside but I kept watching out the kitchen window. Did you know I was there? It felt like I was still being watched but you must have gone inside at this point to write your first letter. The shapes and movement of the hedge tricked me into seeing you though. I thought I could make out hair, eyes. After a few minutes I suddenly saw your hand poke through the hedge and drop an envelope.

It was a letter to me, which I still have.

Then I wrote you a reply but I can't remember what I said. Anyway, that's the story of how we met and began writing to each other.

The end.

Sam

I sit on the swing in the back garden. Mum and Dad brought it with us when we moved here, even though I was already too big for it. I played on it when I knew they were watching, hoped it would stop them getting a divorce if I made them happy.

We used to live in a big house near the Botanics. The house bought with Dad's success. The house where everything went wrong.

That time feels like a dream sometimes, like it never really happened. We don't go near that side of town now if we can help it and, when we do, they don't point anything out. They never say things like 'that was your first house, Sam,' or 'that's where you took your first steps and said your first words and learned to ride a bike.' I guess it reminds them too much. Happy memories and sad ones. Sometimes the happy ones can cause just as much pain as the sad ones.

The swing creaks as I move forward, back, forward, back, forward, back. The chain is old and rusty and black paint flakes from the frame which lifts from the ground as I swing. Forward, back, forward, back, forward, back. I keep it grounded with my feet; my grass-stained toes scraping the lawn.

I watch the bedroom window as I swing. The curtains are closed, the glass misty with condensation, smeared with handprints.

What's he thinking right now? Can he still think? Probably not.

Reanimated human corpse.

Mute and mindless.

Unthinking.

I've been googling the word zombie a lot these last couple of days.

Maybe he can think? Maybe he's wondering why we've locked him up? Or maybe's there an innate desire to eat us which doesn't require any thought process?

The curtains move every so often. Sometimes I think they're about to be torn down from the wall. Mostly he hangs about on the other side of the door.

The wind chimes jangle from next door. I look away from the window. Alice's gran is out feeding the fish in her pond. I hope she doesn't notice me. I don't want to have to speak to her. Maybe I should just go in before she spots me? What's the least desirable option right now, speaking to her or going back in the house? Her garden's usually a bit of a jungle, plants and bushes and trees, but at this time of the year, when everything's dead or dying, I can peer through the hedge.

Just like Dad. Turning brown, shrivelling up and... what? How can he be dying if he's already dead? Would his bones crack like a dead twig or is there still blood inside? Would it drip out or is it congealed mush?

I take out my phone. Google.

Decomposition of a body.

Stages of decomposition.

What happens on a body farm?

What happens to your body after you die?

Human death and decay. Warning: Graphic Images.

I put my phone away again. I don't think I'm quite ready to follow any of those links yet.

Tertiary colours, that's what Mrs Everitt called them in Art. Everyone knows the primary colours: red, yellow and blue. Then when you mix them up, you get your secondary colours: green, purple and orange. Once you mix those up though, it's all browns and dirty greens and rusty oranges. Tertiary colours. Dad's in his tertiary phase right now.

Alice's gran is wearing a hat like a tea cosy. Probably knitted it herself. Or maybe Alice crocheted it. She's into that right now. Making these wee things called granny squares. She says she's going to join them all up into a blanket for the baby. Sometimes I think she's more excited than I am about the arrival of my little sister.

Alice's gran looks like Paddington Bear, in her yellow wellies and old duffel coat. There's a gust of wind and all the windmills she has in her garden rustle and spin. I think she's talking to herself, or maybe to the fish. I can see her lips moving but I can't hear anything. I used to think she was a witch, casting spells.

'A white witch maybe,' Mum said. 'Harmless'.

'Probably would have been burnt back in the middles ages.' Dad replied.

'She's been very kind since we moved in.'

The wind chimes jingle again. Alice's gran is standing at the hedge. She's been looking at Mum and Dad's bedroom window. Then she sees me and waves.

I wave back.

'Everything alright?' She asks.

'Yeah,' I nod.

She smiles and wanders away. I keep swinging, forward and back, forward and back, forward and back. It's cold but I don't want to go back inside. I don't know what it is, the noise of us, the smell of us. If we're in the house, it sends him crazy. I wonder if Alice's gran knows something is going on? Maybe she can hear him groaning and knocking things over? Or maybe she's starting to notice the smell? It's spreading through the house. Mum's been spraying perfume and air freshener, but it doesn't work.

Alice's gran wanders around pulling out weeds, pruning the tops of things. She puts me on edge. I wish she would go back inside. I keep expecting her to come over and ask what's happened to Dad.

My eyes are drawn to the old post box in the hedge. Alice's gran made it for us years ago. It's totally falling apart now, it's been exposed to the elements for too long. It kills me a little. Why do important things never last, but dumb old lifeless things endure? All that plastic in the ocean, killing sea creatures, turning up in the stomachs of fish and birds, getting in the food chain. Lego and rubber ducks that never decompose washed up on beaches.

The wood on the post box is rotting and split and covered in moss.

Not that me and Alice use it anymore. Emails and texting took over. I still like the thought of it being there though. I used to check it every day if Alice had been at her gran's, sometimes more than once.

That's where we met. Through that hedge. It was smaller then. Alice's gran has let it get out of control. I still remember that nervous thrill when I set those cuttings on fire and the whole box went up in flames. The panic as I realised the fire was completely out of my control, then the relief as it calmed down again and I watched the newspaper articles burn away to nothing. Alice called me an arsonist. I'd never heard that word before and I thought she'd called me an arse.

I guess I was that too.

I waited ten minutes after I saw her leave that first letter. I was desperate to read what it said but I didn't want to look like I `was. When I went out, I imagined her eyes on me. I tried to act cool. Walked straight past the letter like I didn't even know it was there. Then on my way back. Oh, what's that? Look around, side to side.

Lift it, read the single word on the envelope.

Sam

Feigned surprise.

It took ages to write my reply. I was intimidated by how confident Alice was. How fierce, how beautiful. I wanted her to like me. For us to become friends. Even if she did kind of irritate

54

me too. I threw so many drafts in the bin before I came up with something. Then I worried she might have gone home before I could leave it, but I watched from the kitchen window and five minutes later she picked it up.

Alice really came along at the right time. I was so worried Mum and Dad were going to split up and I kept obsessing over what would happen when they did. The thought of having to choose who to live with kept me awake at night. It was worse than the bullying and all the other shit that came from Dad's exposure as a drugs cheat. Alice made me think about her instead.

I miss the letter writing now. There's something about getting an actual letter that is so much more exciting than a text or an email. I used to love coming in from school and seeing the flag sticking up on the mailbox.

I'd never tell Alice that though.

Instant messaging isn't the same. You can't doodle on an email, see the crossed-out words, the smudges. There's less of her personality, even although it's her fingers tap, tap, tapping the keyboard. There's an absence that wasn't there with letter writing.

I still have every letter she sent me. The coloured scraps of paper, the homemade envelopes, the drawings, the poems. That one where she used her rainbow biros. It's funny reading them now. It reminds you of stuff. Things you did, places you went. The things you were into that meant everything then but makes you cringe now.

The curtain twitches and draws my attention to Mum and Dad's bedroom again. What must it look like now? We hear him smashing stuff. Mum can't even get in to get her clothes, she keeps rewashing the same couple of outfits over and over and over.

We need to do something with him. Move him or secure him or something. We can't just leave him like that.

I take out my phone. Look at the time. Mum will be home soon. I should go in so she doesn't see me sitting out here on the swing.

I don't move though. It's cold and I'm hungry and bored as fuck, but I still can't bring myself to go back in. I'll wait till I hear the car in the front drive.

I log into YouTube.

Matted hair, thick prominent veins all over her face. Black blood dripping from cracked lips.

Hissing. Ripped shirt sleeves. Shiny skin, dark circles under his eyes. Arms outstretched.

Milky eyes, thinning hair. Receding gums and brown teeth. One leg dragging behind.

I call Alice instead. It rings a few times then goes to voicemail.

What is she doing? What's stopping her from answering her phone?

I start to text but it goes on for too long so I decide to email her instead.

From: samredpath08@gmail.com

To: alice_gryffindor4@gmail.com

Subject: Bored!!!!

Hey Alice,

I just tried to call you, but I guess you must be busy. I'm sitting on the swing in the back garden.

I stop for a moment. She'll wonder what I'm doing out here.

I start to delete the last sentence.

I'm sitting on th

I stop myself again. Why shouldn't I tell her? She's my best friend after all. Plus she's going to wonder why she can't come over to the house the next time she's at her gran's.

I'm sitting on the swing in the back garden. You may be wondering why I'm out here in the cold and the dark.

Stop.

Mum would kill me if she thought I'd told anyone. I told her I wouldn't. Not even Alice, she said, and I agreed.

I'm sitting on the swing in the back garden. You may be wonde

But then Mum's not here. She's out and I'm stuck having to deal with this on my own for another evening.

I'm sitting on the swing in the back garden. You may be wondering why I'm out here in the cold and the dark. You probably wouldn't believe me if I told you the truth. I can hardly believe it myself. I'll just come out with it. I think my dad is a zombie. See, I told you. I bet you're laughing at me now. Think I'm being an idiot. I promise I'm not. Alice, I'm deadly serious. This last week has been the shittest time of my entire life. And you know I've had some shit times.

I keep writing. I have no intention of actually sending it now. I'll just delete it once I've finished. The act of writing, putting it in black and white, is cathartic.

Basically I woke up the other morning because Mum was crying, like full-on hysterics. She said Dad was dead. Alice, you know I wouldn't joke about something so awful. I went to see him and he was dead. He was lying there and he just looked totally wrong. I've never seen a dead body before but I'm sure of it. Then he suddenly started moving and trying to bite us. Now he's locked in Mum and Dad's bedroom. He's going mental and that's why I'm out here on the swing, because I can't face being in the house right now.

I swear it's true. You can't tell anyone. Mum made me promise to keep it a secret and she'd kill me if she knew I'd told you. I don't know what to do, Alice.

I don't even know if I should send this email or delete.

I feel like the worst person in the world. Betraying Mum and using this all to get attention from Alice.

I hear the car. Mum's pulling into the driveway. I look down at the email and scan the last line.

I don't even know if I should send this email or delete.
Send. Discard. Send. Discard. Send. Discard.
'Sam, is that you? What are you doing out here?'
I jump off the swing, walk towards Mum.
Send. Discard. Send. Discard. Send. Discard.
'Nothing.'
I glance down at my phone again as I press Discard.
Sending...
Wait. What?
Shit. Shit. I try to close it down but it's too late.
'Sam, what are you doing? Come in the house.'
I open the Sent Items folder.
There it is.

From: samredpath08@gmail.com
To: alice_gryffindor4@gmail.com
Subject: Bored!!!!

Hey Alice

15th March 2013

Hi Sam (my gran told me your name – although, like I said, I am psychic. You look like a Sam).

It's Alice here. You know, the girl from before who gave you the hose. Sorry if I annoyed you. Mum says sometimes I don't know when to leave things alone. I really did believe you'd regret burning all that stuff though and I like to stay true to my beliefs – the apocalypse is coming…

Anyway, would you like to be penpals with me? Gran says letter writing is a dying art.

Please reply,

Alice

X

Jude

I google B&Q, type chain into the search bar and hit enter.

Scroll down the first page of the fifty-five products available, before I click View All instead.

Bath plug and chain.

Chainsaw chain.

Door chain with brass effect.

I'm not really sure what I'm looking for. What I'm even doing for that matter. At least I am admitting to myself that we can't go on as we are. Chaining him up might be the only solution right now.

If we want to feel safe in our home.

Jesus, I can't believe this. That we need to protect ourselves from Adam.

It's just a short-term solution. I can get through this if I keep telling myself that. A short-term solution until we figure out what the hell's happening or (please, fucking, God) he gets better.

I stroke my belly to calm myself down. Or at least try to convince my bump that I'm calm. The rest of me can be wired and anxious, so long as the little one inside is floating in an amniotic pool of zen.

Stop. Stop. Stop.

Focus on the chains.

'What are you doing?'

Sam points over my shoulder. I jump, didn't hear him come in. Didn't even realise he was home. He crept up on me like a monster in a horror movie.

Which makes me think of that sign the other day.

Zombie.

I can't get that word out of my head.

'Sam, you gave me a fright.'

He sits next to me.

'Why are you looking up chains?'

'I'm not.'

'Mum, I'm not an idiot.'

'Okay. Sorry. I thought we could use something to restrain your dad. It might make things a bit easier.'

'That's just a bike chain. That one.'

He points at the screen.

Heavy Duty Welded Steel Chain.

I click on it, bring up the product description, read it aloud.

'Galvanised steel, specially designed to give your home an additional level of security.'

We're trying to keep a family member in, not keep strangers out.

'What does galvanised even mean?' I ask.

Sam shrugs.

'Google it.'

'You mean use a dictionary, right? I thought you were all for saving the printed word.'

Sam rolls his eyes.

I bring up a new tab, type in the word galvanised.

We're faced with four different definitions.

1. to stimulate by electric current.
2. *Medical.* to stimulate or treat muscles or nerves with direct current.
3. to startle or shock into˅ sudden activity.
4. to coat metal, especially iron or steel, with zinc to prevent rusting.

'I'm assuming it's number four then,' says Sam.

'I think so.'

'Do you think they'll be strong enough?'

'I don't know.'

They should give more information. Would suit a large dog. Can hold an elephant. Perfect for chaining up your zombie husband.

I stifle a laugh. The fucking absurdity of it all.

I suddenly remember those furry, pink handcuffs we got from Ann Summers when we were first living together, before we had Sam. And the night we got so carried away they snapped. Cheap rubbish. Nothing like these heavy duty chains from B&Q.

I click back to the list of items again.

Chain lubricant.

Jesus. I turn my laugh into a cough, stand up from the laptop and get myself a drink of milk. I need to compose myself.

My stomach heaves and I feel the loss of him grip at me.

I sit back down beside Sam.

'These are the strongest ones, Mum.'

'Is he extra strong do you think?'

'What?'

'I mean, does this thing, whatever it is, make him extra strong, or is it just…'

I falter. How to word it? Sam's my wee boy, I'm supposed to protect him from shit like this.

When he was a toddler, maybe two or three, Adam and I left him with a babysitter. We went to the cinema, got the times mixed up and ended up watching this terrible sci-fi film instead of the film we'd planned on seeing. It was set in the not too distant future and I remember looking at the date that this dystopian world was set in and working out how old Sam would be. My wee boy would be an old man. Sam, so full of joy and innocence and endless wonder, would be at the end of his life. And the thought of it made me so, so sad I couldn't concentrate on the film. I was already feeling guilty about leaving him with a babysitter and, after it was in there, I just couldn't shake the thought. It made me ache inside. I sat in the dark crying because I wanted to stop time.

Now he's a teenager and I still can't stop time.

'Is it just... what?'

'I can't remember what I was going to say.' I lie.

Is Adam just so desperate to get to us that it makes him seem strong? Like those kids who lift cars off their parents. Freak examples of super-human strength in extraordinary circumstances.

'Is he a zombie superhero?' Sam says.

'What?' I stop and look at him.

'Nothing, I didn't mean it.'

'A zombie. Is that what you think he is?'

'I don't know. Maybe.'

'How long have you thought that?'

'I don't know. Not long after it happened, I guess.'

'Why didn't you say something?'

'It's not like I really believe it.'

'Don't you?'

'Do you?'

'I don't know what to believe anymore.'

So, Sam's beaten me to it. He's jumped to the zombie conclusion already. Does that mean it's what Adam really is?

'So, these ones?' Sam points at the screen again.

'Let's just get the strongest ones we can,' I reply.

'We can order online, or click and collect.'

I'm still reeling from the zombie revelation and now he's being so matter of fact about these chains. Like he's ordering a DVD or a t-shirt or something.

There's a crash from the bedroom.

'I think we probably need them sooner rather than later,' I say. 'We should probably look at them first. These specifications mean nothing to me.'

As much as I really would rather not go into the shop, it's what we have to do. Please let them be strong enough. I don't have a Plan B right now and I sure as hell don't know where you get extra heavy duty chains.

'We should look up padlocks too,' Sam says.

I lean back from the computer. He's the one in control here. It hadn't even crossed my mind that we'd need those too.

I watch him type padlocks into the search engine.

Page 1 of 30.

I can't face this.

Buying chains is one thing. Thinking about what happens next exhausts me too much.

'Let's just get one when we see what the chains are like.'

Sam nods.

A sudden thought hits me, and I push Sam out of the way and type in paint. Something B&Qy, something normal.

'Paint?' Sam asks.

'What if our internet usage is being monitored? This is going to look really dodgy.'

'What's dodgy about chains and padlocks?'

'B&Q, also known as Serial Killers R Us.'

'Only if you also buy plastic sheets, a spade, an axe, some bleach...' He lists them on his fingers.

'Okay wise-guy. How do you know so much about this subject?'

'I watch TV. I read books. Why are we even using the internet if you're so paranoid?'

'Because I only thought of that now.'

Why am I being so paranoid?

I've always been a worrier. It got worse after Adam was found guilty and I've never really been able to get it back under control.

I keep imagine people watching us. That Adam is the centre of some awful health scandal. That we'll be taken away, tested, locked up.

That they'll take my baby away from me.

'You just feel guilty because of what we're going to use them for. I feel guilty too.'

His eyes mist and he looks away. Those brown eyes, his dad's eyes. I squeeze his hand where it rests over the mouse.

My baby. Getting older each day. Out of my control.

He shakes my hand off.

'I think we should get a chain long enough to go right round the bed. If we can get him lying down, maybe we could lock him to the bed like that?'

He's been giving this some thought. Too much thought.

'That sounds like it would work.'

Another crash from the bedroom is followed by a dull, moaning.

I want to squeeze Sam so hard right now. I put an arm around his shoulders and pull him towards me.

'Mum, stop it. This is serious.'

It is. We're discussing the fact that Adam has turned into an actual zombie. We've entered our own dystopian future.

'How wide is your bed, Mum?'

I visualise getting the measuring tape from the tool box. That's never going to work.

'It's okay, I'll just google double beds. It is a double right?'

I can't help myself. I burst out laughing.

'Mum, what is it?'

I can't speak. My stomach aches and my eyes are watering. I lower my head into my hands.

'Mum, are you okay.'

'I'm sorry. I don't know why I'm laughing.'

And if they check my search engine now, chains and double bed measurements.

They. I'm imagining men in dark clothing holding guns.

'Just go with what's biggest,' I finally say. 'We can padlock the chains to fit.'

Sam shuts down the computer.

'Okay, let's go.'

Now? Right now?

'Okay, let's do this crazy thing,' I reply.

Our family catch phrase. Used whenever we go somewhere. The shops. The pool. The park.

B&Q

Just another family outing.

Maybe we should include Adam? Get him to pick out his own chains.

Jesus, I'm losing it.

Sam heads outside while I get my bag, my keys, my jacket. I stand at the front door, gather myself. Hear the scraping of fingernails on the back of our bedroom door.

66

'I'm sorry,' I whisper.

I don't take in any of the drive to B&Q. I'm on automatic pilot, pulling into the carpark before I even realise.

'Basket or trolley?' Sam asks at the entrance.

'A basket should be okay? Shouldn't it?'

Sam shrugs and lifts an orange basket from the pile. He extends the plastic handle and trundles it along behind him on its wheels.

It's always so dark in here. The shelves so high, blocking out the light. We're like mice in a maze. I try to work out which aisle we need. I can't get my brain to work.

'Where do you reckon the chains are kept?' Sam asks.

I feel like I'm drunk. Like those sunny afternoons in your twenties when you'd go drinking, then try and do normal things afterwards. Everything hazy. I'm glad Sam's here, even though I shouldn't have brought him.

Pink, furry handcuffs. Pink, furry handcuffs. Pink, furry handcuffs.

That was the last time I shopped while drunk. Buying those handcuffs in Ann Summers. Me and Adam. One of those rare occasions when he had a break from training and let himself go. The wonderfulness of afternoon drinking with the one you love.

'Can I help?' An old guy in an orange apron asks.

'Chains and padlocks?' I reply. ' For a bike.'

'Follow me,' he says.

Sam and I troop along behind him. He turns and smiles every so often, checking we're still there.

I couldn't work here. It's too claustrophobic. No daylight. It feels like everything could topple down on us at any moment.

'Here you are. What kind of bike have you got?' The man asks Sam.

'Eh, it's a hybrid.'

'Ahh, okay. These ones here are a bit more expensive but they're excellent quality. Harder to cut through. That's if Mum's prepared to pay a bit more.' He smiles at me.

'Great, thanks for your help. We'll just have a wee look around.' I say, hoping he'll leave us alone.

'If you have any questions, just ask.'

'No problem, thanks.' I pretend to study the chains. He hovers for a bit until he spots another lost B&Q soul and hurries off to help them instead.

Sam wanders up the aisle.

'I think this is the one we saw online,' he says, lifting a chain. 'It's heavy. I think it would probably hold.'

'Sam, shhh.'

I read the information on the shelf but it still means nothing to me. I take the chain from Sam, but he won't let go of it fully.

'It's heavy, Mum, you need to be careful.'

He's right. I feel the weight of it, even with both of us holding it. This should do it.

'Is this long enough?'

Sam checks his phone.

'Should be. Maybe we should get two. It might hold better if we chain the top and bottom of... the bike?'

I try to picture it.

My husband chained to the bed. Nothing pink or furry in sight. Heavy duty chains. One across his top half, one across his bottom half.

This is so fucked-up.

I nod.

'Yeah, let's get two.'

Everything's starting to blur. The shelves, the chains, the specifications.

The Marley and Marley song from *The Muppets Christmas Carol* pops into my head. When Sam was little, we started the Christmas Eve tradition of watching it before bed. We still watch it now, even though Sam claims he's too old for it. He can sing along with every song. Recite every line. I can hear his wee voice in my head from when he was little. Singing it to himself. Making up his own words because he didn't know the real ones.

I want to stay forever in that Christmas Eve magic.

I want my old life back.

I need to relax.

I need us to get out of here.

We both glance down at the basket.

'I'll go get a trolley instead,' Sam says.

I try to focus. It's like I've stepped off a boat but can still feel the waves.

I add up how much this is going to cost. Nothing like a bit of mental arithmetic to focus the mind.

Jesus, I'll need to use the credit card.

I wander up and down, trying to read the brand names. Maybe there's a cheaper own brand version we can use?

The guilt of that thought tips me. Do I really care how much this is going to cost?

Buying the best quality chains and padlocks is the least I can do for my husband.

I imagine Adam listening into this. He's somewhere between life and death right now, and I can't share any of this with him.

And I didn't even kiss him goodbye. I didn't kiss him on the lips. I kissed my fingertips instead. I didn't even kiss him goodbye.

My legs ache and I suddenly feel short of breath. I squat down on the floor. Stare at the grubby lino.

'Mum, are you okay?'

Sam is pushing the trolley towards me. Leaning on the handle. Riding those waves.

He abandons the trolley, lets it crash into the shelves.

'I'm just feeling a bit tired. And... a bit... sad.'

I shouldn't have said that to Sam.

'Me too.'

He turns his back on me and goes back to get the trolley. I know what's going on. Don't let Mum see you cry.

Not my little boy anymore.

Sam fills the trolley with chains and padlocks. He helps me up, takes my arm, and we walk towards the check-outs.

'Let's do self-service, okay?' I say.

I can't face having to make small talk with anyone.

I feel under scrutiny us as we scan the chains. I'm fearful I might blurt out the truth if someone asks what we're doing.

Sam pushes the trolley out to the car and we load everything in the boot. I watch the car sink with the weight of it all.

I turn the engine on. My bump pushes against the steering wheel and I have to adjust the seatbelt so it tucks in underneath. I won't be able to reach the pedals soon, the seat is pushed so far back.

I breathe in, out, in, out, in, out, as Sam takes the trolley back. Compose myself. I'm Mum and I'm okay. I'm Mum and I'm okay. I'm Mum and I'm okay.

Don't think about what we have to do next, just focus on getting us home.

The Story of How We Met by Alice Wilson.

Okay, so this is my side of the story of how we met. I suppose it all started that day I found you burning the newspaper cuttings in your garden. But I'd seen you before. Gran and I watched you move in. She recognised your dad, told me who he was. I know nothing about sport! I saw you a few times after that in the garden, on your swing, coming home from school, that sort of thing.

Gran said I should go and say hello, but it never really seemed like the right time.

Then that day arrived!

I was looking out the bedroom window and that's when I saw you come out with a shoebox. When you started setting fire to it, I had to see what was going on.

I didn't plan on speaking to you, so I crept out and hid behind the hedge. I thought you were a bit crazy to be honest, I wasn't sure I wanted to be friends with a twisted Firestarter!

Anyway, I hid behind the hedge so I could watch what you were doing. I still couldn't really work out what you were burning.

Did I really say I was psychic? What an idiot! If you want to know the truth, a couple of the charred cuttings floated over the hedge so I could see they were about your dad.

Then you totally freaked out because you thought the whole garden was going to go up in flames!

That's when I decided to try and stop you. Gran had been going on about how history is recorded and how the way that happens has changed. How everything is online, digitally archived; blogs instead of diaries, printed newspapers disappearing. It's okay while we can access it but what if it all disappears? What if there was some crazy zombie apocalypse and we lost electricity and access to the net. Would history just disappear? Should we back everything up on hard copy just in case? Future generations wouldn't be able to find out about their past or their family trees. Anyway, I tried to explain this to you, but I'm not sure I did a very good job of it as you didn't seem all that bothered.

I also knew you'd regret burning all that stuff. Even if you were mad at your dad, I'd seen you with him so I knew you loved him deep down. I could tell he was a good dad even if he had done something totally stupid.

I've never really told you about my own dad, but that's because he left when I was two, so I don't remember him. I've seen photos but that's it. I'm always curious about other people's dads, because I don't know anything about my own. Mum never talks about him and I don't like to ask in case it upsets her. Gran never mentions him either. It's like this weird family secret or something. Not that I'm all that bothered. If he didn't want to stay in touch, then I don't want to know him. But they act like he never existed. Like I'm the immaculate conception!

Anyway, this is meant to be the story of how we met, not the story of my life!

This is how I remember our first conversation going.

Me: Hi

You: Hmmmmmmppphhh (meant to be grumpy noise)

Me: I'm Alice

You: Why are you in the witch's house?

(You were very grumpy and rude!)

Me: She happens to be my granny and she's not a witch.

You: Silence (grumpy face)

Me: You shouldn't burn those stories. You'll regret it.

You: What do you know?

Me: You're destroying memories.

You: Silence (grumpy face)

Me: I know why you're doing it, but you'll just feel bad later

You: Shut up. It's nothing to do with you.

Me: I know. I'm just trying to help.

You: Silence (grumpy face)

Me: Silence too (no grumpy face though!)

You: Are you still here?

Me: This is my granny's garden. I can stay here as long as I like.

You: You don't know anything about me.

Me: I know who your dad is. He made a mistake. But you don't get that far without talent. That's what my granny said.

You: Silence (grumpy face)

This went on for a bit and then I went to get the hose. I'd totally forgotten about those friendship bracelets! We used to make them in school all the time.

Me: Here, take this.

You: You're as weird as your gran.

Me: For the black marks, dumbass.

You tried to scuff them away with your feet and just ended up getting your trainers all black.

Me: Just take it.

I pushed the hose through the hedge and eventually you took it, so I went and turned the tap on. Then I watched as you washed the path clean. I turned the tap off and came back to get the hose.

Me: A thank you would be nice.

You: Thank you (not in a voice that meant it!)

Me: See you later.

You: Yeah, whatever.

I went inside after that. Gran asked what I'd been doing so I told her I'd been speaking to you but that I didn't really like you.

She said you'd had a hard time of it and that whenever she'd spoken to you, you'd been really nice. She said that boys can be a bit shy and awkward and that you'd probably be a bit defensive after all that had happened with your dad. That made me feel guilty, so I decided to say sorry. And that was my very first letter to you!

Imagine if Gran had told me just to ignore you. We might never have become friends. This whole story would have ended right on the first page. Instead it continues and continues, chapters and chapters, for as long as we remain friends (so forever, dumbass!)

I left the letter outside for you and then I waited at the kitchen window until you went back out into the garden again. At first I thought you hadn't seen it, but then you spotted it and took it inside. Then you took sooooo looong to reply, I thought you were going to ignore me. I decided you were rude after all. But as it turned out, you weren't rude and you did reply! Yay!

And that is the true story of how we met and became friends forever!

Xxxx

P.S. The end

P.P.S. Of the story, not our friendship!!

xxxxxx

Sam

I glance over at Mum. Try not to make it look like I'm staring at her. She was starting to freak out a bit in B&Q and it scared me. She seems better now, not as uptight.

She turns the radio up.

'...*Science and Security Board have announced that the Dooms-day Clock is now sitting at two minutes to midnight. The closest it's been to midnight since the cold war in 1953. Is the end of the world nigh? Let us know what you think...*'

We've certainly moved closer to midnight the last couple of days. I didn't realise the whole world had too.

'*We've got Bill from Cumbernauld up next. Bill, do you agree with what our previous caller had to say?*'

'*Not at all. We need to do more to improve security in this country. We should be installing more CCTV cameras, monitoring phone calls, internet use.*'

'*But isn't that a violation of human rights?*'

'*Nonsense. We keep pandering to these so-called human-rights. If you've nothing to hide, it shouldn't worry you.*'

'We were sure our phone line was tapped when I was a student.'

I didn't realise Mum was listening so closely.

'How come? Could you hear people listening in?'

'No, there were strange clicking noises and it would go all echoey.'

'What did you do?'

'My flatmate tried to take the phone apart one night.'

'Did you find anything?'

'No, I don't even think she managed to get into it.'

'*There's one man to blame and that's the complete idiot sitting in the White House. The man's a moron and that's putting it nicely.*'

'*Remember you're on the radio, Angus.*'

'Who do you think it was?'

'I don't know. We lived in a privately rented flat, down in Dumb-iedykes, so it was probably for a previous tenant. They wouldn't have heard anything interesting from us.'

'...heard from Angus earlier on and he wasn't holding back. Do you agree with him, Louise?'

'Oh, most definitely. It's not just him though. The majority of politicians are power hungry egocentrics who only care about themselves and their own agenda. Look at the complete and utter mess that Brexit is.'

'Surely, they're not all like that.'

'Well, I do like Nicola. The sooner we get independence the better.'

'Okay, Louise. Let's not get into the independence debate right now, we've had numerous phone-ins about that already and I'm sure we will again...'

'I used to let them know I knew though.'

'What?'

'The people tapping our phone.'

'How come?'

'I'd say stupid things down the line to them: I know you're listening, that sort of thing.'

It's weird to think of Mum back then. I've seen photos of her and Dad from before I was born, but trying to imagine her having a life without me. I can't do it. A whole different Mum from the one that I know.

Sometimes I wish I could go back there and watch her and Dad, see what they were like. Spy on them, like watching through the Pensieve in *Harry Potter*.

'Next on the line, we've got Stevie from Blairgowrie. Stevie, what's your take on it?'

'The single most dangerous thing affecting the planet right now is climate change and the sooner we agree on that and try to do something about it, the better. It's time to start taking it seriously.'

Mum reverses into the driveway.

'Whoa, you're awful close to the house.'

'When did you become the driving expert? I'm fine. Let's just get these inside before anyone sees us,' she says, glancing around.

'Okay,' I reply, although I doubt anyone is going to pay us much attention.

Maybe the neighbours already know anyway? I still haven't had a reply from Alice since I sent that email and I'm starting to dread what she's going to say. Mum's going to go mental if she finds out.

Mum opens the front door and I lug the chains out of the boot and dump them in the hallway outside their bedroom. We both stand and look at them.

Dad's up and about as always.

'Let's have something to eat and work out the best way to do this.' Mum says.

'I thought we knew what we were going to do.'

'Yeah, we know the whats, but what about the hows? He's not just going to lie on the bed and let us strap him down?'

I follow Mum into the kitchen. She shuts the door. I've noticed she's started doing this recently. Whichever room she goes into, she closes the door behind her.

Mum puts the radio on. Trying to drown out the noise he's making. The phone-in is still going on.

'...to recap we're discussing the announcement that the Dooms-day Clock is now sitting closer to midnight than ever before. Can we stop it? Or do we just wait until midnight strikes and Armageddon hits. Stevie had the novel idea of putting David

Attenborough in charge of everything. Kirsty from Lochgelly, what do you think?'

'I've been reading about these cyber attack things and it's got me very worried. We rely too much on technology. Everything's on the computer. One attack could bring down the NHS, *the government, our electricity. I mean, what would we do? We'd never cope. Look at that snow. People running out of bread and milk. I make my own bread, but young people don't know how to do that...'*

'What do you fancy? Cheese toastie?'

'I'm fine with just a sandwich,' I say.

'Nah, let's have a toastie. I'm in the mood for one.'

'Don't let me get in the way of a pregnant lady and her cravings.'

It's a diversionary tactic. Toasties will take longer. She'll make us wait until she cleans the machine afterwards. Delaying the inevitable.

I sit at the breakfast bar, watch as she spreads the bread with butter. Both sides, front and back. I've never understood why you have to do that for a toastie but, according to Mum, you do. She slices the cheese, peels the bread from the counter where it's stuck, waits for the red light to turn green before she loads in the sandwiches. I'm sure she normally just shoves them in regardless of the red light, but I can't be sure.

'...load of nonsense. It's phone-ins like this causing all the trouble. The Doomsday Clock is actually accelerating the possibility of Armageddon as it provokes all these knee-jerk reactions, shock headlines in the tabloid newspapers, people panicking. It all contributes to the already fragile situation...'

'So, you do agree we're living in a fragile situation?'

'Well, yes, of course, but...'

Mum squeezes the lid of the toastie maker down, squashing the bread until she can clip it closed. While we're waiting, she pours us both a glass of milk. The cheese sizzles and melts, drips out the side of the machine and onto the counter.

Mum opens the toastie maker. Closes it. Waits a few minutes. Opens it. Closes it again.

'They look okay, Mum.'

'I'll just give them a couple more minutes.'

Eventually she turns off the machine at the wall, scrapes the toasties out with a knife and brings them over to the breakfast bar. The cheese on the outside is crusty and yellow, I pick at it while I wait for the inside to cool down enough to eat.

'...*Lynn in Peterhead. Lynn, what do you think of Jimmy and his view that God has a divine plan that we cannot interfere with? That a Day of Judgement is something we can't hide from.*'

'*I don't know where you dug him up from. Religion is one of the main reasons why we're in such a mess, people fighting over a load of old hocus pocus...*'

Mum takes a drink of milk, then grabs my hand, presses it against her belly.

'Can you feel that? I think the cold milk woke her up.'

I shake my head.

She presses my hand deeper.

Then I feel it, a twitch, then another.

'I hadn't felt her at all today, I was starting to get worried,' Mum says, rubbing her belly.

She lets go of me and I take a bite of my sandwich. The cheese is stringy; it trails down my chin and burns my lips.

'*Is there anything we can do? Can we turn back time?*'

'*At the end of the day, the human race is just a type of animal. And, like all animals, we'll eventually go extinct. Look at the dinosaurs. They didn't have any of this nonsense about terrorism and climate change to deal with and they still went extinct. It's just what happens.'*

'That's quite a bleak point of view.'

'I'm just telling it like it is.'

There's a bang from the bedroom. Loud. Loud enough to be heard above the radio. Mum doesn't acknowledge it.

'...always down to Russia and America. They're the common denominators in all this...'

There's another bang against the bedroom door.

'How do you want to do this?' Mum says.

'We need to get in there so we have to make sure he's away from the door,' she continues.

'One of us could go outside and bang on the window?'

I've been watching zombie clips on YouTube. People bang on fences, make noise, light a fire; all to attract the zombie's attention, lure them away.

'Okay, that sounds a good idea.'

Once we're in, I have no idea what to do. Winging it seems the best option.

If Dad really is a zombie, then I guess we could just knock him over. I watched a *Making of The Walking Dead* and they said that, one on one, a human should always win an encounter with a zombie. Zombies are too slow, too focussed on one thing, too clumsy.

'We have to try and get him onto the bed. Maybe push him over?' Mum suggests.

'Yeah,' I reply.

'You go and knock on the window, okay?'

'Why me? I'm stronger than you. What about the baby?'

'You're knocking on the window, Sam.'

'But, Mum...'

'...this is not a negotiation, Sam,' she interrupts me, 'you're knocking on the window.'

We finish our toasties in silence. The melted cheese leaves fatty puddles on our plates. Mum puts the plates in the dishwasher, then starts to wipe down the toastie maker with kitchen roll.

I feel a bit sick.

'You need to be careful, Mum,' I say.

'I know. Right, come on.' Mum stands in front of me, 'let's get this over with.'

We sit in the hallway and unlock the padlocks, loop them onto a link in the chain. All we have to do is get the chains round him while he's lying on the bed.

All.

Like it's nothing. A piece of piss.

Dad's bumping himself against the door, like a wind-up toy that can't change direction.

'We need to do this,' Mum says. 'We need to secure him. For his sake.'

'I know.'

'You need to be prepared, Sam. He might look... or act... it's not your dad.'

It's easier to do this if he behaves like a monster.

Mum runs a hand up and down the door.

'This door isn't strong. If we don't do this soon, he'll break it down.'

'Mum, I still think you should knock on the window.'

'Sam, I told you.'

'I don't think you should go in there at all. I can get help. Ask Alice?'

'Sam, you haven't told her, have you?'

'No, but I'm sure…'

'You can't tell anyone. Promise me.'

'Okay.'

'Promise me.'

'I promise,' I say.

Does a promise count if I've already broken it?

'If anyone found out, they'd take Dad away, God knows what they'd do to him. They might take us away for testing too. They could hurt the baby.'

'Testing for what?'

'This isn't an everyday illness, Sam.'

'I know, but they might help him?'

'Sam, we need to be together on this. If you don't want to do this, just tell me. We're in it together, okay?'

'We can't leave him chained up forever, Mum.'

'I know. But let's just deal with this one day at a time, okay?'

'Okay. Let's do this crazy thing.'

Our family motto, spoken for the second time today.

Mum's right. What happens next is too hard to think about, it's best to ignore it right now.

'We both know what we're doing then? You go outside and knock on the window.'

There's no point arguing.

'I won't go in until I'm completely sure it's okay.'

'And leave the chains till I get back, they're too heavy for you.'

'I will.'

'Promise me, Mum.'

'Yes.'

Neither one of us is being entirely honest today.

I head through the kitchen, unlock the back door. Something stops me. I turn back and go to the cutlery drawer, take out a sharp knife. I hold it for a moment, but can't bring myself to imagine the act of using it. I don't think I could, even if I had to. I slip it back into the cutlery drawer.

Out in the back garden, I start to tap on the window.

Nothing happens, so I knock, harder, harder, harder.

I jump back from the window, as something suddenly moves behind the curtains. There's a moments grace, before one whole curtain is torn down and Dad's there under it, flailing around like some terrible Halloween ghost.

My heart's thumping.

He walks into the window then stumbles backwards. I peer in. The first time I've seen inside the bedroom since it happened. What a fucking mess.

Dad's hitting himself against the double glazing. It's like we're playing a game of monsters peekaboo. I will him to throw off the curtain and grin at me. Nothing wrong. It was all just a game. Instead he's angry and confused, unable to free himself. Like a trapped wasp.

A flash of movement from the other side of the room and I realise Mum's in there. The curtain monster thrashes and turns.

Fuck. I realise where I am and run back inside the house. Mum's trying to drag the chains with her, but I take them off her and pull them into the room myself.

The smell hits me as I enter. I gag then try to hold my breath against the funk of it. I can tell by Mum's face that she's doing the same. The curtains reel and twirl, like some strange country dancer. He stumbles towards us, sensing us close.

'Quick, now, while he's trapped,' Mum says. 'Watch out for the glass on the floor.'

I give him one massive shove in the chest so he falls backwards onto the bed. Then I climb on top of him and try to pin him down with my knees and hands, hoping his teeth aren't close. He's soft underneath me and his skin slips and moves as if it's not attached to anything anymore.

'Sam, careful,' Mum's got one of the chains and she tries to lift it onto the bed. It's heavy though and takes her a couple of shots. Dad's rolling and bucking, it's all I can do to stay on top.

'Too much crap,' Mum gasps.

She drags stuff out from under the bed, shoeboxes, CDs, books. At last she disappears underneath, the chain slinking behind her.

'I'm stuck,' I hear her shout, 'the bump.'

I feel the mattress push from below me as she wiggles about.

'Mum, be careful.'

She emerges, dusty, her hair dishevelled; rushes to the other side of the bed and pulls the chain through.

'That wasn't easy.'

She's out of breath.

'Mum, quick.'

I'm slipping, Dad's too strong for me. I lose my grip and he throws me off. I fall onto the mattress next to him. One arm works itself free and he starts to grab at me.

'Mum, Mum,' I shout and then she's next to me, hitting at the outstretched arm with a high heeled shoe. Dad's nails are brittle, yellow and curling like old-lady toenails. I jump back on top of him and bear down with as much weight as possible. Mum reaches for the other end of the chain, pulls it tight over him and clicks the padlock shut.

I roll off the bed, hit the pile of boxes and shoes and lie there out of breath.

He's trapped now and it drives him mad. I can hear his teeth snapping.

'You okay?' Mum asks.

'Yes.'

'Okay, we still have one to go.'

We work the other chain around him then under the bed, lock it tight. There's one across his chest now and one across his thighs. He's still struggling but the chains seem to hold.

I sneeze at the dust that's visible around us.

I have to keep telling myself that this is real. Dad is a zombie, a zombie that we have chained to the bed. I'm having a weird out-of-body experience. It's like I'm in a computer game. The situation feels so unreal, it has to be a simulation.

We stand together, out of breath. I realise Mum's crying.

'It's okay, we've done it.' I say.

She reaches for the curtains.

I tug her back.

'I just want... he won't be able to brea... it's not fair to keep his face covered like that.'

I don't think she should. I open my mouth to say the words, but something stops me.

I know what Mum means. It's Dad after all. It feels cruel to do this to him. The least we can do is uncover his face. But the curtains might calm him down, act like blinkers.

And there's the other reason. I'm terrified to see what his face looks like. What he's become.

'Okay, I'll do it,' I say.

I lean over the bed and try to get hold of an edge of the curtain, but he's moving so much, I can't. I reach out, pull back, reach out, pull back, reach out, pull back, before I can finally uncover him.

He snaps at me, teeth biting the air.

I can't believe the change in him, in just a few days.

Bulging eyes and a swollen tongue which protrudes from his mouth. His face is bloated and the skin is marbled and covered with blisters. Some of the sores have burst leaving a sheen. He bites down and his teeth crack together.

He stinks too, it makes me heave.

'Sam, come on, get out of here.'

I can't take my eyes off his. The frenzy in them. The deadness. He's looking at me but he doesn't see me.

'Sam, Sam.' Mum grabs me and pulls me out of the room.

Her face is white, like she's about to throw up. She pulls the bedroom door shut and we stand there in the hall, listening to his teeth bite, bite, bite on the other side. The bed creaks under him as he writhes about beneath the chains.

'Mum, I didn't, I didn't really…' I can't get the words out.

'I know, I know.'

She doesn't though. She doesn't know what I'm trying to say.

I kept saying the word: zombie. Zombie, zombie, zombie. I looked up videos on YouTube. But somewhere deep down, a voice kept telling me not to be so daft. That voice is silent now.

Zombie. That's the only word for what Dad is right now.

A monster that you tell yourself doesn't exist. A monster, like a vampire or a werewolf, that blurs the line between horror and real-life; between human and creature.

Mum's hand grips my shoulder, and I realise she's shaking. She's squeezing me, trying to make the shaking stop. I feel the juddering pass from her and ripple through me.

'Mum, are you okay?'

She shakes her head, then puts a hand over her mouth and runs into the bathroom. I hear her puking. I picture that yellow, congealed toastie cheese coming back up. Fatty oil collecting on the surface of the water in the toilet.

I hear her spit, then the tap goes as she rinses her mouth out.

She emerges from the bathroom. She looks old. I've never thought of Mum as being old before.

This is the first time I've noticed it. The lines that gutter around her eyes and mouth. The grey hair. She's stopped having it coloured since she got pregnant.

It scares me more than anything. The realisation that she's decaying too. Not at the same rate as Dad, but it's happening. One day she won't be here.

'I need to lie down for a bit,' she says and shuffles into the living room where she collapses onto the sofa.

I stand in the hall. I can smell Dad on me, the stench of him, mixed in with the puke from the bathroom. I want to shower, wash everything off, but I go out into the garden instead. Inhale the fresh air, breathe in, out, in, out, in, out.

I look at the bedroom window with the curtains missing. The glass is all steamed up. I go back into the house and get an old sheet from the airing cupboard and a box of drawing pins.

I brace myself for the smell as I head back into the bedroom. stand on a chair and pin up the sheet over the exposed panes. Just in case someone decides to come snooping.

Dad's still snarling and biting, his eyes on me the whole time, his neck bulging as he stretches towards me.

What a fucking mess. Shredded bedclothes. Scratch marks raked down the back of the door. The photo of the three of us at North Berwick, that Mum had on her bedside table, torn into pieces. The table lamp upended, bulb broken and lampshade ripped. Mirrored wardrobe smashed, glass everywhere.

I step down from the chair and start to gather up some of the shards of mirror. I hold them carefully, the edges sharp and ready to slice. I try not to look at my reflection, remembering something Alice's gran said about it being bad luck to see yourself in a broken mirror.

Fuck it. What could be worse than what's already happening to us?

I look at myself in one of the bigger shards. The cracks radiate across the glass and split my face into segments. I don't join up anymore. I'm distorted. The pieces of my face are misaligned and out of sync.

I wonder if Dad still has a reflection. Did he shatter the mirror just by looking at it with his monstrous face, or is he like Dracula, his reflection disappeared? I walk over to him and hold the mirror above him. He's still hissing and biting at me. I can't get the angle right though and I don't want to cut myself.

Then another thought takes hold as I hold the shard of glass above his head. It would be so easy just to... just to...

No. I turn away from him. Carry the pieces of mirror outside and dump them in the glass bin.

As I come back in, on the way to my room, I notice the key still in the door to Mum and Dad's bedroom. I guess we don't need that now. I walk over to it and place my hand on it when a groaning noise from inside stops me. I leave the key where it is and turn it to lock the door.

Hi Alice,

Thanks for your letter. You were a bit annoying, but that's okay. I was in a bad mood so I probably found you more annoying than you actually were.

Yes, we can be pen pals if you like, although it seems a bit pointless when your gran lives next door and we can actually just talk to each other.

It might be fun though anyway.

Sam.

P.S. Sorry if the paper is a bit messy, my hands are still covered in soot.

Jude

I stand outside our bedroom. I can hear him in there. The chains, the snarling, the moaning. He goes quiet sometimes, but he never really stops. Always awake. Never at peace.

If he were a dog or a horse, we'd put him out of his misery. But he's not. He's my husband and he's Sam's dad and he's...

Well, we don't know what he is right now, but it's too early to consider euthanasia.

I can hear his jaw working, biting down on air, teeth grinding together. It reminds me of when Sam was teething. Anything that came near his mouth, he would ram in there and try to chew. Spoons, bottles, fingers. And nothing ever satisfied him, nothing. He would get so frustrated and upset that he'd end up screaming the place down.

Zombie baby. Shit, I'd forgotten about that. For a few months, Adam and I referred to him as the zombie baby. The way he would burrow his face towards you, his wee gums bite, bite, biting. If you put a finger in his mouth, he'd clamp down on it, gnaw on you. It was fine when it was just his gums but, when he started to get teeth, it could be really painful. The white points rooting from underneath. He could pierce the skin, leave you bleeding.

Zombie baby.

Zombie.

I miss Adam. I fucking miss him. The pain can't be articulated, it's just noise that comes out of me. I can't think of a future without him. I got used to him going away for training camps and competitions, though I never liked it. That was nothing like this though. We could still speak to each other. I knew he was thinking of me wherever he was. I can't accept this is it, for good. That we've lost him. It's only in the last year or so that I've felt like we finally got the real Adam back.

I mean he's right there, on the other side of the door. Except he's not. It's not Adam. What's happened to him? Why is this happening to us?

I wouldn't even care if he stayed like that, the eyes, the teeth, the skin. I don't care what he looks like, or what he smells like. If I could just get him back, the essence of him. If I could just have a conversation with him.

I don't understand any of this.

I've gone over it again and again. When I found him, he was dead. I'm sure he was.

I've been so close to phoning someone: a doctor, an ambulance. But something's always stopped me. He'd be taken from us, tested, cut open probably. Then they'd want to test us too. The woman he slept with, his son, his unborn baby...

I won't let them harm Sam or our baby.

And now we're in so deep I can't see a way out.

He's dangerous. That's what makes me so sure he's not there anymore. My Adam, our Adam.

If we tell anyone the papers will find out. It will be like before, only worse.

I only just held it together last time.

Mark Rogers. I'm sure I saw him yesterday. On the corner of the street as I pulled into the drive.

I don't know what's real anymore.

I'm Adam's wife and I'm thinking it: wondering if the stuff he took made this happen. If it's some horrible, delayed side-effect. If I can think it, then it won't take much for someone to print it. We'll be hounded again.

People will be scared of him. Hell, I'm scared of him. I love him but, the way he is right now, he's terrifying.

The living dead are the stuff of horror films. But this is real horror. And there's nothing I can do to stop it.

I lean my cheek against our bedroom door. Can he sense I'm here? I hear a raspy gurgling in his throat. Heavy, excited, like he's aroused, desperate to get at me. A primal noise from deep inside him, a sound he never made, not when he was training, pushing himself to the limit or when he was in pain, or when we had sex. It's nothing like the guttural, animal sounds I made myself in labour. Noises I didn't even realise I could make.

He just wants to get close so he can bite me. And it's not even me that turns him on anymore. It's anyone. Any scent of skin. I'm not a significant other. I'm food. Sam's not his son, he's food. The man who held a facecloth on my forehead as I pushed out our firstborn, the man who cried at *The Lion King*, the man who cut a smiley face into Sam's toast every morning for five years because that's all we could get him to eat for breakfast, now wants to sink his teeth into us.

We have to sneak around our own home trying not to make too much noise in case we rile him up. And here's me, waiting until Sam's at school, just to sneak a moment with Adam. A closed door between us.

The baby kicks and I rub my tummy. Almost like she knows; reminding me I need to be careful.

'Don't worry,' I whisper. 'I won't let anything harm you.'

I turn the key.

He's hyperaware of any noise, any movement. I should leave him alone.

I realise I'm gripping the door handle. I let go and can still feel it throbbing in my palm.

I push the door open.

Every time I do this I regret it. When I see how much he's changed, how he's deteriorating. But I can't fight the urge to be close to him. To check on him. There's always that glimmer of hope that maybe...

I step inside the room. The movement, the light from the hallway, whatever it is, sends him crazy.

I brace myself for the smell, pull my top up over my nose and mouth, gag anyway. No matter how much I prepare myself, my body's natural responses take over.

The smell's getting worse. Nothing masks it.

I hear a buzzing. Jesus, there are flies in here. They crawl on his face. It makes my stomach lurch.

How do they even find him? How do they know he's here? Especially at this time of the year.

We keep him hidden.

Our secret.

Our skeleton in the closet. Everyone has one.

If we leave him here, is that what will happen to him?

Will he rot away until he's a skeleton we can hide in the cupboard?

Then we could see him in his most basic form. The shape of his skull. His jawline. The crack in his fibula from where he broke his leg when he was a kid.

Christ. I don't think I can bear that.

He keeps changing. His colour. His shape. He's green now, grey in patches, like a piece of marble. He's expanded too, bloated and swollen.

'Adam, it's me, Jude.' I whisper.

I spot his phone lying among the mess, pick it up and put it in the back pocket of my maternity jeans. The Lycra waistband suffocates my stomach. I can feel the sweat prickle all the way up to my boobs.

I reach out to touch him and feel his skin slip underneath me. I pull my hand away again.

'Adam, I miss you so, so much.'

I feel my throat constrict and fight back the urge to cry.

Adam's jeans and an old NIKE t-shirt lie on the floor. The ones he threw off before putting on his pyjamas and getting into bed. I pick up the t-shirt, sink my face into it, but his smell has gone. His actual smell. Everything in here smells of rotting flesh now.

He always smelt so good. Even after he'd been training or in the gym, dripping with sweat. It turned me on.

How did it become this putrid?

This is what we are. Cells in decay and musky degradation. We're not clean or minty or lemon fresh. That just masks the real us. The organic, biological processes that we don't want to be reminded of.

I pull Adam's t-shirt over my head and slip it down so it clings over the bump. This t-shirt that once held his warmth. His body.

They always do this in films; clutch an old t-shirt, breathe it in before breaking down. It's never some crazed woman, crying so much she can't see, snot running into her mouth. The husband isn't chained to the bed and the room doesn't smell like this.

I lift his jeans, slip my hands in his pockets. A few coins, a tissue, an old receipt, a half-eaten pack of chewing gum.

Nothing out of the ordinary. Nothing to tell me what happened. What did I expect? An empty bottle with a skull and crossbones on the side?

I walk to the head of the bed, swat away flies. Adam's head snaps towards me. His fingernails are ragged from clawing the bed-sheets. The sheets we marked with our sweat, our sex and now the juices rotting out of him.

Maybe if I stroked his hair it would help?

'Don't you recognise me at all.'

His jaw works up and down, up and down, up and down. Part of his top lip is missing and I can see his teeth, his receding gums.

His skeleton already starting to reveal itself.

'Adam.' I finger his hair. It's slick, unwashed.

He worries his head like a dog with a rag. He's so aggressive. I remember those first few months when we first started seeing each other. The way he would bound around me like an over-excited puppy.

I keep my hand just out of biting distance.

I doubt he'd let go if he got hold of me.

Biting distance.

Something Sam said. I'm not even sure I believe it, but I don't want to risk anything.

Would we really turn out like him if he bit us? Is that how it spreads or is that just the stuff of comic books?

Is that how it happened to him in the first place? You'd think he would have mentioned being bitten.

It's not like I can check for teeth marks now.

His teeth look pretty rotten. A couple have fallen out. If nothing else, we'd get a nasty infection.

Do I believe in these zombie rules? The rules of a fictional world.

It's all too real though. All too fucking real.

I reach out a hand again. His teeth gnash, gnash, gnash, his groans get louder and louder and louder.

'Adam, I miss you, I want you back.'

He bites down so hard that his crown falls out, rolls down his chin and bounces off the bed.

I kneel down, pick up the tooth and place a hand on the bed to help myself up to standing again. The covers are wet. I cradle the tooth in the palm of my hand. The way I handled Sam's first baby tooth when it fell out. I still have it in an envelope in my jewellery box. Bits of body which have dropped off, but so precious to me. I don't think you can buy a special keepsake box for your husband's false tooth.

I stand at the end of the bed. Try to touch his feet. He kicks me away though, his overlong toenails, yellow and brittle. I read once that nails don't keep growing after death, it's just that the skin retracts so they look longer.

But he's not dead, is he? I just don't know.

He's moving. The bed is shaking with the effort he's putting in. How can he move if he's dead?

'Stop it, stop it. Adam, stop it.'

I just want him to lie still. To let me touch him. Let me help him.

I miss how we'd lie in the dark, arms, legs, feet touching, talking as we drifted into sleep. The warmth, the safety of it.

'Adam, please.'

I grip his ankles but he's moving too much and his skin's soft. I can't hold on. My fingers sink like he's an overripe pear and I drop the tooth. I scrabble about for it. Where did it go? I can't believe I've lost it. I wanted to keep it. I wanted to keep it safe.

It's so cloying in here. And he won't stop trying to bite me.

'What's wrong with you? Why are you doing this?'

The smell of him. Oh God, the smell of him. I run from the room, slam the door. Get to the thermostat in the hall and turn off the heating. Try to stop the rotting. I keep going, out the back door, down the path until I reach the bottom of the garden. Breathe in the fresh air, breathe, breathe, breathe.

'I'm sorry, I'm sorry,' I whisper as I lean against the hedge.

It's not his fault. Not his fault. Not his fault.

My clothes stick to me with my own sweat. That Lycra waist-band, so stretchy and giving but the most uncomfortable thing I've ever worn. I'm still wearing his t-shirt. My hands are sticky. I hold my fingers under my nose, I can smell him on me. I hate myself for thinking it, but it's disgusting. I'm disgusted by the smell, the sight of him. I promised. In sickness and in health. In sickness and in health. But what kind of sickness is this?

I head back into the kitchen and scrub my hands until they're red. I sit down at the breakfast bar, feel something uncomfortable in my back pocket.

His phone. Adam's mobile phone.

I slip it out of my pocket, stare at my reflection in the dark screen.

Press the button on the front.

4% battery power left.

I know his passcode. After all those years of secrets, we made a pact to keep nothing from each other, not even a pin number. The home screen is a photo of me and Sam; nothing special, just sitting next to each other on the sofa.

I bring up his messages.

There it is. The last text conversation I'll ever have with my husband. Staring back at me in light blue speech bubbles.

The banality and the intimacy of it makes me ache. When he typed these words, he was my living and breathing Adam.

On my way home. See you soon. Xxxxxx

Don't forget the milk. This baby is driving me mad with indiges-tion! Xxxx

Okay! This baby is going to come out hairier than a gorilla! Xxxx

Thanks! Be safe, see you soon. xxxx

I scroll through his other texts.

Sam.

Have you got your house key? Xx

Yes but I forgot my PE *kit*

It's on your bed. When do you need it? I could drop it off at the school? Xx

This afternoon

Okay, I'll get it there by lunchtime. Be more organised! xx

Then a few from his friends, his agent, his clients.

Can we meet for lunch next week? A few things to run by you.

Meet you at the gym at 9am.

Check your emails, Adam. Sent you a couple of things that need answers asap.

Nothing about feeling unwell. About being bitten by some rabid monster. Nothing to suggest what was going to happen.

I wish I didn't have his mobile. I wish I hadn't found it. I want to be able to text him and have the messages go somewhere unknown. A place hidden from me. Somewhere I can pretend he's reading them.

I drop the phone as it starts to ring.

It buzzes on the lino for a few moments and I can't bend down fast enough to pick it up and see who's calling before it runs out of battery and goes dead.

I clamber off the stool and pick it up. Turn it over in my hand.

The screen's splintered like a spider web. Fuck. I've lost his tooth and now I've broken his phone

I sit back down and turn the phone over so I don't have to look at the damage I've caused.

Where's his charger? It might be in the bedroom somewhere or in one of his bags. The phone went off before I was ready. I'm not ready to do this. Shut him down. Turn him off. Acknowledge the end of him by letting him go. This is what happens nowadays. So many things need closed down. Facebook, Twitter, mobile phone, emails. All these things we leave behind.

How do you even go about shutting down someone's Facebook? Do you need to provide a death certificate or do they just take your word for it?

I take out my own phone. Open the Facebook App and click on Help Centre.

How to report a deceased person or arrange for a Facebook account to be memorialised.

FAQS.

Memorialised accounts are a place for Friends and Family to gather and share memories or pass on their respects. Key features include – The phrase 'In Remembrance' will be shown next to the account holder's name.

Jesus, I don't read any further. I get that people need a place to share their grief, but this is just too much. Do we really want to be immortalised on Facebook of all places?

Can't believe it's been a whole year. Miss you hun xxxx

Happy birthday. I know you'll be partying up there with John and Aunty Norma xxxx

Since the day you got your wings, life has never been the same xxxx

Spelling mistakes, emojis and those godawful social media philosophical phrases.

If you keep chasing yesterday, you're going to miss tomorrow.

Everybody wants happiness, nobody wants pain, but you can't have a rainbow, without a little rain.

Life isn't about finding yourself. Life is about creating yourself.

I shut Facebook down. What about when your loved one is living dead?

I guess they don't have an FAQ for that.

Some people post their whole lives on Facebook but that's not for me. Maybe I'm just too old for it.

Just chained my husband to the bed as he's trying to eat me and Sam, lol!

I'm starting to sound like Sam and Alice. We're all creating this huge digital footprint for ourselves. What happens when technology lets us down? Do we disappear altogether, along with our online tributes?

I read the last text conversation with Adam again. This time from my phone.

Don't forget the milk. This baby is driving me mad with indigestion! Xxxx

Okay! This baby is going to come out hairier than a gorilla! Xxxx

I close it down again. It hurts too much looking at it. Thinking of me in that moment. Oblivious to the future. I wish I could be that me again.

I can hear his voice in my head. A voice that over time will fade. His face, his voice; they'll both disappear from my subconscious. Even if I don't want them to. I won't be able to stop it. We like to think we're in control but our bodies dictate everything.

On my way home. See you soon. Xxxxx

Our last text conversation. But what was our last actual conversation. Words we spoke to each other, face to face. I can barely remember.

I think I'd mentioned the milk again. Asked him to pick some up on the way home.

And he had. He'd remembered to get it.

Our last conversation was me nagging him to get milk. Milk which he never even got to drink himself.

A sob starts in the back of my throat and I swallow it down, feel it catching on every ridge on the way back to my stomach.

So much left unsaid. Half-finished stories, half-listened to conversations, all those unanswered questions. I should have paid more attention. Put the fucking mobile down and actually listened to what he was saying, even if it was just something totally banal.

All the stuff I put off. The things I'll ask him later. In the morning. When we're old and have more time to ourselves.

Not just the stupid, mundane questions, like where he put the superglue, or how to work the radio in the bathroom. All the other stuff too. The big stuff, the important stuff. The stories he's told me time and time again but I always forget so make him repeat. The ones about his childhood, about how he got that scar on his back, about when I had Sam and he came home and got the house ready for us, about the training camp he went on to South Africa.

So much of what I am disappears with him.

We can piece together parts of his life, Sam and I, but the true, definitive story is lost now. He's the only one who can tell that.

At Adam's dad's funeral, I remember the minister saying that those of us in attendance all shared a different part of his life. That collectively we could keep him alive as we were all there at different points and could remember different things. Together we could tell his story. I remember taking comfort from that at the time. But now, now it just feels like bullshit. The only person who can tell our true story is us. And when we go, it goes with us.

Adam's true story died with him.

But he's not dead. He's not fucking dead. Not as we recognise death to be. He's not lying still with his eyes closed. He's moving and making noises and... I don't know what the fuck he is right now.

And maybe we have it too, Sam and I. Maybe it's nothing to do with being bitten. That's just TV and horror stories. We could be breathing it in from the air he breathed out. Picking up his germs from door handles, from wearing this t-shirt. Contagion on our hands, face, lips.

What is it?

Something new. Maybe they'll name It after him?

Adam's Disease.

Or maybe he's not the first known case? Maybe it's already being covered up? Sam and I will vanish, or be shot in our beds to hide the trail.

I shake my head. Fuck sake, Jude. I know it's a dark road you're on right now, but let's not go any darker.

I lift the t-shirt over my head, keep it there. I start to get claustrophobic. The air is stale. I can't breathe properly. I don't allow myself to escape though. I stay inside. Imagine his touch. The arms inside these sleeves. The warm chest, breathing in and out, in and out, in and out, filling the space. Giving the t-shirt shape. His shape.

Fall From Grace by Adam Redpath

It wasn't easy. I had to hide it from Jude and Sam. Not only the actual administering of it – injecting myself in the stomach, rubbing creams into my forearms, swallowing tablets, putting drops under my tongue – but also the cost. It's not cheap being on one of those programmes. They don't just give away that stuff for free.

I made up all kinds of stories. I'm not proud of the way I lied to my family. Locking myself in the bathroom to inject. Hiding the drugs at the back of my wardrobe. Pretending I was taking supplements, vitamins, herbal remedies. I even set up a secret bank account in order to finance it all.

I was on a very strict calendar and a multitude of different drugs. I had to follow it completely and not allow myself to miss anything or take the wrong thing on the wrong day. It was incredibly stressful and that, combined with the many side-effects of the drugs, made me aggressive and bad-tempered. I suffered from headaches, stomach cramps, paranoia, and my family bore the brunt of that.

Sam walked in on me one day; I'd forgotten to lock the bathroom door. I panicked and lost control and pushed him out of the way so he wouldn't see anything. He fell and started crying. I was so ashamed of myself that I shouted at him. I can still see his confused face as he ran from me. That was one of my lowest points, my own son scared of me like that. Me, unable to control my temper. I was a different person on that stuff, it changed me. At the time I didn't realise. It's only looking back that I see how badly it affected my personality.

Sam

Alice's gran opens the front door.

'Hi Sam, you know where she is,' she says, as she lets me in.

No matter how often I'm at Alice's gran's house, it always feels weird. Her bungalow is pretty much the exact same as ours but flipped round the other way. I always imagine our houses like one of those butterfly paintings you'd do as a kid: where you painted on one side of the paper then folded it over. When I'm over here it feels like I'm in a parallel universe, or someone redecorated our house without telling me.

Alice's gran definitely does not have the same taste in décor as Mum though. She has all these crazy, abstract paintings on the walls, including ones she's done herself. There are candles and incense sticks on every shelf, plants on every windowsill. Flowing rugs and throws hang from chairs and doorframes and there are lots and lots of cushions. Alice says her gran rarely sits on the sofa, always prefers a pile of cushions on the floor.

I wander down the hall to Alice's room, which in our house is our office. There's a desk, a computer, a printer where her bed is; stacks of Dad's autobiography, Mum's work stuff piled against the other wall. Alice's room is the only one in her gran's house that's really changed over the years. Since we've been friends, I've watched it evolve alongside her, seen the posters change from *Harry Potter* to Jon Snow in *Game of Thrones* to Jodie Whittaker as the Doctor.

Last year I helped her paint the walls purple.

Alice lies, propped on one elbow, on her purple duvet cover. There are balls of wool on the bed next to her. She's been making more granny squares for the blanket. I don't know how many she's managed yet or how big this blanket is going to end up. They're all different colours. Blue and pink and yellow and green and red and orange, and purple of course.

'Hey, Sam,' she says.

'Hey, how's it going?'

'Good. Do you like this one? It's a new pattern.' She holds up a granny square.

It looks exactly like all the other ones to me but I nod. I sit on her desk chair, use my feet to swirl me from side to side, side to side, side to side, not allowing the chair to do a complete spin.

This is the first time we've been together since I sent that email about Dad. She replied to me eventually, but I don't think she really believed me.

Okay, I'm not sure how to reply to this one! Have you fallen and hit your head or something? Haha! Only joking. Of course I believe you. You need to come over and explain properly. I'll be at Gran's after school on Thursday.

It's kind of the elephant in the room. I'm feeling fidgety and full of this weird pent-up energy. I wait for her to bring it up. Maybe she's waiting for me to bring it up?

'Do you think I could see your dad?' she suddenly asks.

'Don't you believe me?'

It comes out more defensive than I'd meant it to.

'If you don't want me to, that's fine.'

'No, you can, if you want to.'

If I'm going to prove to her I'm not making it up, then I suppose this is one way of doing it.

'I'm not just being voyeuristic, I thought it might help. Give you a second opinion. Not that I don't believe you.'

I make a mental note to look up voyeuristic later. I don't want her to think I'm a total idiot.

It would be good to have someone else see him. I know what I see when I look at him but, when I'm away from him, I doubt myself.

There's another reason too. One I'm ashamed to admit out loud, but has been whispering to me ever since I sent that email; not completely accidentally despite what I've tried to convince myself. I want to create this shared secret, a closeness that belongs to just me and Alice. There's a part of me that hopes she'll be so shocked or scared or sorry for me, that she'll hug me or kiss me. Or...

I feel like a total shit for thinking these thoughts, for using Dad like this. It would really hurt Mum if she could hear inside my brain. I can't help it though. I don't want to think these things, but I have no control over them. The voice inside my head just keeps talking and I can't shut it up.

'Only show me if you're really sure and you really want to,' Alice says.

'I am. I mean, I do. Only you can't tell anyone and you can't let my mum know. She'd kill me if she knew I'd told you.'

'You know I wouldn't say anything. I promise.'

I feel so guilty.

'Do you want to go now?' I ask.

'Oh, okay, if you think so.' She moves but doesn't sit up.

Maybe she didn't mean it after all.

'Only if you want to.'

'No, okay, hang on.' She sits up and flexes her fingers, 'my hand's gone dead.'

She blushes, looks away. 'Sorry, bad choice of phrase.'

'Don't worry about it,' I reply.

It's just a saying. It's not as if her arm really is dead. Alive and dead at the same time. Like Dad.

Zombie. Zombie. Zombie.

Alice gets up and slips on her Converse.

'I'll just let Gran know where I'm going.'

'Don't tell her.' I blurt out.

'As if. I'll make something up. Are you sure you're cool with this?'

'Yeah, sorry.'

I'm so not cool with this, but I want it to happen anyway.

I follow Alice into the kitchen. Her gran's standing at the cooker. It smells really good in here, makes me hungry.

'Is it okay if I go round to Sam's for a bit?'

'How long's a bit?'

'I don't know. I was just going to borrow a DVD?'

'Horror or comedy?' her gran asks, looking at me.

'Eh, neither,' I reply.

I like Alice's gran, but I never know whether she's joking or being serious.

'Okay, but don't be too long, I'm making lasagne for dinner.'

'I won't.'

Alice and I head out the front door, onto the pavement and back into my front garden.

I start to have second thoughts as I unlock the front door. This is a bad idea. I shouldn't be doing this. It's happening too fast.

What if we go in and there's nothing wrong with him? He's just sitting there having a coffee, or watching old races on YouTube? That weird obsession he used to have. Punishing himself. Reliving old glories. He'd look up from the screen and it was like he'd never met you before in his life.

Alice would think I was a liar, that I was just making everything up.

Shit. What's wrong with me? For a moment, I almost wanted Dad to remain a zombie rather than look a dick in front of Alice.

I hesitate, grip the handle of the front door; ashamed of the smell, the mess. Mostly of myself for using Dad like this.

'What is it?' she says.

I open my mouth. Undecided about whether to apologise about the stink, set the scene, or just say I've changed my mind. Instead I shake my head, let us both into the house.

I lead Alice to the bedroom, turn the key and push open the door. Quickly before I change my mind. So I don't have to explain. Not that I could if I wanted to. The only thing to do is let her see for herself.

She grips my arm and we shuffle into the bedroom.

I watch her face, wait for her reaction. I can tell she's holding her breath but doesn't want me to know she's holding her breath.

'You okay?' I ask.

She nods.

There's a lamp switched on. Mum must have come in here and changed the bulb. The other one smashed by Dad when he was free range. Funny, the way we both keep coming in here without telling the other one.

He squirms on the bed. Alice's grip tightens. I don't think she realises she's holding on so hard, maybe doesn't even realise she's got me at all.

I take another step forward but Alice tugs on my arm. I hear her gag as she's forced to take a breath.

'That's close enough, Sam.'

'It's a bit gross, isn't it.'

'No, it's not that.' she's whispers. 'I thought it would be cool, exciting. I wasn't even sure that I really believed you. But now. Oh, Sam. It just makes me feel so sad. Your dad.'

One of the chains sinks into him, his flesh ripe and worn down, like the hero rubbing rope against a rock in a movie to get his arms free.

He gets more agitated as we stand there. Tries to lift his head, snaps his teeth, groaning at us.

'Shut the door, Sam. It's not fair.' Alice pulls me back out of the room. She stares at the closed door, the noises still coming from inside.

'I can't stay in there. It's too sad. Watching him like..., like an animal in the zoo or something.'

I feel like an even bigger shit now.

Alice hugs me suddenly. I'm knocked off balance and we rock against the doorframe before I steady myself and hug her back. Her hair tickles my nose, she smells of peppermint.

I'm getting a hard on, so I let go of her, break the moment before I want to.

Think of Dad. Dad. Dad.

Zombie. Zombie. Zombie.

'I didn't really believe you. I thought you were just being an idiot.'

'It's okay. It's not like it's an everyday situation.'

'But you're right. Zombie. That's the only way to describe him.'

We head out into the back garden.

She sits on the swing and I stand against the frame, feel it lift as Alice sways backwards and forwards, backwards and forwards, backwards and forwards; I use my weight to ground it, keep it from tipping.

'Are you alright?' I ask.

She puts a hand up to her cheek. It's shaking. I want to reach out and hold it, but I'm not brave enough.

I didn't really think about what seeing him for the first time could do to someone. I've gotten so used to him. I'd forgotten she knew him too.

That sounds so bad. Have I really got so used to the sight of him that it doesn't affect me anymore? I've become immune to the horror of it.

'Do you ever think…'

'What?'

'No, never mind.'

'Tell me,' I say.

'You're going to hate me for saying this.'

'No, I'm not.'

I could never hate her.

'I keep thinking of that rabbit in Gran's garden. Do you remember?'

'The one she smacked over the head with a rock.'

'Yeah.'

'Do you think I should do that to my Dad? Put him out of his misery?'

'Not when you say it like that. It sounds so bad when you say it out loud.'

That rabbit still haunts me. It was just a wee one. We didn't know what happened to it, maybe a cat got it or something, but Alice and I found it lying in her gran's garden. It was terrified of us as we stood over it, even though we were trying to help. Its fur all matted, its eyes darting this way and that. Its little heartbeat, so quick, fluttering inside its chest. Alice ran to get her gran and she told us to go inside and then she put it out of its misery.

'I was so angry with Gran that day,' says Alice, 'I thought we should take it to the vet or call the SSPCA or something. I couldn't believe it when she came in and said she'd killed it.'

'It probably wouldn't have survived.'

'Yeah, but she was so brutal. For all her weird hippiness, she's got an edge to her. Your dad was super nice to me that day.'

'My dad?'

'Yeah. I was really upset. Gran just put it on the compost heap. I wanted to give it a proper funeral. Your dad came out and I was a total state. I couldn't dig deep enough and I was scared to touch the dead rabbit. He dug the hole and helped me bury it.'

I feel like I might cry and I have to look down at the ground, hide my face. My dad. A fallen hero to so many but not to Alice. I didn't even know he'd done that for her.

'I want to help him, Sam. What can we do?'

'I don't know.'

She looks at the bedroom window.

The sheet is still pinned up.

It used to be Mum and Dad's room, but it's not anymore.

It's not even really his room.

The room.

I wonder if the reality of seeing him is worse than she imagined? I'm too scared to ask. I don't know what answer I'd prefer.

'Can you still hear him?' she asks. 'I feel like I can but I don't know if it's just in my head.'

'I can always hear him now. I don't know what's real anymore.'

An earworm, burrowed deep inside my head. Like the worms that would burrow into him given half a chance.

'I'd better get back,' Alice says, 'before Gran sees me out here on the swing.'

She doesn't move though. Just rocks backwards and forwards, backwards and forwards, backwards and forwards; the chain creaking.

'This swing is going to collapse underneath you one day,' says Alice. 'It's like one of those old abandoned fairgrounds you see photos of in Chernobyl or somewhere. Right, I'm definitely going now.'

She still doesn't move.

'Hang on a second,' I say and run inside to my room. I can still hear Dad. We've riled him up. She's right. It's cruel to peer at him like that.

I grab a DVD, head back out.

'Here, you'd better take this in case your Gran asks,' I say.

She looks at it.

'*Iron Man?*'

'Sorry, I know you don't like Marvel movies, but I just grabbed the first one that came to hand.'

'Alice, dinner's ready.' Her gran shouts from the back door. 'What is the attraction of this old swing?'

'Coming, Gran.' Alice gives me a look and walks down the side of our house, avoiding having to go inside. I see her cross over the pavement to her side of the fence.

'You two look very serious,' Alice's gran says as she waits for Alice.

I shrug, sit on the swing, rock myself backwards and forwards, backwards and forwards, backwards and forwards.

'Do you want to join us for dinner?' she asks.

I do. That lasagne smelt amazing. But I don't want to act like anything is wrong.

'No, I'm fine. Mum'll be home soon. And Dad.'

'How are they both? I've not seen them for a few days. Not long to go now.'

'They're fine.'

She nods.

'Where are you all?' She says.

'What?' I reply, then realise she's wandered off to her bird table, is addressing the sky.

She picks up a handful of seed, then sprinkles it back down again.

'I usually have to put food out every other day, but nothing's touched it this week,' she says.

'And my fish,' she glances at the pond, 'all hiding at the bottom for some reason. We must be in for a hard winter.'

I don't know what to say, but she doesn't seem to be looking for a response from me anyway.

'Back, Gran.' Alice appears at the kitchen door. She waves to me before they disappear inside.

I stay on the swing, wish I'd said yes to that lasagne. I'd be sitting in that warm kitchen now, next to Alice. The smell of food all around me instead of this smell of decay I have trapped in my nostrils.

Backwards and forwards, backwards and forwards, backwards and forwards.

Creak, creak, creak, creak.

Faster and higher, faster and higher.

The frame tips and I use my weight to settle it again. Alice is right; it's going to collapse underneath me one day.

I rock slowly now.

Backwards and forwards, backwards and forwards, backwards and forwards.

No birdsong. Just the grind of the rusty chains.

Hi Sam,

How's it going? It's 7:12pm and I'm at home. You'll never guess what I found out about my gran today – it is literally the grossest thing I think you'll ever hear. I couldn't believe it when Mum told me.

So I had a big fight with Mum and Pete again after school. He was being such a dick and acting like he was my dad. Telling me what to do and not to speak to my mum like that, blah blah blah. Anyway, I lost it and yelled at him that he wasn't my dad and to shut up and then I packed a bag and said I was going to Gran's. Mum said I wasn't. I said I was, etc etc – you get the gist. Then she said, you can't go because she's not in anyway. She's at her naked swimming class. Then she and Pete burst out laughing and I started crying and ran out of the room because they were totally laughing at me, especially Pete. Oh my God, I HATE HATE HATE him soooooo much!!

Mum must have felt bad because she followed me and was acting all nice again. She tried to hug me and was all like I know it's difficult, and I know Pete can be a bit much but he means well and I'll have a talk with him. Blah, blah, blah.

A bit much!? He's a dick! I never said that out loud though.

Anyway, then she said we could have a girls only day at the week-end. I was still a bit pissed off with her but I said okay. Then I asked her what she meant about naked swimming and that's when she told me. It turns out that Gran does actually go to a naked swim club!

It's in Haddington wherever that is. Mum says they don't adver-tise it on the pool timetable in case a bunch of pervs turn up.

She says she drove Gran to it one day. The staff lock all the doors and then all these old men and women start turning up. Mum had to wait outside in the car while they all swam naked for an hour. She was asked to leave the building unless she was participating!

Who knows why they want to swim naked but, you know Gran, always into weird stuff.

By the end of it though, Mum and me were in hysterics and Pete came in and Mum totally ignored him when he asked what we were laughing about and he went away in a proper huff – haha, serves him right.

Anyway, this has taken me forever to write, so I'd better go!

Alice

Xx

P.S. Don't tell anyone I told you about this!

Jude

He's quiet today. Well, as quiet as he ever is. My phone sits propped up on the breakfast bar. The baby monitor app that I downloaded is open. One of the girls at work gave me the camera. It links to the app on my phone. There are all sorts of functions, mostly so complicated that I can't work out how to use them. You can see at a glance what the temperature is. Play lullabies or switch on a nightlight at the touch of a button. Take photos and videos. There's a walkie talkie function and it even sounds an alarm if it thinks your baby has stopped breathing.

It's nothing like the basic monitors we had when Sam was born. When the slightest sound would send us racing to his cot. This new one can connect to your TV. You could probably leave a baby alone in the house with it, and pop to the shops and back, it's so advanced.

Adam is moving on the screen on my phone. I set up the camera in there this morning, after Sam left for school. It's up high on a shelf, hidden so Sam won't see it. I'm not really sure why I'm being so secretive about it.

I need to get out of my dressing gown and jammies, but I can't motivate myself to get up. I can't stop watching.

Adam writhing and squirming on the bed. Grunting and moaning. Movement and noise that would send you sprinting to his side if he was a baby, but which I simply stare at. I don't really need the phone to hear him, he's in the walls of the house now like damp, but I leave the volume up anyway. That low, guttural moaning, the grinding teeth. The chains rattling like some fucking ghost in a Dickens novel.

'Marley and Marley'

That song has been replaced recently by another one.

'Zombie' by The Cranberries.

It came on the radio the other day in another glorious moment of synchronicity. Dolores O'Riordan's voice screaming the chorus.

Zombay. Zombay. Zombay, ay, ay.

Maybe it's all in my head too?

I press the microphone symbol.

'Adam,' I say.

He reacts to my voice, thrashes his head around, trying to locate the source.

He's deflated now, a popped balloon. And he looks dark, purple in places. His hair is starting to fall out too. Sometimes if I look closely I can see maggots squirming inside him.

'Adam.' I say again.

'Adam. Adam. Adam. Adam.'

This would be funny if it wasn't so fucking awful. Like teasing a dumb dog. I'm loathe to admit it but there's a part of me enjoying this. Getting some sadistic pleasure from hurting him, the way he's hurting me right now. God, what sort of person am I?

I don't really understand why there's a microphone function. Would you really use it with a crying baby?

Sorry, darling. I can see you've spat up but Mummy's having a cup of tea.

I know you're hungry, but it's three in the morning and Mummy's sleeping.

I'm not coming. I'm watching Love Island.

I get up from the breakfast bar. I need to step away from the phone. This is not me. What's happening?

I look out the window. A magpie lands on Sadie's bird table. It glances around, pecks and flicks at some of the seeds and bread lying there, makes that grating, rattlesnake sound that magpies do. It lifts its head towards me.

Sam said the birds had stopped coming. Told me Sadie had noticed it too.

He's drawing connections where there are none.

I lift my hand to salute the magpie but stop myself. Something about the way it's looking at me, head tilted to one side.

How does that rhyme go again? One for sorrow, two for joy. I scan the sky, the trees. Any sign of another one?

Sadie told me the Scottish version of that rhyme once, but I can't for the life of me remember how it goes. We were chatting over the fence as we often do. I don't know how we got onto the subject of magpies, let alone superstitious rhymes.

How does it go again?

I'm sure it starts with one for sorrow.

Sorrow.

I guess that's about right.

I remember Sadie telling me that magpies can be seen as representations of the devil. Some old religious tale. What did she say again? She mentioned Jesus on the cross and a magpie being capable of human speech. It's why she hangs up all those CDs and mirrors in her garden, to ward off the evil spirits.

I wander back over to the breakfast bar. Finish my toast, drop the phone into the pocket of my dressing gown.

The magpie's in our garden now. Watching me. Watching our house.

I stoop to open the dishwasher, stack my plate. Fill my glass with more cold milk. Adjust the magnets to straighten up the baby scan picture on the fridge door. I turn to face the window again.

The cup falls from my hand and shatters. Milk splashes all over the place.

The magpie's sitting on the windowsill. It cocks its head, swivels its dark eyes as it watches me. Its wing and tail feathers shimmer metallic blue like tinsel.

I wait for it to speak to me. To say something.

I know it's just a bird, but the fright it's just given me. Even my legs are shaking. I can feel my heart pulsing in the tips of my fingers, throb, throb, throb, throb.

I'm trapped in my bare feet, surrounded by broken glass. My belly is so huge I can barely see the floor where I'm standing. My eyes keep going back to the magpie. I have the feeling it can only move when I look away.

Jesus, Jude. Get a grip. You're not Tippi Hedron. It's just a bird. Just a bird. Just a bird.

No matter how much sense I talk to myself or how rational I try to be, that bird is freaking me out and I want out of this kitchen right now.

The window's shut. The back door's locked. But I don't feel safe.

Peck once for yes, twice for no. I'm scared to say it out loud. I'm pretty sure that bird would do what I asked.

Just a bird. Just a bird. Just a bird.

Adam's louder now. The smash has woken him. Woken him? From what? He doesn't sleep. What a stupid thing to think. Roused him? Fired him up? Excited him? Nothing sounds right. There are no right words to describe what he is at the moment.

Zombay. Zombay. Zombay, ay, ay.

That song again. Burrowed into my brain.

I take the phone from my pocket. There he is. Struggling to get free.

The magpie bobs its head, quizzical. It takes off from the windowsill. Where's it going?

I put the phone away. I don't care how irrational I'm being, I need to get out of this kitchen.

Zombay. Zombay. Zombay, ay, ay.

Zombay. Zombay. Zombay, ay, ay.

'Jude. Stop it. Just stop it,' I say aloud. 'The magpie has gone. It was just a bird. Stop being such an idiot.'

I close my eyes. Do my pregnancy yoga breathing. Innnnn. Ouuuuut. Innnnn. Ouuuuut. Innnnn. Ouuuuut.

I manage to contort myself enough that I can bend down and pick up the glass, transfer it onto the counter.

Tap. Tap. Tap. Tap.

I feel around, trying to get every bit of glass.

Tap. Tap. Tap. Tap.

My knees crack as I stand and I make my own groans.

Tap. Tap. Tap. Tap.

What the fuck is that?

I can hear it in stereo. Through the phone in my pocket but in real time too.

Tap. Tap. Tap. Tap.

Where is it coming from?

I clear a few more bits of glass. I've managed to get most of it now. I wind paper towel around my hand and start to mop up the milk. It seeps through the paper towel, the puddle barely disappearing. I stand on a dishtowel instead and use my feet to move it around. The lino's sticky and the soles of my feet cling and peel.

Tap. Tap. Tap. Tap.

That noise again.

Tap. Tap. Tap. Tap.

I think I know what it is but I can't bring myself to check.

I squirt washing up liquid onto a sponge and try to wipe the stickiness from the floor.

Tap. Tap. Tap. Tap.

I place one hand on my phone but don't take it out of my pocket.

Tap. Tap. Tap. Tap.

At the bedroom window.

Tap, tap, tapping at the glass with his beak.

Is he trying to get in or is he trying to let someone out?

'Jude. I said, stop it.'

I lean against the counter. I'm getting myself all worked up.

Tap, tap, tap, tap.

'Stop it. Stop it.'

I don't know who I'm talking to. Me or the bird.

Just a bird. Just a bird. That's all. Birds land on the windowsill all the time. I'm being irrational.

You're allowed to be irrational when you're pregnant. When your husband's a zombie.

Zombay. Zombay. Zombay, ay, ay.

One for sorrow, one for sorrow, one for sorrow.

Tap, tap, tap, tap.

I need to get out of here. Out of the kitchen. Out of the whole goddamned house.

I walk towards the door.

Fuck.

Fuck, fuck, fuck.

I've stood on a piece of glass. I pull it out of my sole and there's blood all over my fingers.

Tap, tap, tap, tap.

I hobble to the counter for more kitchen roll and watch the blood soak into it as I hold it against my foot. Just as bloody useless as it was with the milk. My iron levels are already low enough without this.

It stings. I can feel tears coming but I try to swallow them back down.

Tap, tap, tap, tap.

One for sorrow. One for sorrow.

'Shut up, shut up, shut up!'

I limp to the back door and open it, waving my arms at the magpie sitting on the bedroom windowsill.

'Get out of here!'

I pick up a stone and throw it at the bird.

It takes off, disappears into Sadie's garden.

I go back inside and lock the door. I'm out of breath and I'm shaking.

'You're okay, you're okay, you're okay,' I tell myself. 'It was only a stupid, fucking bird.'

I turn on the cold tap, lean my head underneath and let it pour into my mouth and over my face.

There's still milk all over the floor and the blood from my foot gives it a pinky, marbled effect. It's like one of those art projects from primary school. I should get a straw and blow on it, watch the way it swirls and collects.

I stick a plaster to my foot. There's still milk everywhere. Floor, walls, fridge, skirting boards, cupboards. Drops of it cling and run down every surface.

It must be impossible to get away with bloody murder. There would always be a trace left to incriminate you.

There's milk and blood all over my dressing gown and jammies. I can feel sweat collect under my over-sized boobs. I strip down in front of the washing machine, shove all my clothes inside. My bare belly protrudes in front of me.

Shit, the phone. I reach inside the washing machine again, feel for my dressing gown pocket. Adam is rolling from side to side, rhythmical, a pendulum. Like that poor polar bear at the zoo who used to swim round and round and round in her tiny pool.

Zombay. Zombay. Zombay, ay, ay.

I need to have a shower, get dressed, get out of here.

I can feel the throb in my foot every time I take a step and the plaster comes off as I stand in the shower. Blood flows out of the cut again and down the drain.

I get out, sit on the toilet seat, and hold a towel against my foot until eventually the blood stops. I leave the shower running. It's such a waste of water but it drowns out everything else in the house.

I'm exhausted. I sit there and try to come back to myself again. Sort out my breathing. My heart rate. My head. I close my eyes and tune in to the water pounding from the shower. Let the steam build up around me, clouding the windows, the mirrors, condensation on the tiles and the door. It's warm and I muffle myself with it as if I'm wrapped inside a big roll of cotton wool. Safe in the centre. Safe from whatever is happening outside.

25/01/14

Oh my God Alice!!!!

Why did you even tell me that!? That is literally the grossest thing I've ever heard. I do not need those kind of images in my head.

What is the actual point of swimming naked anyway? Can't they just have a bath? My dad always used to go on about being stream-lined on the track and not creating any drag – there's got to be a lot of drag in a naked swimming group. Remind me never to go to Haddington Pool – no offence, but your gran can be so weird sometimes!

Sorry to hear you had another fight with Pete. He is such a tool. I hope your mum breaks up with him soon. You know you can always come over here if you need to get some space.

This week has been pretty boring for me. Not much to report. Mum and Dad had another big argument last night so that was fun... not! Some newspaper wanted to interview him because the Com-monwealth Games are in Glasgow. I don't know why? It's not like he's going to be running at it. He's not even going to go and watch! Mum got all upset because Dad was considering doing it and then Dad got all defensive. The usual shit. I wish people would just leave us alone.

Sorry, that turned into a bit of a rant there! Have you seen *World War Z* yet? I got it on DVD for Christmas and I've just been watch-ing it tonight. It's quite good, but I'm not sure I believe in zombies that can run!

Anyway, I'm going to go and watch the end of it. Write to you soon.

Sam

X

Sam

Alice and I sit on an old tartan rug under the blossom tree at the bottom of her gran's garden. The branches are bare, the pink petals blown around the garden months ago. Most of the plants look dead right now.

A breeze lifts the wind chimes which tinkle above us. Mirrors and old CDS hang from the branches. They swing and spin on fraying thread casting flickers and shadows.

Fairy lights illuminate the faded paintings Alice and I made on her gran's fence a few years ago. Our handprints and footprints in red, yellow, blue, purple. I placed my hand a certain way, so that I could make the fingertips touch Alice's.

I remember the way the paint oozed between my fingers. Mum went mental because I left prints all over the bathroom.

Alice is making more crochet granny squares although it's getting too dark for her to see properly. I try to follow what she's doing but her fingers move too quickly. She's wearing fingerless gloves. Balls of yellow and red and purple wool lie scattered on the rug.

'Mum saw a magpie in your gran's garden the other day.'

'Uh, oh,' Alice replies, 'I better not tell her, she'll freak out.'

'I still don't get why she loves nature but hates magpies.'

'We've been over this a million times.'

'It doesn't make any sense though. How do the mirrors work again?'

'The magpies don't like the reflection of the light or something. I don't know. I didn't hang them up.'

I think Mum's been listening to Alice's gran too much. She was in a really weird mood after she saw that magpie.

'Did you know magpies can recognise themselves in a mirror,' I say.

I googled them after Mum said one had been tapping on Dad's window. I thought she was exaggerating.

'No,' Alice replies.

She's concentrating on her crochet and holds it up in front of her face.

'We can go in if you want to.'

'No, it's fine. I can just about see. It's just because this wool's dark.'

'Only a handful of animals can do that. Dolphins, elephants, chimps, humans,' I say.

'What?'

'Recognise their reflection.'

'And magpies.'

'Why do you think they hate reflective stuff if they can recognise themselves?' I ask.

Alice shrugs.

'Maybe they're really self-conscious.'

'Do you think they're evil?'

'They attack baby birds, that's pretty evil.'

'Yeah, but loads of animals attack baby birds. It's on *Springwatch* all the time. Magpies are actually really smart. They can…'

'…what's all the interest in magpies? Shhh for a second, I'm trying to count.'

She runs the wool between her thumb and forefinger, counting stitches.

I glance over the fence to our back garden. With the foliage starting to die you can see the bedroom window clearly.

'Do you think your dad would recognise himself in a mirror?' Alice asks.

'Who knows? He smashed the mirrored wardrobe in there. I don't think that was anything to do with his reflection though. Just general zombie rage and clumsiness.'

The word comes out naturally. Zombie.

I can't help looking at the window. I keep expecting to see something.

I've got my own bedroom key now. I found it on that old keyring. Sometimes at night, if I'm really struggling to get to sleep, I lock myself in.

'Where is your gran anyway?'

'At one of her Friends meetings.'

'What are they discussing this week?'

'I think this week is..., eh... which Friend you'd most like to do.'

My gran's in a group called the Friends of Corstorphine. I like to think they start each meeting with a rendition of 'Smelly Cat' before they drink coffee from over-sized mugs and discuss the important topics of the day, like whether Ross and Rachel were actually on a break or what happened to Ben after season 8. Unfortunately, the reality is not so interesting. They're just a group of volunteers who help look after Corstorphine Hill, the tower and the walled gardens and stuff.

I hadn't even realised there was a tower up there until Alice told me about it. One day she borrowed the keys from her gran and took me up there to see for myself. The tower's hidden amongst the trees, you don't see it until you're almost on it.

You get this amazing, panoramic view of the city and you can see the bridges across the Forth and right across to Fife. It's pretty cool.

'Gran likes Chandler, I think.'

'Don't. You'll make me picture it!'

I squirm on the blanket, start to feel aroused. I'm glad it's dark enough that Alice can't see anything. I'm totally grossed out that the mention of Alice's Gran with Chandler has this reaction in me.

Alice laughs and pushes me over. Her touch doesn't help and I back away, even though I like the feeling of her fingers on me.

She gives up on the crochet and lies back on the rug.

I lie down next to her. We're both in jackets and hats and scarves but we're lying out like it's the middle of summer. I can feel the cold ground through the blanket. I think of buried bodies, rotting as worms curl through them. A shiver runs through me. Someone walking over my grave.

'Does your gran still have keys for the tower?' I ask.

'Yeah, I think so. Do you want to go up there again?'

I don't answer. I've had a crazy idea and I'm hoping she'll follow my train of thought.

'It's shut over the winter, isn't it?'

'Yeah, but that's okay. We could still go up there. One of the perks of having a Friend for a gran.'

I think of the chains digging into Dad, of sitting in the garden all winter because I hate being in the house, of locking my bedroom door at night.

I think about Dad escaping when Mum's alone in the house or when the baby comes home.

We have to move him. Even if it's only for a few months until we work out something more permanent.

Alice picks up her crochet again. I lean on my elbow and watch as she winds and knots the wool around the hook.

'I still can't work out how you do that,' I say.

'It's not difficult. I can show you if you like?'

'Not just now. I can't be bothered concentrating.'

'It's getting too dark anyway. I keep getting mixed up.'

'I suppose we should go in.'

I don't want to move though. It's nice being out here with her. Like that time we went on a trip up Blackford Hill to the observatory. Afterwards we lay outside in our winter coats watching the stars.

'I'll just finish this row,' she says.

I'm about to tell her about my plan to move Dad but I stop myself. It's such a crazy idea. She'll probably think I'm an idiot.

'Stop staring, you're making me self-conscious.' Alice says.

'Sorry, I'm just trying to work out what you're doing.'

'It's not as complicated as it looks. I told you I'll show you how to do it.'

I roll over onto my back.

'What is it, Sam? You're being weird.'

'Nothing. Just Dad, you know.'

My excuse for everything these days. My get out of jail free card with Mum and Alice.

'I've been thinking about Dad and how he can't stay in the house.' I say.

'I was thinking that too. I didn't want to say anything though.'

'How come?'

'Well, he's your dad. You'd have to call the police or something. It could get messy.'

'What if we moved him somewhere ourselves?'

My hat's getting itchy and I scratch underneath it.

'Where?'

'What about the tower? Nobody ever goes there in the winter, right?'

Alice stops what she's doing. I can see her working it out in her head. It doesn't sound so crazy now I've said it out loud and she's not laughing at me.

'Just in the short-term,' I say. 'I know we'd have to move him before it opens again.'

'I don't know. People with keys might still go there. I don't want to hurt any of the Friends.'

'No, I don't either. I just don't know what else to do.'

'It might work. But how would we get him there?'

We. Does that mean she wants to help me?

'I don't know. I'm just thinking aloud. It's a dumb idea.'

'No, it's not dumb. I guess I could check with Gran how often it's used during the winter?'

'At least that gives us a place to start.'

'Okay. Leave it with me. Do you want to come inside? It's freezing out here.'

We stand and she lifts the blanket before we both head into her gran's kitchen.

'Do you want a hot chocolate?' She asks. 'I feel like the cold is in my bones.'

'Yeah, thanks,' I say. 'You should have said earlier that you were cold.'

'It's okay,' she shrugs. 'I like being outside.'

'I'm freezing all the time now because Mum's turned the heating off.'

'Why did she do that?'

'I think it's to stop the... to slow down what's happening to Dad.'

I can't say the word.

Decomposition.

To slow down his rotting.

'Oh right. Sorry.'

I shrug.

She pours milk into a pot and turns on the gas hob underneath it, then scoops chocolate powder into two mugs and stirs the milk with a wooden spoon.

I watch her then pretend to look at something on my phone when she turns to face me again.

Her bag of wool is lying on the table. I wind an end round my finger and cut off the blood supply, watch the tip as it goes purple. I unwind it again, my finger white and marked from the wool.

'Don't drop my stitches,' she says.

'I won't.'

She waits for the milk to bubble before she takes it off the heat and pours it into the mugs. She hands me one and a teaspoon and sits beside me at the table. I stir my drink and watch the granules dissolve, turning the milk brown.

Alice takes a ball of wool and a new crochet hook out of her bag.

'Look it's totally easy. This is how you start. You just need to make a chain.'

She fixes the wool to the hook and starts to make loops in it.

'See, you just wind over and pull through, wind over and pull through. You try.' She hands me the wool and I drop the hook.

'That's okay,' she slips the hook back into the wool. Her fingers brush against mine. I fumble, try to make a chain but I can't concentrate with her so close.

'Almost, like this.' She takes my hands, tries to guide me.

It's like an electric shock. I can't help the way my body reacts to her and I don't want her to see, so I push her away, when all I want is for her to keep touching me.

'It's too difficult,' I say.

'You're not even trying.'

She puts the crochet down and takes a sip of hot chocolate.

'You want sugar?' She asks.

'Nah, that's okay,' I say. I can feel prickles all over me.

'Ray has, like, six sugars in his hot chocolate, it's gross,' she says.

'Who's Ray?' I take a sip but it's too hot and it burns my tongue.

'Simon's son.'

'I thought you said he was a dick?'

The electricity fizzles out and everything starts to droop at the mention of Ray.

'He is.'

So how come you're having hot chocolate with him?

I ask the question in my head but don't say it aloud.

I'm in a bad mood now. Annoyed at the mention of Ray and frustrated at my reaction to her teaching me crochet.

'Do you think your dad's the only one?' She asks.

'Only what?'

'Zombie.'

'How should I know?'

'I was thinking that maybe there's more. He could just be one of them. You know the start of something.'

'The start of the apocalypse?'

'Well, maybe. The end of the world has to start somewhere.'

'Great, so now my dad's responsible for the end of the world?'

I take another drink. It's cooled now but my burnt tongue makes it taste funny.

'I've been checking online and in the news, just in case anything similar comes up.'

I have too, but I don't admit it. I take another drink of hot chocolate so I don't have to speak.

In amongst the fake zombies, the YouTube clips of old movies and episodes of *The Walking Dead*, I've been checking for real ones. I've not found anything though. There's zombies in nature, certain ants and wasps and caterpillars. Then there's voodoo and witchcraft stuff from places like Africa and Haiti. But whatever it is that Dad is. I can't find anything like that.

'It's the sort of thing they'd cover up though,' Alice goes on. 'They wouldn't want to cause mass panic.'

She doesn't notice I'm pissed off and that makes me even more annoyed. I don't know where this anger has come from. I was fine a few minutes ago.

'Maybe they're right?' I reply. 'Humans are idiots. We can't even cope with a few inches of snow.'

'I guess.'

'And we're selfish in a crisis, fighting each other for the last roll of toilet paper. I hate the human race. They're fucking idiots. They believe everything they're told even if it's bullshit.'

I don't know why I'm getting so worked up, why I'm arguing with her.

'Not everyone's like that,' she whispers into her hot chocolate.

I take another drink, gagging as I accidentally swallow the skin.

My dad is special and she's trying to take it away from me. Suggesting that he's just another victim, part of some world-wide conspiracy.

I used to be so proud of all he'd done. Cocky with it too. I joined an athletics club and swaggered around imagining that everyone was talking about me – that's Adam Redpath's son. The other kids were much better than me though and the coaches joked about me having my dad's eyes but not much else.

Sometimes the other kids would ask him for photographs and autographs. I liked the attention at first but then I got fed up. I felt like telling them they wouldn't be so star struck if they knew he'd farted while watching TV or how he picked his nose in the car. Then I'd feel guilty for betraying him.

I love him but sometimes, in my darkest thoughts, I hate him too.

'I'd better get back, Mum'll be home soon.' I gulp down the rest of my drink.

'Okay,' Alice replies.

I dump the mug in the sink and head outside. The hurt look on Alice's face makes me feel better. I don't know why. We never usually argue.

I'll probably regret it later but for now I let the anger take over.

I kick Dad's door on the way to my bedroom. Make as much noise as I can to rile him up. I put my headphones on and listen to Biffy Clyro so I can't hear him. I lie on my bed with my eyes closed and let the music drown out everything.

Fall From Grace by Adam Redpath

I felt guilty. Of course, I did. I'm not a complete monster. I let my team mates down, especially the guys who ran the 4x400m with me. They had to give their medals back too, had their titles stripped from them. They had to go through that humiliation and disappointment because of me and the choices I'd made. For a long time I was so ashamed that I couldn't face them. I was scared of them; of how they'd react to me. Guys I'd thought of as not just team mates, but friends. Eventually I did try to apologise. They weren't interested of course. I couldn't blame them. Mark Rogers went from being a relatively unknown athlete to a household name overnight. A spokesperson against not just me, but drug cheats in general.

'I don't think I'll ever be able to forgive Adam Redpath. That moment on the podium as part of the relay team was the pinnacle of my career. I planned on passing my medal onto my children, my grandchildren. Instead I had to hand it back like I was some cheat myself. He knew what he was doing and the risks involved. He should have pulled out of the relay squad but he wanted it all. And because of that we were all left with nothing. We could have won silver or bronze, maybe even gold, without him. This is the reality of taking drugs and cheating to win. You bring everyone down with you.'

Jude

I'm due to test a canoeist this afternoon.

Siobhan Carmichael.

I'm parked a few streets away from where she lives because I left earlier than I needed to.

I google her on my phone. European Junior Champion. World Junior Champion. C1 Slalom, whatever that means.

It's good to have some prior knowledge before you turn up on the doorstep as it can help to put them at ease. It's not the most natural situation in the world, having someone watch you pee into a pot.

I'm not allowed to be too familiar though. I can't ask for autographs or selfies, can't accept gifts or become friends.

I used to be a lot more chatty with the athletes I tested, but I closed down a bit after what happened with Adam. I know I have a bit of a reputation now for being aloof, but it's hard to put yourself back out there after something like that.

My finger hovers over the baby monitor app. I press it but shut it down before it has time to fully open. I need to relax.

I drop my phone in my bag and recline the chair. I turn the radio up. It's Janice Forsyth on Radio Scotland. She's talking to some author about their new book. I let the conversation wash over me, tuning in every so often.

'…so your main character has quite an unusual job, doesn't she?'

'Yes, Maria's an obituary writer.'

'So what inspired that?'

'Well, I actually worked as an obituary writer myself for a local newspaper.'

'I suppose some people might think that's a bit morbid, but it sounds fascinating to me.'

'Yes, a lot of it is very sensitive, dealing with bereaved relatives, that sort of thing, but it's also a privilege to pay tribute to all these amazing lives.'

This is too close to home. I should turn the radio off. I want to close my eyes but, if I do, I'll fall asleep. It's hard enough trying to get comfortable at night with the indigestion, the cramp, the bump, but it's even worse when…

No, don't go there, don't go there.

I should be preparing myself for what's ahead. Stockpiling nappies. Packing a hospital bag. Sorting out which baby clothes we can reuse. I haven't done any of that though.

Sam's old cot is lying in pieces in the spare room. Adam and I were going to sort the nursery out together.

I float along like a piece of driftwood.

'So, tell me, you must have some great stories from your time as an obituary writer.'

'Yes, no two days were ever the same. We once had an obituary handed in by four daughters about their dad, and they had clearly hated him. They were using his obituary as some sort of catharsis for the years of pain they'd experienced.'

'And did you publish that?'

'No, I took the decision not to. I'm not sure it would have helped anyone really. It was sad and the poor girls were obviously hurting but we couldn't do it. That's part of what I try to explore in the book. That the way you behave after a loss is not the way you would behave at any other moment in your life. You make peculiar decisions when you're vulnerable. Grief brings out the stranger in us but it also reveals our most true selves.'

I see someone approaching in the wing mirror and I check it's not the canoeist. My job has so many rules. If she knew she was about to be tested she could take a masking drug or diuretics or drink lots of water so her urine was too dilute. It's harder for a woman to swap a urine sample but I've heard of male athletes using a prosthetic penis.

I don't know what Adam did to avoid being caught. He was so ashamed, I don't think he told me everything.

I check the time. I hate being late for anything.

I was fifteen minutes early on my wedding day. It never occurred to me that I should keep the groom waiting. When the limo pulled up in front of the hotel some of my guests were still arriving. The best man came out and gave the driver twenty quid to go around the block a few times. Adam always used to tease me about it.

You're the only bride I've ever known who turned up early!

You're lucky I wasn't some bridezilla!

An image of a zombie bride pops into my head; the dress torn and bloody; long fingernails with chipped red polish; matted hair; snarling...

I shake the image away.

'...and you've been writing since you were five? Is that right?'

'Yes, I was quite a precocious child. I used to write poems and stories and then make my family listen to readings.'

'Well, you must be well-practised then. In fact, let's have a wee reading from you now. This is from the start of the book, yes?'

'Yes, this is the first paragraph.'

'Great.'

'Maria held the piece of paper in front of her. It was from David. His obituary. He'd written the whole thing himself...'

I lift my phone out of my bag. My thumb hovers over the app but I resist and check my paperwork instead.

If Siobhan doesn't answer the door, I have to collect anti-doping intelligence. It makes me sound like a spy, but really I just have to check that nobody's hiding inside trying to dodge the test. Three missed tests counts as a doping offence and the athlete can be banned for that.

'And is it fairly common for people to write their own obituary? Does that not put people like you out of a job?'

'A lot of people, if they know they're dying, will write their own obituary. Just like a lot of people in that situation will plan their own funeral. It gives them some form of control and makes it easier for their loved ones. We always give them a fact check though so the obituary writer is still needed.'

'Aye, and would there ever be a case where someone made it up? Gave themselves this fabulous life.'

'You'd be surprised. I remember one guy wrote that it was now time to reveal he was a superhero and not an accountant.'

'I suppose that brings a wee smile to the faces of those left behind.'

'Yes, definitely.'

'Well, listen, thanks for speaking to us today, Joan. That was fascinating. And it's out... now?'

'Yes, released last week.'

'Great, that's Ghost Writer by Joan Fernie. Okay, now as the book's set on Mull, here's the Mull Historical Society to take us to the news with 'Animal Cannabus'...'

I turn off radio and clamber out of the car with my stuff. It's cold but this wee bump is like Sam as a baby, an internal hot water bottle.

Sam still doesn't seem to feel the cold. Good job, I suppose, as he seems to be spending a lot of time outdoors these days. He thinks I don't notice, but mums have a sixth sense.

Home doesn't feel like home anymore. It's like walking through a forcefield. Everything muffled and distorted. The colours, the smells, the sounds. I never thought home with Adam would feel like that.

I stop at a pedestrian crossing and push the button to cross. A wasp is stuck inside the box, must have flown in but can't get out again, like a Chinese finger trap or a lobster creel. I watch as it hits itself against the plastic, over and over and over again. I can hear the buzzing loud and angry. I'm hypnotised by it and have to pull myself away to make the appointment on time.

Siobhan's flat's on the third floor. My legs are burning and I'm panting like a heavy smoker by the time I get to her door. I take a moment to compose myself before I knock.

My auto-pilot kicks in when she answers the door.

'Hi, my name is Jude Redpath from UK Anti-Doping. I'm here to see Siobhan Carmichael.'

I produce my ID card and Siobhan lets me in. I follow her into the living room and she lifts old magazines and books from the sofa, makes space for us both.

'I need to notify you formally that you've been selected for a drugs test. You're required to provide a sample of urine under my supervision. Failure to provide this is a doping offence. Do you understand?'

'Yeah.'

I don't think she's really listening to me. On auto-pilot too.

I reach into my bag and take out a selection of pots.

'If you could choose one you're happy with,' I say.

'This one,' she takes the one nearest her.

'Are you ready to provide the sample.'

She nods and I follow her into the bathroom. As she passes the bath, the shower curtain ripples and I see the mildew which creeps up it.

'If you could just adjust your clothing so that I can get a clear view of the sample being given.'

She pulls her jeans down then lifts her top and tucks it into her bra. Her stomach is like a piece of ribbed cardboard. A sparkly, butterfly charm dangles from her pierced belly-button. I don't think my stomach has ever been that flat.

I used to have my belly button pierced but I took it out when I was pregnant with Sam and it closed up. It felt like I'd lost a part of myself. I cried when I discovered I couldn't get the barbell back in. I still miss fiddling with it, like a stress-ball.

I realise I'm staring.

'Whenever you're ready,' I say.

Siobhan pulls down her pants and squats over the toilet holding the pot. I watch as it fills before Siobhan finishes and puts on the lid. The pot is warm as she hands it to me and I give it a quick scan for hair or blood.

I think of all the urine samples I've had to give throughout the pregnancy; from peeing on the test all those months ago to the specimen bottle I take to every midwife appointment. How did we discover we could learn so much from piss?

It takes a while to get through all the paperwork but eventually we're done and Siobhan lets me out again.

I never mentioned any of her achievements that I'd looked up on Google earlier. I probably made the whole experience more formal than I needed to. In the old days, I would have chatted. My appointments used to last longer. Now I'm in and out.

I like the distance that my job gives me. I see inside people's houses and we share an intimate moment but I never get close to anyone.

I cross the road on the way back to the car but stop at the pedestrian crossing again and press the button. The wasp is still trapped inside but it's not as frantic now. It hits against the plastic a few times but quickly gives up.

Fall From Grace by Adam Redpath

The story was so big, it even made *Panorama*. It turned out that my coach, Kennedy, was guilty of numerous doping violations. He had been part of a group helping to distribute illegal performance enhancing drugs to athletes here in the UK and also in America.

The programme makers hassled me for weeks, trying to get me to give an interview. I declined though. I swore not to watch the programme when it was aired but I couldn't help myself. None of us came out of it with any reputation left.

Sam

Date: 14/10/18

From:samredpath08@gmail.com

To: alice_gryffindor4@gmail.com

Subject: Squirrel

Hey Alice,

I went for a run along the canal after school today. Better than another evening on the swing! I was running across the viaduct near the visitor centre when I saw this dead squirrel in the water.

It was lying on its back with its tail floating up and was all bloated and swollen. I was going to take a photo but this guy walked past and I felt like a twat so I kept on running. Sorry, I know that's a bit weird. I just wish someone else had seen it.

Hope you're okay,

Sam

X

I read over the email to Alice again but still don't hit send. It's a bit weird emailing about a dead squirrel. I don't want her to think I'm a total loser.

It looked really beautiful though, despite the fact that it was dead. Its arms were floating out on either side and its tail still looked soft, the way hair goes in water. I can't get it out of my head.

It's been a while since I've been running and that viaduct always makes me dizzy. It's narrow and cobbled and so high up. I can't help but look through the gaps in the railings even though it makes me feel like I'm already falling. Mum calls it the scary bridge and refuses to walk over it.

I read over what I've written again. Add an extra bit at the bottom.

Sorry, I know that's a bit weird. I just wish someone else could have seen it.

Also, it made me think of this joke: why do squirrels swim on their backs?

To keep their nuts dry!

Haha! :-)

Hope you're okay,

Sam

X

I've had no contact with Alice since we had that weird argument.

I looked up her Facebook profile earlier. There was a selfie of her and Ray, taken in her bedroom in Ray's house. Alice said her mum stays there most of the time now. Ray was the one taking the selfie, a big stupid grin on his face. Alice and I don't do selfies. I'm surprised she agreed to be in it.

I clicked through onto Ray's page. Most of it was hidden, but I could see a few posts and photos. I don't get why she's hanging out with him so much. He's everything that usually annoys her about people. You only have to look at his Facebook page to see that.

I looked at the photos of him. There were a couple of him at parties, the same stupid grin on his face. A few of him competing in those Tough Mudder competitions. Lots and lots of his car.

It was because of those photos that I went running along the canal today. I'd stood in the mirror, flexed my non-existent muscles then lifted my t-shirt to expose my white, hairless, chest. I'd ended up doing fifty sit-ups then digging out my old athletics kit and going for a run.

It was a pretty dumb idea.

I haven't told Alice that the reason I spotted the squirrel was because I got as far as the canal, thought I was going to puke, and walked home.

I read over the email.

P.S. Sorry for being a bit of a dick the other night.

I add the line then delete it. It was partly her fault so I don't know why I should apologise.

Sorry if it got a bit weird the other day.

I delete that too.

I'm just going to act like it never happened.

I want to mention moving Dad but I'm not sure how to word it. Maybe she won't want to help if she's mad at me.

P.S. Just wondered if you'd had any more thoughts about our plans for a visit to the tower?

Send.

I open up another tab and log into YouTube; look up zombie videos again.

A bloated, fat, zombie. Naked and rubbery, being pulled out of a well on a chain. His body is ripped in half and his guts spill out.

A zombie hanging from a noose, spinning round and round on the branch it's attached to.

A notification flashes up from Alice.

Date: 14/10/18
From:alice_gryffindor4@gmail.com
To: samredpath08@gmail.com
Re: Squirrel

Hey Sam,

How's things? I started writing you an old-school letter at, well, school today, haha! But I got caught by Mrs Brodie and sent to the front of the class so I never finished it. I was just about to email you when I got your message – spooky or what!!

I thought you hated running! What were you doing that for? That squirrel sounds like Lady Ophelia! We're doing Hamlet *in English right now. You should have taken a photo though. I'd like to see it.*

And that joke, oh man, that was bad. But you know what it made me think of... wait for it, you're not going to like it... Gran's trips to Haddington Baths!

I've been thinking about the tower visit. It'll be easy to get Gran's keys. She leaves them hanging up at the front door. I tried to suss her out about whether anyone was likely to head up there over the winter but I didn't want to make it too obvious. I think it'll be okay though.

We just have to work out when and how...

Alice

X

She's not mad at me. Maybe I was just imagining it all? I'm kind of on another planet right now.

That picture of her with Ray flashes into my head. Maybe she's only fine with me because she's all loved-up with him? What if she tells him about Dad, wants to bring him with us when we go to the tower?

The thought of her with him makes me queasy.

Now we're okay, we can instant email again. I don't have to worry about how much time I leave between replies just to make it look like I have a life.

Date: 14/10/18
From:samredpath08@gmail.com
To: alice_gryffindor4@gmail.com
Re: Squirrel

Hey,

Hope you didn't get into too much trouble. I think we probably want to go at night or really early in the morning – less people about, less chance of being seen, etc. It will be dark though so we should probably take a torch or whatever. We can make a list of stuff we might need. This could be pretty dangerous, are you sure you want to come with me?

I don't know what to do about Mum. She'll never agree to it. The only thing I can think of is to move him while she's away and then try to explain later. What do you think?

I wonder if she's working away. Hang on, I'll go and look at the calendar in the kitchen.

Right, back now. It looks like she has a couple of overnights at the end of the month – the 21st and the 31st. Halloween, spooky!

Sam xx

I get a horrible feeling when I think about what we're planning. Especially when I think about how hurt and upset Mum will be. Not only have I told Alice, but now we're making plans that I know Mum would never agree to.

I hate the part of me that's excited by it all. That loves having a secret with Alice. That relishes the prospect of doing something crazy with her. That ignores the fact that my dad's the monster.

Zombie Barbie, tiara balanced on peroxide blonde hair. Smeared lipstick, perfect white teeth covered in blood.

Man in green hospital scrubs on a deserted Westminster Bridge.

Date: 14/10/18
From: alice_gryffindor4@gmail.com
To: samredpath08@gmail.com
Re: Squirrel

Sam,

Of course I'm coming. You can't do this on your own! I know what you mean about your mum though. If you want to change your mind, I'll understand. I've just had a brilliant idea though, we could do it on Halloween. I'll make some excuse so I can stay at Gran's then we can both dress up so we look like we're going guising or to a party. What do you think? Am I a genius or what??

Alice

Xx

Date: 14/10/18
From:samredpath08@gmail.com
To:alice_gryffindor4@gmail.com
Re: Squirrel

Hey,

No, I'm not changing my mind. We have to do this. That sounds a good plan. It's so crazy it might work. I think if we can get him off the bed and padlock the chains around him, then we should be able to lead him, like Michonne in The Walking Dead.

Should we dress up as zombies or just a random Halloween costume? What time do you think?

Sam

Xx

The plan becomes more real with each email. I distract myself with videos on YouTube and tell myself this is the right thing to do. I'm full of doubt. How much of this is for selfish reasons? Because I hate having him in the house. Because I want to go on an adventure with Alice.

This could all go horribly wrong.

Zombies feeding on the cooked flesh of people burnt in a car explosion. One gnaws a hand like it's a chicken leg.

People board up windows and doors with 2x4s. The zombies break through the slats and grab at anyone who gets too close.

Date: 14/10/18
From: alice_gryffindor4@gmail.com
To: samredpath08@gmail.com
Re: Squirrel

I don't think we have to dress as zombies. Gran usually goes to bed around 9:30pm, so I'll wait for her to do that and then come and knock on your bedroom window. Make sure you're in your costume before I come over. It takes about half an hour to walk normal pace so, even if we triple it, that's an hour and a half. Plus an hour at the tower. Then we can run home if we need to. We should be back by 1am.

What we might need:

Torch

Water

Keys!!!

Halloween costume (what will I wear?)

Not sure what else?

How will you tell your mum after? She's going to notice...

Alice xx

A zombie bites into a woman's ankle. The muscles and tendons stretch and pull like Highland Toffee.

A zombie with melted skin bites into a bald head as if it was an apple.

Zombies in a frenzy trying to get at people locked inside a car. They climb onto the bonnet and the roof; the bodywork dents beneath them.

Date: 14/10/18
From: samredpath08@gmail.com
To: alice_gryffindor4@gmail.com
Re: Squirrel

Hey,

That sounds like we have a plan. I'd better go for now as Mum's just come in. I think we should wear lots of layers if we can to protect us, just in case.

Have a good night!

And thanks for your help!

Sam

Xx

P.S. Not sure what I'll tell Mum…

Part of me isn't sure this is even going to happen. It's one thing making these plans by email but another thing actually doing them.

I think about Alice's list.

What else would we need?

A knife, in case it all goes wrong?

A zombie girl uses a trowel to stab her mother, protracted screams as red paint spatters on white walls.

A man being chased by a zombie on an American football field. He stumbles and falls and the zombie rips open his neck.

A girl leaves her dad sitting on the stage amongst the scenery for a school play. He's been bitten on the ankle.

I shut down my computer and head into the kitchen. Mum's rummaging in the freezer and she jumps as I open the door.

'Sam. Don't sneak up on me like that,' she says. 'What do you want for dinner?'

'I don't mind.'

'Spaghetti Bolognese?'

'Yeah, fine.'

She brings out a Tupperware from the freezer with frozen Bolognese in it. She puts it in a pot over the hob and jabs at it with a knife to try and break it up.

As it heats up, she puts her shopping away and I open a bag of crisps and sit at the breakfast bar.

Mum pours herself a glass of milk, jabs at the Bolognese some more, then turns to face me.

'Sam!' she gestures at the bag of crisps.

'I'll still eat dinner.'

'So, how was your day?' she asks, as she puts on water for the spaghetti.

'Fine,' I say.

'What did you get up to?'

'Not much. School.'

'How's it been since you got home?'

'Fine.'

She drinks her milk and refills the glass.

I wander over to the calendar and pretend to read it.

'Are you working away on Halloween?' I ask.

I try to make the question sound as casual as possible but I'm sure the guilt is giving me away.

Mum glances at the calendar.

'Yeah, I'm meant to be. Why?'

'No reason, really.'

I'm so rubbish at this. I should have come up with some sort of story before I started asking her questions. She's going to get suspicious.

'I've told them I can't do overnights anymore but there's a couple they've already booked. Would you rather I was here on Halloween?'

'No. I'm not scared or anything.'

'There's no shame in admitting you're afraid, Sam. I know I am.'

'Of Halloween?'

'Well, no, not of Halloween. But of what's happening right now. I'll tell them I can't do it.'

'No, don't do that. I'm okay.'

Mum stirs dry spaghetti into the boiling water.

'Are you sure, Sam? You know you can always talk to me.'

'I know.'

'Please don't keep things to yourself.'

'I know. Get off, Mum.'

I push her away as she tries to kiss me.

I check my emails again after dinner but there's nothing from Alice, so I log back into YouTube.

A woman struggles with a zombie in a forest. A samurai sword flashes and the head of the zombie tumbles to the ground.

Men throw records at two approaching zombies. The records spin and shatter and a shard gets lodged in one zombie's head.

The zombies in these clips are people in make-up and fake blood. It's comic book violence, some of it so over the top it makes me laugh out loud.

A baseball bat swings and the zombie is spun to the ground.

A car door is slammed repeatedly on a zombie's head.

A girl pushes down on one end of a see-saw and the other end smashes up into the zombie's head.

These zombies behave to a script and do what they're told to by the director. Violence doesn't seem real when it's aimed at a zombie.

A clown zombie at the fairground has a test-your-strength mallet swung against its head.

Bill Murray, pretending to be a zombie, is shot in the chest.

Something changes when the violence is human. It's not funny anymore.

Girls dressed in red gowns, sitting on a sofa, waiting to be raped by soldiers.

A group of vigilantes led by a man with a rifle slung over one shoulder. Another man lies dead, a gunshot wound in his forehead.

A baseball bat wrapped in barbed wire is brought down on top of a head.

Dad's not going to behave the way zombies on TV do. What does it matter if we get killed off? They're not going to dedicate a whole episode of *Talking Dead* to us. I could be responsible for getting Alice killed.

How do I explain that afterwards?

But what if something happens to Mum or the baby? How do I live with myself knowing that I had the chance to move Dad and I didn't take it because I was scared and unsure.

I've already lost my dad. I can't lose my mum too.

Zombie is shot in the head. Blood and brains splatter across the wall.

Zombie is shot in the head. The road beneath the slumped body is a pool of black.

Zombie is shot in the head. It disintegrates like a melon.

I'm so confused. I want to do the right thing, but I don't know what that is.

Zombie is shot in the head.

Zombie is shot in the head.

Zombie is shot in the head.

I think I'm going mad. I do. Maybe none of this is happening after all. Maybe it's all in my head.

It's like that episode of *Buffy* I watched with Alice. Buffy's in a padded cell and her parents try to persuade her that all the vampire slaying is just a delusion. The episode flickers between Sunnydale and the psychiatric hospital until you're not sure what's real anymore.

Zombie is shot in the head.

Zombie is shot in the head.

Zombie is shot in the head.

I lock my bedroom door and wrap myself up in my duvet. I try to shut out everything else.

I breathe in and out, in and out, in and out. Try to calm myself down.

This is why I need to do something.

I have to get him out of the house.

I can't have him here.

For the sake of my own sanity.

Fall From Grace by Adam Redpath

I remember exactly where I was when I got the news. Jude, Sam and I had gone for a walk along the promenade at Portobello.

My mobile rang and it was a number that I didn't recognise so I ignored it. They rang back immediately so I answered. I was booked to go on *A Question of Sport* that month and I thought it might be the arrangements for that.

Although I lived with the constant fear of being caught, I was unprepared when it finally happened. The official on the other end of the line said the words I'd been dreading.

I'm afraid that the urine sample taken on the 24th October has tested positive for a banned substance.

The shock must have shown on my face, as I remember Jude took my arm and asked if I was okay. I walked away. I didn't want her and Sam to find out like that. We'd been having such a good day.

I can't really remember the rest of the conversation. I just kept saying 'okay' over and over to the official speaking to me. He told me I'd have to attend an official hearing and I was advised to bring my solicitor. I remember being surprised that it had escalated so quickly.

What haunts me most from that day was the look of concern on Jude's face. She knew something wasn't right and her only concern was for me. I felt sick knowing that I'd have to go home and confess everything.

Jude

I jump as the living room door opens and grab at my phone. I manage to shut down the baby monitor app before Sam sees it.

I don't even know why I keep watching it. Adam never changes.

I tell myself it's to keep us safe but underlying all that is something more murky. I miss him and it's becoming an obsession but, like all addicts, I tell myself that I can stop at any time.

'What are you watching?' Sam asks and sits next to me on the sofa.

'Some documentary about 9/11.'

'That's cheery.'

'It's not really about the attacks. I almost shouted on you earlier as I thought you might find it interesting.'

I paused the TV but stopped myself from shouting Sam's name. Everything is done at a whisper these days. I worry that we don't talk as much as we used to for fear of rousing Adam. He can recognise our voices and it makes him worse.

It reminds me of when Sam was a baby and was so responsive to my voice. He would wake at the sound of it, turn his head if he heard me, cry out if he was being held by someone else and I spoke.

'How come?' Sam asks.

'There were hundreds of safety deposit boxes in the Twin Towers which were destroyed when they came down. Obviously that's nothing compared to the human lives lost, but all sorts of heirlooms and historical documents were lost forever.'

Sam nods his head but doesn't give anything away. He becomes so animated when he's having a conversation with Alice but he never gives that kind of reaction when it's me.

'They said not all the contents were disclosed because they might have been illegal or top secret, so they don't know exactly what they lost.'

I stop talking at a noise from Adam.

I can't stop thinking about those undisclosed safety deposit boxes. What did they hold? Will one of life's mysteries now remain forever unsolved?

The programme shows footage of people going through the metal boxes that they'd managed to retrieve. From the outside the boxes don't look all that damaged but they're black inside. A guy wearing a mask and latex gloves sorts through the contents. Some of it is melted together. It reminds me of that fairy tale about the little tin soldier and the toy ballerina who end up in the fire.

The TV shows a lady holding a blackened diamond brooch.

I was one of the lucky ones. I never thought we'd get this back. It belonged to my grandmother who fled Nazi Germany. I was going to get it repaired but then I changed my mind. It survived one of the most horrendous events ever to happen to America, just as my Grandmother survived the Holocaust.

In the grand scheme of things, these artefacts are nothing compared to the lives that were lost but I still feel sad for them. It's such a weird human trait to transfer emotions and personalities onto inanimate objects.

The programme shows a battered, spherical sculpture, standing in a park in New York. It's discoloured and dented with holes in it.

The sculpture, which stood in the plaza of the World Trade Centre, endures as a symbolic reminder to all those who lost their lives, just like the treasures which were destroyed in the safety deposit boxes. Some of which were never inventoried and have now been lost forever.

The programme then shows for the third time the footage of the plane hitting the second tower, before the credits roll. Footage shown over and over but still hard to comprehend.

'I'm sure it'll be on catch-up if you want to see the start,' I whisper.

I want to engage Sam in a conversation but the thought of aggravating Adam stops me. A flash of anger rushes through me. This is my home. Why should I be prevented from sharing time with Sam?

'I wonder what secrets were lost that day.' Sam says.

'I guess we'll never know.'

'All those stories gone forever.'

That must happen with any tragedy. People are taken with things unsaid, stories untold. And the ones who are left behind, their lives are changed forever too.

'Do you think they pretended something in the safety deposit boxes was destroyed when actually it had survived?'

'I suppose that could have happened.'

'Is destroying the truth the right thing to do?'

'What do you mean?'

'Nothing.'

'Tell me, Sam.'

'Dad,' he says, not making eye contact.

'What about him?'

'By keeping him secret, we might never know what happened to him.'

He's right. We might never know the answer. And would knowing really help anyway? The need to have answers to everything is another of those human traits. We ask why to questions that can never be answered. We try to find comfort in meaning but sometimes discovering the truth makes it worse.

'Just forget I said it,' Sam says.

'No, it's good to talk about this. We might never find out what happened to him. Do you want to know?' I ask.

'I don't know. I keep changing my mind.'

'I feel the same.'

'Is it wrong to keep him a secret?' Sam asks.

'Not if we're trying to protect him.'

'But what if...'

'What if, what?'

'It doesn't matter.'

'Tell me, Sam. We've got to be together on this. If you're having doubts, you've got to let me know.'

'What if more people get sick because of him and we could have stopped it.'

'He's not going to make people sick while he's locked up.'

'Never mind.'

'Tell me.'

'He can't stay here forever. We can't keep him locked up for years.'

'We'll think of something, Sam, don't worry.'

I'm lying to both of us though, and I'm sure Sam knows it.

What is this doing to Sam? I should have phoned 999 when it first happened. Why didn't I do that? I still don't really know.

Maybe I should do it now? Take this out of our hands and let strangers make the difficult decisions.

But then all those other doubts come flooding back. The ones that stopped me before. And they're worse now because we've left it too long.

I don't know what to do. I really don't.

'I don't think he'll get better,' Sam says, his voice breaking.

I can see his face reflected in the television.

'I don't either,' I reply.

I pull him into a hug. He resists at first but then he relaxes and buries his head into my shoulder. I feel his stomach convulse against my bump. He tries to stop himself but he can't stop the tears.

I squeeze him and let him cry it out and before long I'm sobbing too.

I don't know how long we stay like that but eventually I feel Sam stiffen up again. I loosen my grip and he stands from the sofa.

'I'm going to bed,' he says and leaves the room.

I pick up the remote control and flick through channels, but I don't take anything in.

What do we do with Adam? Finish him off the way they do in zombie movies then bury him in the garden?

I don't want to admit it but it's taking its toll on me. I never appreciated how tough being pregnant at my age would be and that was before Adam.

I listened and nodded to the midwife when she told me all the risks but I kept thinking those won't happen to me. I'm different from those other geriatric mothers. Adam and I laughed afterwards when I told him she'd called me a mother of advanced maternal age.

I can't deny it though, it's so much harder this time around. I'm exhausted all the time. I'm worried about everything. I'm trying to work as long as possible so we can be financially secure while I'm on maternity leave. I'm terrified of something happening to the baby. And that's before you factor Adam into this and how utterly shit scared I am of doing this alone.

My heart is pounding and I can feel it pulsing in my ears. My leg spasms with cramp and I cry out at the pain and shock of it. I rub my calf muscle and the cramp subsides but the pain inside me doesn't.

I pull a cushion over my face and whisper into the fabric.

'Don't worry, it's going to be okay. Don't worry, don't worry, don't worry.'

The material presses against my nose and mouth, smothering, but not enough to suffocate.

People do that for their loved ones. Hold a pillow over their heads, give them pills. And not just on TV shows like *Casualty*. It happens in real life. Little old men appear in court for ending the life of their dearly beloved wife of sixty years. We put the needs of our loved ones ahead of our own. We take away their pain and suffering even if it brings the same things down on us.

Or we should anyway. That's what unconditional love is.

The classic zombie method is to stab the brain.

Can I do that? Am I strong enough to do that for Adam?

For Sam?

Fall From Grace by Adam Redpath

One question I'm always asked is why take the risk? Why voluntarily take something that can cause such damage to your body and cause such horrific side-effects: risk of heart attack, stroke, hallucinations, diabetes, baldness, infertility, brittle bones, death.

Looking back now, I can't understand it myself. I was such an idiot. At the time there were so many different reasons to do it though – fame, money, to ensure my family had the best of everything. I was reaching the end of my career too, and I was starting to panic. I didn't want to get slower and retire; I wanted to keep going.

I was lucky. The side-effects I experienced were horrible but they weren't as serious as they could have been. Sometimes I'd be doubled over with stomach cramps or forced to stay inside with chronic diarrhoea. My appetite increased too and I was starving all the time. It took all my willpower to stay on a healthy diet and not give in to crisps and Mars Bars. I did sometimes wonder if it was really worth it, but then I'd see my times coming down and the titles being added to my name. With the medals and the fast times came the attention, the advertising deals, the prize money, the sponsorships. It was a hard thing to give up once I'd experienced it. Everyone became used to me winning and I couldn't let them down.

The more successful I became, the more clauses were added to my sponsorship deals. I had to remain in the world's top three for my event of the 400m. I had to remain British record holder for that distance, otherwise they'd take the money away. I'm not asking for pity, but the pressure I was under was immense. I couldn't see a way out.

Sam

'Hey Sam-I-Am.'

Mum's started calling me by my childhood nickname again. Apparently I loved the book *Green Eggs and Ham* when I was a kid. I don't correct her, even though I told her and Dad to stop calling me that years ago.

She looks tired as she comes into the kitchen.

'Pour me one of those, will you?'

She dumps her bag and sits at the breakfast bar. I pour her a glass of milk and sit beside her.

'Thanks,' she takes a big glug of it and wipes her mouth.

She undoes her ponytail, slips the hairband onto her wrist. She tries to shake her hair loose, combs it with her fingers, but it remains kinked and hangs limp around her face.

'Who were you testing today?' I ask.

She's not supposed to tell me but she always does if I ask.

'A runner called Stacey Heggie.'

I just want a normal day where Mum and I talk about everyday things.

Mum rubs her belly and takes another swig of milk.

'She's moving again. Here, feel.'

She presses my hand against her warm belly.

I feel something thump against my hand and look at the scan picture on the fridge. I feel the thump again but then the baby stops kicking. It feels weird touching Mum's belly when nothing's happening so I pull my hand away.

'What do you want for dinner?' she asks.

'I don't mind.'

'How about pizza? Something easy?'

'Yeah, okay,' I nod.

'What have you been up to?'

'Not much really. Homework, on the computer for a bit.'

This is what I want. Normal, everyday, boring conversation between mother and son. Mum nods but she's not really listening to me. She doesn't get up to get a pizza from the freezer. Instead she's looking out into the hallway towards the bedroom.

'How's he been today?' She asks.

I've been trying to ignore him but I can't tell Mum that.

'The same.'

What does she expect? It's not like he's in a coma or got fucking cancer or something. He doesn't have good days and bad days.

There are no good days.

Sometimes I wish he would escape. An excuse to finish it once and for all.

Mum finishes her milk and stands up.

'I'm just going to get changed,' she says.

'Okay.'

I sit at the breakfast bar and wait for her to come back.

And wait.

And wait.

What is she doing? I thought she was just getting changed?

I wander into the hall. She's standing outside the bedroom door.

'Are you okay, Mum?'

'Yeah, fine. Sorry. I'll go and get changed.'

I head back into the kitchen. She's been standing at that door for the last fifteen minutes. What did she think was going to happen?

When I was younger we'd play this game called 'Threefold Time' at the dinner table where we all had to tell three stories about our day. It was fun when I was little but, when I got older, I thought it was stupid and we stopped. I'd give anything for Threefold Time now.

Mum is still standing in the hall. Is this the new fucked-up version of family time?

I kick my chair over and storm past her into my bedroom. I want to yell at her but I can't forget what Dad said.

We have to be patient. It's harder to have a baby at her age.

Where's my pizza? She said she'd make one for us. I'm here. I need her. And I'm fucking hungry. For food. Not for human flesh. She's meant to be looking after me. What's going to happen when the baby comes?

I lie on my bed and work myself up into a rage. I go over all the things I'm going to say to her. I'm more determined than ever to get him out of the house. Roll on Halloween.

There's a knock on my bedroom door.

'What?' I answer.

'You ready for that pizza now?'

She opens the door and her eyes are all red. Her hair needs brushed. Her hands shake.

'Yeah, okay.'

I don't say any of the stuff I want to. I act like it's all okay.

Because she's my mum.

And I love her.

I'm struck again by how old she looks. Not just old, defeated. She smiles at me and her face crumples. And I feel like an even bigger shit for being angry with her.

I follow her into the kitchen. She's struggling to pick up the chair I kicked over.

We have to be patient. It's harder to have a baby at her age.

'Sorry, Mum, I'll get that.'

She looks grateful like it wasn't me who kicked it over in the first place.

'Sit down, I'll get it.' I say.

She's got frozen garlic bread and a pizza on baking trays and is kneeling down to put them in the oven. She waves me away and I'm hit by a blast of hot air as she opens the oven door and slides them inside.

She wobbles as she stands up and I take her elbow.

'I'm fine, I'm fine. My balance is all over the place right now. Don't know where my centre of gravity is anymore.'

I have to get Dad out of here. Away from Mum. Away from the baby. Mum needs to rest, to think about herself. To come in from work and take a bath, not stand outside the door of someone who only answers in grunts.

Alice and I have got a plan worked out now. It sounds totally doable by email, but who knows what will happen when we try to execute it.

Execute.
Execute.

Let's get one plan out of the way for now...

I'll wait till Gran falls asleep then I'll knock on your bedroom window.

If we can lock one of the chains around his chest and pin his arms to the side then we can lead him where we want him to go.

I'll hold him down and then you wrap the chain round him.

We've got just under a week to get everything sorted. I still don't know what I'm going to tell Mum when she comes home and finds him gone, but I'll deal with that when it happens.

The oven timer beeps once before Mum switches it off. Yet another thing that riles Dad up. Gone are the days when it used to beep for ages before one of us would finally get to it and stop the dinner from burning.

I feel myself getting angry again. Why use the timer if you're just going to stand right next to the oven? I get us both another glass of milk while she slices the pizza and garlic bread.

She brings the food over to the breakfast bar and we sit side by side. Mum has a slice of pizza and picks at a piece of garlic bread, leaving the hard crust and only eating the doughy insides, while I eat the rest.

'I think I'm going to get an early night,' she says. 'I'm exhausted.'

'Okay.'

'Can you lock up?'

'Yeah.'

'Night, night, Sam-I-Am.'

She kisses me on the cheek as she leaves the kitchen.

'Night.'

I wipe the kiss away.

She acts like this is normal.

Dad told me I had to look after Mum. Getting him out of here is looking after her.

We have to be patient. It's harder to have a baby at her age.

I check the back door and switch off the kitchen light then go to lock the front door. The chain's already on and the door's snibbed. Mum did it even though she told me to lock up. That's just fucking typical of her. What's the point anyway? The real danger is what's inside, not outside.

In my bedroom, I log into YouTube again.

Baseball bat swung at a zombie's head.

Zombie doused in petrol and then set alight.

A wire is pulled tight around the neck of a zombie and slices the head off.

I search Netflix for something else to watch but give up and go back to YouTube instead.

A man lies on the ground while zombie after zombie falls on top of him. He shoots one in the head, then another, eventually lining up two heads and taking out both brains with the same bullet.

A foot stamps on a zombie's head. It bursts like a water balloon.

I check for any emails from Alice but there's nothing.

I skim over the last few we've sent each other.

I meant to tell you about this programme on 9/11 that Mum and I watched.

We could lead him like Michone in The Walking Dead.

I know it's a TV *show but I think it might work.*

Every time I go up there, I imagine what I'd do if I came face to face with an escaped animal from the zoo.

As if we don't have enough to worry about!

We should wear lots of layers of clothes.

What if we cover his head with a hat or something? So he can't see anything. I've got loads of old ones from when I was learning to crochet.

It could just be a meerkat.

Animals that are locked up want to escape. It's instinct.

What's the motivation. They have food, shelter...

Make sure the batteries in your torch won't run out.

They're not free. I had two hamsters and I looked after them really well, but they both escaped. And when I found them and made the cage more secure they found another way to escape.

It's not brains. It's instinct.

We should take some water with us too.

What would you do if you came face to face with a lion or tiger or bear?

Oh my.

That's not an answer.

Run? Climb a tree? Get eaten, I guess.

Should we take a knife?

A machete comes down on top of a zombie's head and slices it in two.

A zombie's head is slammed in a door. Blood and brains splatter everywhere.

A bullet is fired at a gas tank. Zombies are torn apart in the explosion and fly through the air in a wave of flames.

5th September 2014

Hey Sam,

How's it going? I'm in, you guessed it, Science again! Mr Bennett is so clueless about what's going on. We're doing questions in our book right now. Rachel and me are taking it in turns to find the answers. Right now I'm waiting for Rachel to find the answer to question 15. Oh, she says she's got it now. I need to go and write it down and then it's my turn for question 16.

Hey, I'm back. Rachel and I have finished the questions now, so I can write to you properly instead. Oh wait, Mr Bennett says we have to go over the answers. Sorry!

Me again! I'm at Gran's now, I'm waving through the wall at you. It's now 4:18pm by the way. For some reason Gran is listening to the *Sound of Music* on her record player – she is so weird sometimes. She's making scones and singing away to herself in the kitchen! Anyway, the *Sound of Music* gave me an idea. I'm going to write down all my favourite things and then you have to write back with yours, okay?

Film: *Heathers*

Music: Regina Spektor

Drink: Banana milk

Food: Nachos

TV Show: I can't decide between *Buffy, Dawson's Creek, Gilmore Girls* and *ER* – Mum has all of these on DVD and we watch them all the time!

Book: *Harry Potter and the Prisoner of Azkaban*

Colour: Purple

Season: Autumn

Day of the week: Friday

Actor: Ryan Gosling

Actress: Jennifer Lawrence or Winona Ryder

Sweet: Maltesers

I can't think of anything else and Gran's scones are ready – yum!
I'm going to post this now and eat some scones!

Bye!

Alice

xx

Jude

I lie on the double bed in the hotel but I can't get comfy. I've propped myself up on pillows, stuck rolled up towels under my knees, changed into my jammies, but nothing works. My bump is getting so heavy now and my boobs are huge and make my shoulders ache.

I've spent most of the day doing drugs tests on Judo players. The competition went on all day and we had to test all the finalists. My throat hurts from having to say the same script over and over and over again. I probably could have driven home but I was selfish. I wanted to relax, have a bath, and I would have arrived home too late to do either. Despite the peace and quiet, I still feel on edge. I spent about twenty minutes running a bath but only stayed in for about five.

I flick through a magazine but I can't concentrate. I read the same article four times and still don't know what it was about. Nothing penetrates the brain.

Penetrates the brain.

I can't stop myself from playing out the scene. I've been doing it a lot the last few days. Taking a knife and stabbing Adam in the head with it. Ending it once and for all.

Zombay. Zombay. Zombay, ay, ay.

Every time the scene plays, I'm stabbing my normal Adam in the head, not the monster. Sometimes he's sleeping. Sometimes he's standing in the kitchen with his back to me. Sometimes he's driving the car.

I switch on the monitor app. He's moving from side to side on the bed. His mouth opening and closing.

I don't even know if stabbing him in the head would work and, even if it did, would it help or just create a whole host of new problems?

What would we do with the body? I couldn't face cutting him up into…

At least the way he is now, people will believe our story and not think we'd murdered him.

The baby presses on my bladder and I need to pee again. I try to avoid looking in the mirror. The bags under my eyes look like I've been punched and my hair is so grey. Aren't I meant to be blooming right now?

I have a bottle of blue milk chilling in the mini bar. I took out all the wee bottles of spirits to make room for it and now they're lined up on the desk like a row of shots. I pour myself a glass of milk and lie back on the bed.

What time is it anyway?

7:02pm.

I open my contacts. Facetime Sam.

'Hey.'

'Hi Sam-I-Am, how's it going?'

'Fine.'

'What are you wearing?'

'It's a Halloween costume. I'm Batman. Isn't it obvious?'

'Sorry, yeah, course it is. Just can't see very well on this screen.'

I shouldn't have said that. I hope I've not made him all paranoid about his party with Alice now.

'Okay.'

'Have you had some dinner?'

'Yeah.'

'What did you have?'

'Some cereal and some toast.'

'That's not a proper dinner.'

'I'm fine.'

'Will you get food at the party?'

Jesus. I hear myself and realise how old I sound.

'What?'

'At the Halloween party? What time are you and Alice heading out at?'

'Oh yeah, probably. Not till later.'

'Not too late, Sam. It's a school night remember.'

There it is. I'm officially no longer cool. Was I ever cool?

'I know.'

'And no drinking, okay?'

I might as well go the whole hog now.

'Mum.'

'Sam.'

'I won't.'

'What's Alice going as?'

'I don't know.'

'You guys spend all week texting and emailing. What do you even talk about?'

'Just stuff.'

'Okay, be careful. Look out for each other.'

'Yeah.'

'My hotel's nice but I'm shattered after work so hopefully the baby lets me get some peace. She keeps pushing on my bladder.'

'Too much information, Mum.'

'Okay, Sam-I-Am. I'll let you go and finish getting ready. Text me when you're home so I know you're safe, okay.'

'I will.'

'And everything else is okay? You know?'

'Yeah, yeah, it is.'

'I love you.'

'Me too.'

'Bye, darling.'

'Bye, Mum.'

I feel so lonely when I hang up. I'd hoped to have a proper chat but he's in one of those moods. The joys of communicating with a teenage boy. Sometimes he'll get into some really deep stuff with you but, if he's nervous or worried about something, he clams right up. It must be the party. The pressure of trying to impress Alice. I hope that girl doesn't break his heart. He's so hung up on her.

I wish I could phone Adam and share this with him. I feel so homesick here in this hotel room, but it's for a home that doesn't exist anymore.

Text me when you're home safe. What a stupid thing to say. Home is the one place that doesn't feel safe anymore.

I can feel the tears coming and get up for the TV remote control to distract myself.

I flick through the channels.

I should have gone home after I finished work today. I should have asked them to get someone else to cover for me. I should be taking the midwife's advice. It's only a few weeks now until I'm on maternity leave.

What kind of mother am I? Leaving my son alone on Halloween, just so I can try to escape for a night.

I hope he has a good time at the party.

I switch the baby monitor app on again and prop my phone on the bedside table.

I finish my milk and need to pee again.

While I'm up, I brush my teeth. I might as well go to bed. I want to leave early tomorrow and sleep is a welcome respite. It's the only time I can forget what's happening.

I check my door's locked but it's hard to tell in these hotel rooms. I look out the peephole at the empty hallway and it makes me uneasy. I imagine someone out there. An eye peering back at me.

I get the chair from the desk and prop it in front of the door. Just in case. Maybe I'm extra jumpy because it's Halloween. Which is stupid, because nothing could be more terrifying than what is happening at home right now.

Back in bed, I flick through channels again. No scary movies for me tonight.

Friends.

That'll do. I've seen each episode so many times I can let it wash over me like background music.

I turn the volume down slightly before I turn off the bedside light and close my eyes.

I don't know what time it is but I need to pee again. The TV has switched itself off and the room is in darkness. I stumble, disorientated, to the bathroom but forget about the chair in front of the main door and bash into it.

I switch the light on and it's so bright that I have to shut my eyes. I feel like I've been asleep for hours. Sam was meant to text me when he got home.

I swipe my phone into life when I get back to bed and the baby monitor app instantly loads up.

I'm about to turn it off when I see something.

I must be half asleep. I thought I saw someone moving about in the bedroom.

Maybe Adam's escaped?

No, he's still chained to the bed.

It takes me a moment or two to work out what I'm looking at. Like an ultrasound of the baby. I don't see it at first, but then it all becomes clear.

I grip the phone.

Sam.

What is he doing?

Someone else is there too. Who is that? And what are they wearing?

It looks too big to be... no, it is. It's Alice.

Alice. What is she doing there? Sam's told her. Did he get drunk at the party and let it slip? He promised...

Suddenly his broken promise is the least of my worries.

'Sam, Sam.'

Wait. There's an option to speak to the baby on this thing. How do you do it again? I see a microphone symbol, press it and speak into my phone.

'Sam. Sam. What are you doing? Get out of there. Sam.'

He stops for a moment but I don't think he can hear me.

I have to phone him but that means closing down the app. Leaving me blind to what's happening.

I watch in shock, unable to do anything as he and Alice approach the bed.

You can't help by watching. Turn it off. Turn it off and phone him. Do it now.

I swipe to my last few calls.

Tap on Sam's name.

It rings and rings then goes to voicemail.

'Oh for fuck sake. Sam, pick up, answer the phone.'

I try again but the same thing happens.

Maybe he doesn't have his phone on him?

I try one more time.

Fuck. I have to know what's happening. I open the baby monitor app.

It's worse than before. Sam's on the bed, straddling Adam. Alice puts something over Adam's head. It's a hat. She's pulled it right down over his face.

Oh my God. They're going to... I can't watch this. They're going to execute him right in front of me.

Wait. Where's Alice gone?

Suddenly Adam's legs are free and Sam is thrown like a ragdoll. He and Alice are pushing Adam down onto the bed. He's too strong for them. They're going to get themselves killed.

What do I do?

Phone Sadie? Phone 999? Neither of these options are appealing but they're preferable to seeing my son killed. I feel so helpless.

I start to pull on clothes. I need to get home. I need to get home right now.

I can't stop myself from watching. I have to see what happens.

Why are they unchaining him? They wouldn't do that if they were planning on ending it. Are they just tormenting him? Maybe they're drunk and this is some stupid Halloween prank. Sam wouldn't be that daft, would he? But he's so infatuated by Alice. He'd do anything for her.

I pick up the hotel phone and try to dial Sam's mobile again. It doesn't work because I haven't pressed the number for an outside line. I lift the handset and turn it over. Where are the goddamned instructions? How do you get an outside line? I try random numbers, 1, then 9. One of these must get me to reception.

I keep watching the phone app. Sam struggles with Adam on the bed. Alice has disappeared again. What are they doing?

I scream out loud as Adam tries to bite Sam on the arm.

'Hello, you've reached reception...'

At last.

'...I'm sorry but there's nobody here at present...'

For fuck sake. What sort of hotel is this?

I switch the app off and try Sam on my mobile again.

And again.

And again.

Shit. Shit. Shit.

This time it doesn't even ring but goes straight to voicemail.

Fuck. What do I do? What do I do?

I open up the app again.

Sink back onto the bed at what I'm seeing. I can't... I...

It's worse than before.

An empty bed.

An empty room.

They've gone.

They've all gone.

Hi Alice,

Thanks for your letter. I saw you and your gran having dinner in the kitchen when I went to get it. I'll try and write a quick reply so that you can get it tonight too! I just got in because it was parent's night at my school so I had to hang around for ages while Mum and Dad went to speak to all my teachers. It was so boring. School was totally boring in general today. I had a Geography test first thing which I totally failed because it was so hard and I did zero work for it. Then I had PE and they made us run laps of the track even though it was freezing and actually hailstoning at one point!

Anyway, I liked your list of favourite things, although your taste in TV is shocking! Why are you watching all that old crap, you need to watch some more up to date TV and your Mum needs to get some new DVDs! Anyway, here is my list.

Film: *Avengers Assemble*

Music: Foo Fighters

Drink: Irn Bru

Food: Pasta

TV Show: *The Walking Dead*

Book: I'll come back to this one.

Colour: Blue, I suppose. Don't really care.

Season: Summer? Never really thought about it but summer = summer holidays!

Day of the week: Saturday

Actor: Not sure, but I quite like Daniel Craig as Bond.

Actress: Scarlett Johansson

Sweet: Most of them!

Sorry for the rubbish hand writing, I'm trying to write this fast so I can post it to you and Mum keeps shouting me for dinner!

See you soon,

Sam

XX

Sam

I sit in my bedroom with the lights off and the curtains open, waiting for Alice.

It's been over forty-five minutes since she texted me.

Gran just gone to bed with a Horlicks, give me half an hour or so... x

I've been in my Halloween costume all night. Good job I dressed up as Batman rather than the zombie costume I was thinking about. Mum would not have been impressed if I'd answered the phone like that. I've got to let her believe everything's okay tonight. Not give her any excuse to come home early.

When I younger, guisers would come to our door on purpose so they could see Dad. He'd play along, open the door wearing his medals, give them a snack size Mars Bar and an autograph. After the drugs scandal they'd still come to see him, but for different reasons. Some of the older ones would throw eggs at the windows, toilet paper our car. We'd hide inside and not answer the door.

I guess we've always preferred hiding away to sharing our problems. Us versus the world.

I check the time again.

10:47pm.

Where is she? I've got myself all geared up. I don't want to do it on my own but I will if I have to.

Where are you? X

My finger hovers over the send button.

Maybe she's fallen asleep?

I take off my Batman mask, make myself my fourth coffee of the evening. While I'm waiting for the kettle to boil, I fill the kitchen sink with cold water and dunk my face into it. I try to keep my eyes open but it's impossible.

I used to do that when I was younger to wash the sleep away. Dad raced abroad a lot and he always had races that were on overnight because of the time-difference.

I think this had better be my last cup of black coffee. I'm getting anxious and twitchy. I head back to my room but I can't stay still, keep pacing up and down, checking the contents of my rucksack, glancing at the window.

If she doesn't come by the time I've finished this coffee then I'm going without her.

I try to visualise what we're about to do, but I can't. All I know is that I just want it over with. I can't wait to be back here in my room later with it all behind me.

It sounded so easy when we were planning it.

Make sure the batteries in your torch won't run out.

We should wear lots of layers of clothes.

We could lead him like Michone in The Walking Dead.

It was like we were the Famous Five, sneaking out in the middle of the night to investigate a mystery.

Five Hide their Zombie Dad in a Tower.

I open my window and peer out. It's freezing. I've got loads of layers on under the rest of my Batman costume, but I can feel the chill against my face. I put my mask back on but it doesn't offer much protection. I hoped all the extra padding would look like muscles but I just look like Bruce Wayne's let himself go.

Layered up for protection. I saw that in one of the YouTube videos. Harder for a bite to reach the skin.

Where's Alice? Why isn't she here yet?

I panic that she came when I was making coffee and I've missed her. I check my phone but there's nothing.

I go through my bag again.

Head torch. Regular torch. Rope. Water. Ginger Beer. Sandwiches and fresh eggs from the kind farmer's wife whose land we're camping on...

Kitchen knife.

I don't remember the Five carrying one of those.

I don't want to use it, but I have to be ready.

Just in case.

Dad knows something's up. He's calmer. I can't hear him moving around in a frenzy like he normally does.

Zombie. Zombie. Zombie.

I need to keep saying the word. Not Dad, a zombie. If I don't think of him as Dad, then it makes it easier to do this. And I can. I can do this.

I jump as there's a tap on my window.

'Hey, Batman,' Alice grins.

I lift the mask and rest it on my head.

'What kept you?'

'Sorry, I knew you'd be freaking out. Gran took forever to go to sleep.'

'I'm not freaking out. I thought you were coming as Wonder Woman?'

I clock the boiler suit, the bag on her back.

'Nah, too clichéd. Everyone was dressing up as Wonder Woman. I'm a Ghostbuster instead. Much cooler. You okay? You look a bit...'

'What?'

'Nothing, nothing.'

'I'm a bit wired,' I say. 'Too much coffee. I'll let you...'

Alice pulls herself in through the window. All the times I've fantasised about her sneaking into my room at night, I never thought it would be under these circumstances.

'I could have let you in the front door,' I say.

'I've always wanted to climb into someone's bedroom. It's so *Dawson's Creek*. You're the only person I know who lives in a bungalow.'

'That the only reason you're helping?'

'Of course.' She squeezes my arm, 'Don't look so worried, Batman.'

'Jeezo, did you eat all these yourself?' Alice asks.

My bed is covered in sweet wrappers. Funsize Maltesers, Haribos, mini Twix's, Scream Eggs with the green fondant inside.

'I think Mum felt guilty for leaving me on Halloween.'

'Gran made these amazing cakes tonight with black icing. It's a shame all the kids think she's a witch. I brought you a couple in my bag, but I guess you don't need them.'

I forgot that we're not the only freaks in the neighbourhood. Two for the price of one to the guisers. The drugs cheat and the witch.

We stand looking at each other.

'What now?'

'I guess we do this crazy thing?'

'Come on then.'

We dump our bags in the hall and stand outside the door.

'Ready?'

'Yeah,' Alice nods. 'Wait.'

She leans towards me and, for a moment, I think she's about to kiss me, but she reaches behind my head and slips off the Batman cape and mask.

'These might get in the way. Put them on after, okay?'

'Good thinking,' I say.

'Batman.' She smiles and places them on top of our rucksacks.

'Have you got enough layers on?' I ask.

'As many as will fit under this boiler suit, I'm roasting.' She replies.

'Me too.'

I'm starting to feel a bit queasy. I don't know if it's because of what we're about to do or all the coffee and chocolate I've had. My stomach is churning. I feel like I need a shit, but I've been to the toilet four times already. I hope I don't fart in front of Alice.

Dad's... the zombie's making a weird noise, guttural, a bit like a growling dog.

I can still feel Alice's fingers, wisping the nape of my neck. I close my eyes, try to shake it away. Get my head back in the here and now. I shouldn't be enjoying this.

'Sure you're okay?' She asks.

'Yeah. I'm running on sugar, adrenaline and coffee here,' I say. 'It's a weird combination.'

'The hard stuff,' she replies.

I'm not sure whether she's taking the piss or not. I've never even been drunk before. She probably does think I'm some kind of loser. I bet Ray...

No, come on Sam. Get your head switched on.

'Hey, whatever works for you.' She smiles.

The smile is worse than the teasing. My gut is all over the place.

We need to get moving. If we don't start soon, we'll never do it.

Fuck it.

I push open the door. The light from the hallway spills into the room and onto the bed, where Dad's surprisingly still. What if he's improving or what if...

I'm hit by the stench. It fucking stinks in here. I turn away, gag. I don't want to puke. Alice lifts a hand up to her face, grimaces. I feel guilty again, for being embarrassed by the smell. He can't help it. He's a zombie. At least if I fart she won't think it's me.

Zombie. Zombie. Zombie.

Most Dads embarrass their sons by showing home movies, old photos of them naked in the bath, arriving early to pick them up from a date. Mine does it by smelling like a rotting corpse.

Wait. Not Dad.

Zombie. Zombie. Zombie.

Alice reaches for the light switch.

'Should we switch it on?'

I don't want to. I don't want to see what he looks like, not properly. I don't want Alice to see what he's become. We can't do this in the dark though.

'Yeah,' I reply.

The light comes on and his attention is drawn to the lampshade hanging above him. Then he sees us and begins to shake and snarl as we approach the bed.

He's changed so much since I was last in here. He looks smaller, thinner. Dad has always been fit, but he was strong, toned and muscley. Not anymore. Everything seems loose, his skin papery and formless. He's almost purple in colour. Stuff is oozing out of him too, his nose, his mouth, his eyes. It's like that foamy stuff you get on the beach but it's red and bloody.

For a moment I'm sure I hear Mum's voice and it stops me. It sounds so real but it must be in my head. My guilt manifesting itself.

My phone starts to ring in my pocket.

I dig about for it under my costume.

It makes Dad worse, his movements rocking the bed.

'Turn it off, Sam,' Alice says.

'I'm trying.'

I eventually find it but it's stopped ringing by the time I get to it, so I put it on silent. Almost immediately it starts to vibrate in my hand.

Mum.

'Shit, it's my mum.' I say.

'Just ignore it.'

It rings off, then immediately starts again.

'Sam, come on.'

I switch my phone off and put it in the back pocket of my jeans under my costume.

We stand next to the bed and I try to psyche myself up.

'You think this will work?' Alice asks.

'It better.'

I don't want to touch him. He's viscous and gooey and he stinks.

Alice won't want to come near me if I'm covered in that.

This isn't about Alice. Come on, Sam. You have to do this.

I climb onto the bed next to him and push down on his chest, but my fingers can't grip properly. He's not solid enough. I need to use force, but I'm worried my hands are going to disappear down to the bones. There's no way I'll be able to hold him once Alice loosens the chains.

'I'm going to have to sit on him,' I say, as I straddle his torso.

It reminds me of the countless wrestling and tickling games we would play, only this time he's really trying to hurt me. Too many layers constrict my movement and I'm not balanced very well. He rolls from side to side, trying to bite anything that goes near his mouth. I push down on his shoulders. Feel us both sink. He's all wet. It seeps into my clothes.

Zombie. Zombie. Zombie.

'Sam, be careful,' Alice's voice registers but it's like she's far away.

Dad's eyes are milky, his pupils enlarged. I look into them and try something, so I don't regret forever what we're about to do.

'Dad,' I lean my face close to his.

'Dad,' I whisper.

I wait for some flicker of recognition, but there's nothing.

He's really gone.

Zombie. Zombie. Zombie.

His teeth bite, bite, bite at me, eyes rolling. He doesn't see his son, only flesh. The skin above his lips has disintegrated. I can see some of his jawbone through a hole in his cheek.

Alice grabs my arm as he snaps at me.

'Oh God, Sam. That was close. What are you doing?'

'Sorry, nothing.'

I'd almost forgotten she was here.

She pulls a large, crochet hat out of a pocket and slips it over Dad's head so it covers his eyes. Blinkered. I'm glad his eyes are hidden but I wish it was his whole face.

'Sam, I'm going to unchain this now. Are you ready?'

'Yeah. I'm ready.'

She releases the padlock on the lower chains. I feel it immediately as his legs break free underneath me. He's so strong, so determined. He flips me and I fall to the side. His mouth snaps at my arm, misses, bites down on air.

'What are you doing? Leave his legs till last. We need to pin his arms down.'

'Shit, Sam. I'm so sorry. I didn't think.'

Alice jumps onto the bed and pulls Dad away from me.

I regain my balance, tense every muscle, so I'm a deadweight on top of deadweight.

'It's okay, just do the top chain now. Quick,' I say.

'You can't hold him on your own.' She's rocking up and down, like she's riding one of those bucking bronco machines.

'I'm okay. I just wasn't ready there.'

'You sure?'

'Yes, just do it quickly.'

I can feel the strength starting to leave me, my muscles aching. Flies hover and I want to swat them away but I need both hands to hold him.

Not him, not him. It. It.

I brace myself as Alice climbs off the bed and it becomes one against one again. I hear her fumble with the key and padlock and I'm ready for when the chains slacken.

'Ready?'

'Yeah, go.' I reply.

The chain gives and then Alice is back on the bed again. I allow Dad to rise and she loops the chain around his torso, pulling his arms in against his sides, then tries to lock it in place with the padlock.

'He's moving too much, I can't get it.'

I hold him as tight as I can.

'Almost, almost.'

'Alice, quick. I don't think I can hold him much longer.'

Was he always this strong? Holding back so as not to hurt me when we would play-fight?

Alice's breathing is fast and heavy.

'Got it.' She says.

I'm scared to let go but I don't think there's any strength left in me. I relax and roll onto the floor, my clothes damp and clinging.

He writhes around on the bed. His arms secured but his legs free, the extra length of chain hanging like a dog lead.

'What if he can't actually walk?' Alice says.

She's shaking. I can feel it even though we're not touching. Corstorphine Hill seems so far away right now.

'Only one way to find out,' I reply.

I hand Alice the end of the chain and she pulls on it, while I get behind him and push him up into a sitting position.

He's still trying to bite us and his head jerks from side to side. He senses his new freedom and it doesn't take very much effort to get him up to standing. He sways on the spot, and I think he's about to collapse, but then he finds himself again and shuffles towards Alice. His knees and elbows are stiff but he can move.

'Cool. He can walk,' she says, moving backwards as he stumbles towards her.

Cool. Nothing about this is cool, but the same phrase went through my own head.

'Easy bit over,' I say.

Alice laughs, a nervous laugh, and we half-drag, half-lead him out of the room. I feel something flip in my stomach. He's leaving our home, probably for the last time. I glance back at what's left of his and Mum's bedroom. The bed I would creep into when I was small, and snuggle up between them.

I shut the door.

Alice swings her rucksack onto her back. I slip the Batman mask on so she can't see me cry. I pick up my bag too but leave the cape. It's too difficult to put on while trying to keep hold of the chain and I don't feel like much of a super-hero right now.

'Wait,' I say. 'He's in pyjamas, he doesn't even have any shoes on.'

His toes and the soles of his feet are black.

'Do you want to try and put some on him?'

I play out how we would go about doing that and shake my head.

'No, let's just get going.'

Alice holds the chain and Dad follows her out of the house and onto the pavement. I lock the front door but I can barely see what I'm doing in this mask.

I take the chain from Alice and he follows us as we walk. I can't believe this is actually working. He's going more or less where we want him to.

It's going to take longer than we'd anticipated though. He drags his feet, weaves across the pavement like a drunk, head rolling, reacting to every noise. Fingers at his sides, clutching at nothing.

I hadn't factored in the weight of the chains either. They're so heavy. My arms are burning. I'm not going to admit that to Alice though.

Alice keeps lookout in front, but doubles back every so often to help me tug on the chain when he heads off in the wrong direction.

He growls and snaps, but he seems happier. Like a dog let loose. The smell's not so bad out here either. It lingers but isn't as dense as it was in the house.

He's distracted by lights and pumpkin lanterns which decorate the houses we pass.

Alice glances at her watch.

'This is taking longer than we thought.'

'I know. Do you want to go back?'

'No, of course not. I'm just worried we won't make it in time.'

I've never been out this late before. Or is it early? The streets are deserted but every so often a car or a taxi goes past. I tense up the first couple of times but they drive on.

'I can't believe nobody has stopped,' Alice says.

'Edinburgh's full of freaks. Nobody cares about a couple more.'

Dad's groans get louder, his arms push against the chains.

Alice and I look at each other, then I see them.

'Shit, shit.'

There's a group of guys on the opposite side of the street.

'Just keep going, don't draw attention,' Alice says.

I almost laugh. Draw attention. We're dragging a zombie on a chain.

The guys shout across the road to us.

'What did they say?' I ask.

'No idea,' Alice replies, as we both try to keep going.

'Crap,' Alice says as they stumble across the road towards us.

They're in fancy dress too, a zombie, Darth Vader and Elvis.

Elvis tries to pull the hat off Dad's head as they reach us. Dad's head snaps from side to side.

'Leave him alone,' I pull Dad away.

'Just messing about, Batman,' he replies.

'Come on, guys,' Alice says. 'He's really drunk, we're taking him home.'

'Awesome costume,' says Elvis. 'Are they his real feet? Yours is shite, Steve, compared to this.'

The zombie shrugs. He sways from side to side.

I pull Dad's hat back into place, try to avoid his teeth.

He's getting all worked up, lurches around the pavement, trying to get free of the chains.

'Is he okay? How'd you get his hands to look like that?' Darth Vader asks.

'It's professional make-up,' Alice says. 'He was working at that zombie pop-up bar on the Grassmarket.'

Darth nods. I'm impressed at Alice's ability to lie like that. She's so quick. So convincing.

'We really need to get going,' I say.

'Wait, selfie, selfie,' says Darth.

'Yeah,' says Elvis.

The zombie stays silent. Still swaying from side to side.

Darth rummages under his costume, pulls out a phone. He lifts his mask up from where it's hanging round his neck, does the 'ohber, ohber' breathing like some method actor getting into character.

Elvis laughs and positions himself next to the zombie, while Darth stands in front of Dad and I. He holds up his phone, trying to get us all in the shot. I don't like the way he looks at Alice, the way he puts an arm around her.

'A bit closer, guys,' he directs.

Alice gives me a look and I shrug. Dad won't stay still. All these people around him. It's driving him crazy.

'Whoa, he's a bit aggressive when he's drunk,' says Elvis, taking a step away from Dad.

'His nickname's Begbie,' Alice replies.

Elvis laughs, like he's not sure if she's joking or not.

'Come on, just take the fucking photo already,' he says.

'Alright, alright,' Darth replies.

'Jesus, was that you, Steve? That's fucking reeking.'

'Fuck off, it wasn't me.'

Darth holds his phone at arm's length. There's a click as he takes the photo and then we all break apart. I'm sweating so much under all these layers.

Darth checks the photo, gives us a thumbs up.

'Awesome, guys, awesome.'

'See you later,' Alice says.

'We're heading to a party. Why don't you guys join us?' Elvis asks Alice.

'No, sorry. We need to get going,' she replies.

'I could give you my number in case you change your mind?'

'Fuck sake, she looks like she's still at school,' says Darth.

Elvis shrugs, puts his phone away and the three of them stagger off in the opposite direction.

I'm desperate to get away and I tug the chain too hard at the same time as Dad lunges. He stumbles and falls to his knees, starts to half-crawl, half-drag himself along the pavement.

'Shit, shit. Sorry, Dad.' I say it without thinking.

Zombie. Zombie. Zombie.

I try to pull him up but he won't let me. He won't stay still, keeps fighting against me. I'm pissed off at those guys, for stopping us, for speaking to Alice like that, for making me do this. And I'm pissed off at Dad too.

'For fuck sake, will you just stop trying to fucking bite me.' I lose it and push him away from me, letting the chain fall to the ground.

'Sam. It's okay.'

Alice takes my hands. I can still feel the sensation of the chain, throbbing in my palms.

'I'm sorry,' I say. 'I know it's not his fault but sometimes I really hate him. I hate him for doing this.'

'I know, I know.' She squeezes my hands. They're shaking. I hadn't realised until now.

'It's not his fault, I know it's not but, fuck. I fucking hate this.'

I close my eyes, grateful for the second time tonight that she can't see my face behind the Batman mask. I try to imagine that it's just the two of us. Shut out the noise of Dad in the background. I can't though. I can't relax. I can hear his movements and his groaning and I have to open my eyes and check where he is.

'Let's keep going.'

'You sure?'

'Yeah, let's go.'

Between us, Alice and I manage to lift Dad back to standing.

'That was a good save about the pop-up bar,' I say, as we start walking again.

'Thanks,' she replies.

I notice Alice wipe her hands on her boiler suit. She sees me watching and tries to pretend she's just sorting her clothes.

'You don't have to pretend. I know he's gross.'

'He can't help it,' she replies.

'I guess.'

'This is not how I'll remember him. I know he's all messed up and stuff, and this might be my last memory with him, but it won't be my lasting one.'

'What will?' I ask. 'The rabbit?'

'Partly that, but there's another time I never told you about. It was ages ago. Do you remember that guy, Pete, my mum was seeing?'

'Oh yeah. That fuckface.'

'Exactly. I'd had a big fight with them both and stormed out. I got the bus to Gran's but she wasn't in, so I ended up sitting on the back step. I was really upset and your dad saw me and invited me in for hot chocolate. I felt like a total idiot, but he was so kind. I guess you and your mum were out somewhere. Anyway, that's how I'll remember him.'

I don't answer. I don't think I can trust myself to speak without my voice cracking.

All these secrets that Dad kept from me.

We walk on in silence. The rasping and groaning from Dad our soundtrack.

'I sometimes wonder if it would be easier...' I say.

'What?' She replies.

'Nah, it doesn't matter.'

'I think I know what you were going to say anyway.'

'Do you think it would hurt?'

'I don't know. I think it would be quick though. It's hard to tell when TV is your only point of reference.'

'I still can't help thinking about your gran and that rabbit.'

'It wouldn't be like that though. Your dad's already starting to... it would be softer... the rabbit's skull...'

She's trying not to say that he's decomposing. That his head is just mush and it would be as easy as sinking a teaspoon into an apple crumble.

'Do you think it's wrong for me to think about it? It feels wrong.'

'No, of course not.'

'Yeah, but we haven't had anyone's medical opinion. We've kept him hidden.'

'I don't think it's any different from switching off someone's life support.'

'Forget it,' I say. 'This is getting too heavy. Let's just get him to the tower. One plan at a time.'

We start to speed up. Dad stumbles but keeps up with us and eventually we reach the entrance to Corstorphine Hill.

It's pitch black when we leave the street-lit pavements for the muddy path up the hill.

Alice slips her head torch on then takes the chain while I do the same. Dad still has the hat pulled over his eyes but the beams from our torches attract his attention and he's drawn towards them.

We start to climb. I'd forgotten how fucking steep this hill is, especially the first part. I'm out of breath and can hear Alice is too.

The chain's so heavy and I'm starting to regret all these layers. I think I might pass out.

It's tough going. We both slip and slide in the dark and struggle to bring Dad with us.

'I thought this bit would be easier,' Alice says. 'I'm totally sweating.'

'Me too.'

It drips down my forehead and stings my eyes.

I'm tempted to let go. Set Dad loose and leave him to run wild. Maybe he'd wander and wander until he decomposed completely.

The slope begins to even out and we head up through the clearing towards the Rest and Be Thankful.

My breathing starts to slow and the burning in my legs subsides. I've got a stitch though. I want to press a hand there but I have to keep hold of the chain.

'The sky looks amazing,' says Alice, looking up.

You can actually see the stars. Usually they're lost behind the street lights and the city. It makes me dizzy looking up at them, as if I'm trapped in a snow globe.

I'm not paying attention to Dad and I stumble to my knees as he stops suddenly.

'What's wrong?' Alice asks.

Dad's head jerks from side to side and he starts to pull me towards the fence that runs along the side of the path.

'I don't know.' I say, struggling to hold onto the chain.

Alice turns her head and for a second the beam lights up the terrified eyes of some sort of antelope huddled down on the opposite side of the fence.

'The zoo,' I say. 'He must smell the animals or sense them or something.'

We hear movement as the creature darts away from us.

'I think they can sense him too,' Alice replies.

'I need your help.'

Alice grabs the chain but he's reluctant to come with us and we're both panting with the effort of it.

I concentrate on using all my strength to get Dad up the final bit of the hill. We trip over roots and rocks. Dad stumbles alongside us, illuminated every so often by one of our torches. Like a strobe light, he looms out of the darkness. Pyjamas torn and covered in dirt, the hat still covering his eyes. Hissing and moaning as his jaw opens and shuts, opens and shuts, opens and shuts.

'Do you watch *CSI*?' Alice asks.

'Sometimes, why?'

'I'm just thinking about how much evidence we're leaving.'

'As long as it's not a hand or a foot.'

We both start to giggle, nervous laughter that builds and builds, breaking the tension slightly.

'Stop, stop it,' Alice says, 'I can't do this if I'm laughing.'

I try to swallow down the laughter, but it keeps coming. Escaping my mouth in gasps and squeaks. My stomach aches and my eyes water. None of this is funny, so why can't I stop laughing?

'Come on,' I say. 'We're almost there.'

The laughter confuses Dad. He forgets about the zoo and remembers us instead. It makes it easier to lead him up the final part of the hill, through piles of rotting leaves, to the clearing at the foot of the tower.

I'm totally knackered, everything aches and I'm coated in sweat. My back, my legs, my arse. I'm sliding around inside all these layers.

'I need some water,' Alice says. 'I'm all light-headed.'

She dumps her rucksack next to the tower door and takes a drink from her water bottle.

'Here,' she says.

She holds the bottle to my mouth and helps me drink. Water dribbles down my chin and she wipes it away, her fingertips brushing my lips. It makes me dizzy.

She drops the bottle back into her bag and takes out the keys, then she unlocks the tower door and pulls it open.

'Watch out, there's a big step here,' she says as she steps inside the tower.

'There's a lot more inside,' I reply.

'Good point.'

'I'll go first. I'll take the hat off and he'll follow me.'

'I need to go first.' She replies.

'No, I'm doing it,' I say.

'Someone has to unbolt the door at the top,' she replies. 'There's no point getting him all the way up there and finding the door shut.'

'Oh yeah. I'd forgotten about that.'

'Give me a head start,' she says. 'So I'm ready for you.'

'Okay,' I nod, but she's already away.

Her footsteps rattle the metal staircase as she climbs, the light from her head torch bobbing up and up. I pull Dad inside the entrance and glance around the floor of the tower; there's a broom propped against a wall, an old table, a couple of folded up picnic chairs. Under other circumstances I would be terrified standing here alone at night, on Halloween of all days. But the monster's my dad and I brought him here.

'Right, you're good to go,' Alice shouts from above.

I pull on the chain but Dad's like a dog refusing to walk. What if he can't do stairs? I can't face having to take him all the way back and chain him to the bed again.

'Come on,' I say. 'Come on.'

I pull off Dad's hat. The wool's heavy and wet, soaked with who knows what, and it drops to the floor with a clump. We face each other, my head torch spotlights the black spreading tip of his nose. His mouth, snap, snap, snaps at me.

He lunges forward and I step back onto the staircase.

'Everything okay?' Alice calls.

Dad's head moves as he tries to work out where the voice is coming from.

'He's not coming up the stairs,' I say.

'Hang on, I'll come down and help.'

Dad reacts to Alice's voice again and he takes a step forward. Alice's feet rattle down the stairs. Dad steps onto the staircase now.

'Wait, stay there.' I shout. 'He's following your voice, keep shouting.'

'Hellooo down there. Follow me,' Alice shouts. 'I'm up here!'

He starts to climb the stairs as I ascend backwards.

'Come on, keep going, keep going. I'm up here.' Alice calls.

My legs shake. The staircase is narrow and twists in a spiral up the centre of the tower. I'm usually okay with heights, but the combination of my head torch, the drop, and being followed by him is making me queasy. I can see spots in front of my eyes and I'm terrified I'm going to faint. I want to steady myself with the bannister but I need both hands to grip onto the chain. The stairs creak, the stone walls and narrow, grated windows flashing around me in the beam of the torch.

Alice is still shouting but it's making Dad agitated now.

'Okay, you can stop,' I say. 'He's following me.'

My voice echoes and I swallow down sick.

Dad follows, snarling, as we twist up the spiral staircase.

'Almost there,' Alice's voice is closer. 'Be careful, there's not much room up here.'

The stairs get steeper and narrower as we get closer to the top and I have to turn my back on Dad so I don't fall. I imagine tumbling back down all those stairs. Dad falling over the bannister and pulling me down with him. The vertigo makes my stomach churn.

'You made it,' Alice says, her breath against my face.

My blood is pumping in my ears as she leads me through the door. I pull Dad after us. We're out in the open now, on top of the tower. It's too dark to see any kind of view.

Alice gives Dad a shove and he sprawls onto his front.

'Quick, before he gets up.'

'Wait. Can't we at least unlock him?'

Now that it's time to leave him, I want to delay the moment. We can't leave him like that. She shouldn't have pushed him over.

'Alice, shine your torch on him.'

He struggles on the ground, trying to turn himself over.

'Do you still have the key for the padlock?' I ask.

'Are you sure?'

'I can't leave him like this.'

She fumbles in her pocket, passes the key to me.

I try to unlock him, but the padlock is underneath and he won't stay still.

'Alice, can you help?'

I can tell by her hesitation that she thinks this is a bad idea but she helps me undo the lock.

'That's it,' I say.

Dad slips the chain and Alice screams as he lunges at her. Her head torch goes out and I can see her pushing Dad away in the light of my own torch.

'Alice, Alice.'

Everything is shapes now, flickers of detail. We push and pull, stumble and scrape against stone walls. Dad's arms reach and grab as we try to get away from him. I hear Alice's breath, fast and loud, as she struggles. The thought of ending it now flashes through my head but, like an idiot, I've left my knife in the bag at the bottom of the tower. Finally, I manage to heave him back by the shoulders. We both fall over and he rolls to one side.

'Quick! Now!' I shout, getting to my feet and scrambling towards the door. I hear Alice scream again as she tumbles down the first few steps.

'Alice, are you okay?'

I try to pull the door shut behind me but my hands slip and I can't get a proper grip.

'Alice, you need to bolt the door. I can't let go of the handle.'

'My hands are shaking too much. I can't grip it properly.'

'It's okay, it's okay. Just relax. Take your time. I've got the door.'

I don't think I can hold it for much longer. My arms are like jelly. Come on, come on, hurry the fuck up, I say in my head. If you hadn't shoved him like that, this wouldn't have happened.

She's sobbing now. Sucking in gasps of air as she fumbles with the bolt.

'I've got it, I've got it,' she says as she slides it shut.

I relax, let go, and we both slump onto the landing against each other. Scratches and moans come from the other side of the door.

'Are you okay?' I ask.

'I think so,' she replies.

'Do you think that will hold him?'

'I hope so.'

'What about a padlock?'

'I don't know. I'm not one of the Friends.'

Alice holds my hand and we cling to each other as we make our way down the staircase.

It helps take my mind away from what we've just done.

At the bottom of the stairs, I stop and pick up the hat and slip it in my pocket. Alice lets go of my hand and locks the main door as we exit the tower.

I pull off layers of clothes and stuff them in my bag, gulp down my bottle of water without stopping to breathe. The sweat starts to evaporate and I feel it prickle and chill against my skin.

We walk home in silence. I thought I would feel a release once it was all over but I feel worse than before. Walking home without him. Leaving him there, exposed to the elements. I feel terrible.

Alice hardly speaks. I ask her if she's okay a couple of times until eventually she snaps at me.

'I'm fine. Stop asking, okay.'

It took us almost three hours to get him there and lock him in yet we're back in twenty minutes. We're both filthy, covered in mud and old leaves and who knows what from Dad.

'I'm exhausted,' says Alice.

'Me too,' I reply.

'I need a shower.'

'Thanks for coming with me. I couldn't have done it without you.'

'That's okay. See you later.'

I watch her as she wanders up the path. I will her to turn round and come back. Hug me. Kiss me. Something. But she doesn't. She slips into the house and then she's gone.

I stand on the doorstep and try not to think of a house without Dad. I'm all alone. On the rare occasions this has happened before, it felt like a party. A chance to do what I like. Eat what I like. Watch what I like on TV. Go to bed as late as I want to.

But tonight...

Once inside, I strip down to my boxers and collapse onto my bed. I pull the duvet over myself, let the exhaustion and grief overwhelm me.

Fall From Grace by Adam Redpath

How did a drugs cheat married to a doping control officer get away with it for so long?

I've always been absolutely clear that Jude had nothing to do with it. I made the decision to take banned substances and I kept it a secret from my family. It was really rough for Jude when the story broke, particularly given her position as a DCO. Reporters, strangers on the street, even people she thought were her friends, said terrible things to her and accused her of being complicit.

I think the main reason she didn't suspect me of anything was because she finds the idea of cheating in sport so abhorrent. Never in her wildest dreams would she think her husband was involved. I'm lucky that we have such a strong relationship. We might never have made it otherwise.

I'll admit that I've always been slightly in awe of Jude. We met in Tenerife. I was on warm weather training and she was on a girls' holiday. I noticed her right away and thought she was gorgeous, but it took me a couple of days to find the courage to speak to her. She was having breakfast on her own one morning so I asked if I could join her. Her friends were in bed with hangovers but Jude was up early to go on an excursion to the volcano. She said she wanted to see more than the pool and the bar if she went on holiday. I was on a rest day so I joined her on the trip. At the end of the week we swapped numbers. She told me later she thought she'd never hear from me again. That it was a holiday fling. I called her as soon as I got home though.

She was older than me and she seemed so smart, so sophisticated, way out of my league. What did she see in me?

There's a lot of ego among male sprinters, mind games and strutting, trying to psyche the other guys out. You have to channel that part of yourself or you're beaten before the gun goes off. I'll admit I was a bit cocky in my younger days. I wanted to impress Jude and that feeling has never really left me.

Jude

'Sam. Where are you? Sam, are you here?'

Mud trails across the carpet from the front door to Sam's bedroom. I pick up a discarded Batman mask as I look inside his room. Sam's lying in bed, curled up in the foetal position.

I watch his chest rise and fall, rise and fall, rise and fall. Check his breathing, the way I always have since we first brought him home.

He's okay. Sam is okay.

I relax slightly and allow myself a moment to take that in. He's safe.

I turn towards the other bedroom door. I know without looking that the scene in there will be the same as the one on my phone, but I check anyway.

I push open the door and stand on the threshold of carpet, as if stepping over the crack will kill me. The smell of him lingers on the stained sheets and pillow, but Adam is gone.

I rush back into Sam's room and shake him by the shoulders.

'Sam. Sam, wake up.'

His eyes open, but he's groggy. They start to close again but I pull at him to sit up.

'Sam, where is he?'

I can smell Adam on him. Sam's obviously not showered, just fallen into bed from wherever it was they went.

They.

He told someone else. What else does he share with Alice that he doesn't with me? I'm ashamed of myself but I'm jealous of the hold she has over him, of their closeness.

Sam blinks and runs a hand through his hair.

'Mum, what is it? What time is it?'

He picks up his phone.

'Mum, it's the middle of the night.'

'What did you do, Sam?'

I switch on the bedside light and he puts a hand over his eyes and leans against the headboard. There are wisps of fluffy hair on his bare chest. Not quite a man but not a boy anymore either.

'Mum, before…'

'And you told Alice. You promised me!'

'Mum, calm down.'

'Don't tell me to calm down. What did you do with him?'

'I'm sorry, Mum, I just…'

His hair is all tousled and he looks like he did when he was a toddler and would wake up from a bad dream. I would lie on the bed, curl myself around him, and whisper over and over and over that it was okay, until he settled again.

I sit on the edge of his bed and he pulls his knees up to his chest.

'I saw you.'

'What?'

'I had a baby monitor app on my phone. I saw you and Alice. Do you know how scared I was?'

'I didn't know you had that.'

'That's not the point.'

'You should have told me.'

'Why? So I wouldn't be able to see what you had planned.'

'That's not fair. You've been keeping things from me too then.'

'What did you do?'

'What?'

'With him. Where is he?'

'We just moved him. That's all. You didn't think? You did. You thought we...'

His voice trails off and he's right. I've been thinking the worst. I thought they'd killed him.

'I didn't know what to think.'

'He couldn't stay in the house anymore.'

I'm exhausted and shaky. The adrenaline leaving my system. I put a hand on my belly, rub it. I'm sorry, little one. What am I doing to you?

'Where is he now?' I ask.

'The tower on Corstorphine Hill. Alice got the keys from her gran.'

'Sadie knows?'

I feel my heartrate starting to rise again.

'No, no, Mum. Alice took the keys without telling her.'

'But what if she goes there? Someone could get hurt.'

'The tower's shut all winter. We just need to come up with a new plan before it opens again.'

He looks terrified, like he's expecting me to hit him. The rage starts to dissipate. I was never very good at being the disciplinarian. Even when he was a toddler and we were trying to set boundaries, I'd always struggle if he got upset when I was giving him a row about something.

I lean forward and he flinches as I pull him into a hug.

'I was so worried, Sam. You should have told me.'

All the anger drains out of me and all that's left is exhaustion. I'm so tired right now.

'I'm sorry, Mum. I didn't think you'd agree.'

'That's not a reason to go behind my back. We said we'd be honest with each other.'

'You didn't tell me you had the monitor on your phone.'

The petted lip like a toddler. Caught doing something he shouldn't and trying to pout his way out of it. He's right, I suppose. Neither of us have been entirely honest. Still, I'm the parent. I'm allowed to have the moral high ground here.

'You could have been hurt. You or Alice. How did you even do it?'

'We didn't though. We're both okay.'

I kick my shoes off, prop a pillow behind me.

'We had to do something.'

'I know.' I reply.

My teenage son knows better than me. I've known all along that we couldn't live like this indefinitely. A bit like labour really. I know this baby is going to have to come out of me, but I'm trying not to think about it.

He's right. We can't barricade ourselves away and hope that nobody will notice. The midwives will want to visit when the baby comes. When the baby comes...

I can't even remember how to look after a baby; it was so long ago with Sam. How do I do it without Adam?

One more thing I can't think about right now.

'We can't bring him back either,' Sam says.

'I know.'

'We've got some time now to work something out.'

I close my eyes and slip my legs under the duvet. My little hot water bottle.

'Switch the light off, Sam-I-Am,' I say.

I'm too tired to think about this anymore.

'What?'

'Switch the light off. Let's get some sleep.'

We top and tail in Sam's bed and I move away from Sam to give him room. I know I should get up and go to the spare room, that getting into bed with my teenage son isn't right. I was so worried about him though and I miss human contact.

'Can you hear that, Mum?' Sam whispers.

'Hear what, sweetheart?' I reply, already losing myself to sleep.

'The difference in the house. I feel guilty for enjoying it.'

I rest a hand on his foot.

'Sshhh.'

I can feel it too. The absence of Adam. I can relax, sleep without worrying about what's on the other side of the door. It also makes me ache more than I've ever known. Sleep can't come fast enough right now. I want it to take me completely, just so I can lose this homesick hurt, deep in my belly. The urge is so desperate that it almost wakes me but then I hear Sam's breathing deepen and relax. I tune into it. Count the ins and outs, ins and outs, ins and outs. Feel my fingers start to loosen on his foot as his breathing lulls me down with it.

A car beeps its horn outside and my eyes open. For a moment I'm confused, not sure where I am. I think I'm in bed with Adam. Back in my safe space. I come to, realise it's Sam lying beside me. His body heat stifling, his snoring, his bed. I hate this moment of waking, that every morning I have to remember the truth again.

I find my phone, look at the time.

1:32pm

Shit. How did that happen? I was in one of those dreamless sleeps like I remember having when Sam was a new-born; when, every hour, his cries would drag me awake again from the blackness.

I glance over at him. He has the duvet pulled up over his head. Still fast asleep.

I try to climb out without disturbing him, but I've never been the most graceful, even without my bump. Adam called me a baby elephant. Sam stirs and looks confused as he opens his eyes. We obviously both needed the sleep. It's funny the way that over-sleeping can leave you just as out of it as too little sleep.

'I think we slept in,' I say. 'It's half one.'

He just shrugs. The time doesn't seem to faze him, or the fact he's missed school. If I wasn't here, I think he'd just roll on over and go back to sleep. Instead he reaches for his phone. I watch him swipe the screen, then type.

Is he messaging Alice? I don't ask. I can tell by the way he focusses on the phone that he's not in the mood for talking.

I really need to pee so I rush to the bathroom. That was the longest I've slept in ages but I still feel tired. I splash cold water on my face and go to the kitchen for a glass of milk. I'd better phone Sam's school, make up some story as to why he's not turned up today.

Ten minutes later, Sam appears in the kitchen, dressed in boxer shorts and a t-shirt, hair all over the place.

'I phoned School.' I say. 'I told them we both had food poisoning.'

'Okay.' He replies.

'I feel a bit guilty. Everyone was really concerned to hear that a pregnant lady had food poisoning. I don't know why I said I had it. I just got caught up in the lie.'

He puts the kettle on and tips coffee into the cafetière. He yawns and runs a hand through his hair. He's still covered in dirt and he stinks. I want to know exactly what went on last night but I know better than to ask him right now. He's full of one word answers and attitude.

I'm fidgety, fight the urge to open up the baby monitor app. There's no point now.

Sam makes himself a black coffee. When did he start drinking it black? I bet that's another Alice thing. I wait for him to join me at the breakfast bar but he picks up his mug and heads out of the room.

If he thinks he can ignore me all day then he's wrong. I deserve an explanation. I want to know what happened last night.

'Sam, get back here.'

'What?'

'I want you to take me to where he is.'

It just comes out. I hadn't planned it, but there it is. Saying it aloud feels right. I do want to see where he is.

'I don't have the key.'

'That's okay. I don't have to see him. I just want to see where he is.'

'He's in Corstorphine Tower. You know where he is.'

'I want you to show me.'

'Fine, I'll show you.'

He turns and walks out of the room again.

'Now, Sam. I want to go now.'

'Mum, I'm tired.' He turns and faces me, that petulant toddler look again.

'Now, Sam.'

'I need to have a shower.'

'Fine. Go shower.'

'Fine,' he huffs out of the kitchen.

I get dressed and put on my walking shoes. I've started wearing one of Adam's jackets as I can't get mine zipped up over the bump anymore. While I wait for Sam, I drink a glass of milk and eat a bowl of muesli. My indigestion's getting worse. I'm starting to think it's the sign of a breaking heart rather than a hairy baby. The sweetness replaced by acid and bile. At night, I drape myself over my pregnancy pillow, but it's no replacement for his warmth, the tang of his breathing, his hand on my waist.

'Sure, you're up to this, Mum,' Sam asks as he comes back into the kitchen, 'it's a steep climb.'

'I'm fine. I'll take it easy.'

As I lock the front door, I remember the day Adam and I came to view this house. We bought it on the publicity fallout. The book sales, the interviews and exclusives Adam gave after he was caught. The previous owner had died and their son just wanted to get rid of it.

Sam walks a few steps ahead of me. He's still in a mood. Adam kept joking that he didn't know who had the worst mood swings – his pregnant wife, his teenage son or him when he was on the drugs.

I scan the pavement as we go. I don't know what for. Some trace of Adam?

Pumpkins lie discarded on people's doorsteps; the candles long blown out. It's cold and I slip my hands in my pockets. Feel the scrunch of old receipts and tissues belonging to Adam.

Sam was nine or ten when we moved. He cried all the way home in the car from that viewing. I remember crying myself as we painted the old house before putting it on the market, covering the lines on the wall where we'd marked Sam's height every few months.

We reach the entrance to the hill and start to climb. I have to stop every few steps and catch my breath, still lagging behind Sam who strides ahead.

'You okay?' Sam turns back and takes my arm.

'How the hell did you get him up here?'

I tie my hair back with a bobble from round my wrist, wipe my forehead. Wish I'd thought to bring a bottle of water.

'It's not so steep further up,' Sam says. 'This is the worst bit.'

I look for signs of Adam again. There's nothing though. Just mud, frost, leaves mulching underfoot.

The incline drops and levels out and I start to catch up with myself.

'If you stand over there, you can see the monkeys down in the zoo.' Sam says.

His way of making things better without the awkwardness of having to apologise.

I look where he points but the cages are empty.

'They must be inside.' Sam says and we keep going.

My back and shoulders ache and I stand with my hands on my hips and blow out. Maybe this wasn't such a good idea after all.

'Let's have a seat for a bit.' Sam says. 'The Rest and Be Thankful is just up there.'

I follow him up the slope. Grateful for the break as I sink down onto the bench.

Sam wanders over to the information board.

I glance over his shoulder at the view. There's a golf course below us, but the rest of Edinburgh stretches out behind it. You can see most of the city from here. Arthur's Seat and the Crags dominate the skyline then below that you can pick out the tops of churches and buildings, the Castle, Leith and Berwick Law. You can even see the Forth in the distance, Fife on the other side.

'Read what it says,' I ask.

'It's too long,' he replies.

'Summarise then.'

'This is a place to rest your weary legs and think of travellers who have stopped here over the centuries – or parted like the characters in Robert Louis Stevenson's Book Kidnapped.'

'Keep going.'

'The story starts 400 million years ago when lava cooled... blah blah blah, volcanoes erupted... here we are.'

'Sam. What's that bit down there say?'

'It's a quote from *Kidnapped.*'

'Read it then.'

'When we got near to the place called Rest-and-be-Thankful, and looked down on Corstorphine bogs and over to the city and the castle on the hill, we both stopped, for we both knew, without a word said, that we had come to where our ways parted.'

Kidnapped *by Robert Louis Stevenson.*

'Have you read *Kidnapped*?' Sam asks.

'I don't think so. Have you?'

'No.'

'What have we got to be thankful about?' I ask.

'What?'

'We're at the Rest and Be Thankful.'

'We're not American, Mum, this isn't Thanksgiving.'

'Come on. Humour me.'

'I dunno.'

'Well, I'm thankful that I've got you.' I say.

'I'm thankful I have you.'

'That's a cop-out. You need to think of something on your own.'

'This is stupid.'

'One thing. Come on.'

We've both been sinking and I've let it happen. It's up to me to get us out again. I'm the Mum, I need to be strong.

'For my new little sister,' Sam finally says.

'Good one, Sam-I-Am. I knew you'd get there. Okay, let's keep going.'

'You sure?'

'I'm pregnant, not an invalid. Let's go.'

'It's not far now anyway.' He takes my hand and helps me off the bench. Drops it again as soon as I stand.

I see him in my head, holding hands with Alice last summer. They were in Sadie's garden chair, sharing Sam's earphones. Sam's foot rocked the seat forward, back, forward, back, forward, back. Alice had kicked off her shoes, her bare feet not reaching the grass. It broke my heart a little. I tried to describe it to Adam later, the innocence of it, not at all sexual, but I couldn't get the words right.

They were so peaceful. Their eyes closed, lost in whatever music they were listening to. It was hypnotic. I watched them swing forward and back, forward and back, forward and back, before Sadie brought them juice and biscuits. I wanted to scream at her for disturbing them.

Adam and I never really had any moments like that. Still and silent and perfect, like a scene in a movie. Adam was too restless, had too much nervous energy. Even sitting watching the TV, or asleep in bed, he'd twitch and fidget. I think that's why he was such a good athlete – he channelled all that natural kineticism.

It's funny the way that flesh on flesh can be so different between different people and in different situations; the way it changes over time. The way Sam holds my hand now is not the way he used to when he was a toddler, or the way he held Alice's hand. Or the way Adam held my hand.

'Alright, Mum?'

'Yeah, fine.'

The path's muddy and I try to peer past my bump to avoid sliding or tripping over rocks and tree roots. It's a lot harder when you can't see your feet.

'Just up here.' Sam leads me through the trees towards a clearing. The tower rises into the sky, like a rocket but without its nose cone.

There's an engraving above the door.

CORSTORPHINE

HILL

TOWER

SIR WALTER SCOTT 1771 – 1832

ERECTED IN 1871 BY WM MACFIE OF CLERMISTON

PRESENTED IN 1932 TO THE CITY

BY W.G. WALKER C.A. F.S.A. SCOT

I look up but I'm too close to the tower. It leans over me, leaves me dizzy. I take a couple of steps back, shade my eyes with one hand and look up again. Rectangular windows are cut into the side of the tower. I count them. One, two, three, four.

I start to circle it, soggy leaves sinking underfoot. It doesn't take long to walk right round and so I just keep going. Sam does the same but in the opposite direction. We pass each other every rotation, without saying a word, like orbiting planets. I can't see Adam. I can't hear him. But he's there. I know he is. And I know that he knows we're down here. I can feel it. That eerie sensation of not being alone.

Fall From Grace by Adam Redpath

My punishment was as expected: a two year ban from all competition, a lifetime Olympic ban. I was stripped of all my titles and had my times and records annulled. I had to give all of my medals back. The ones I'd had out on display in a glass cabinet in our hallway. The ones that Sam brought his friends home to see and hold. They would marvel at the size, the weight, the splendour. I felt so pathetic as I emptied the cabinet and packed them into boxes. They left their shapes in the dust on the shelves.

That was all humiliating enough, but even more worrying were the financial recriminations. The loss of sponsorships and advertising – nobody wants to be associated with a drugs cheat. I had to return all prize money. We were left completely broke. We had to sell our house, our car, just to make ends meet.

I thought I might lose my family too. Only Jude knows how close she came to leaving me for good, but I know she seriously considered it. I remember thinking, for the first time, how glad I was that my parents were no longer around to see what I'd done.

I ended up on anti-depressants. I became a recluse. At my lowest point, I ran out to the Forth Road Bridge and thought about ending it all.

Sam

'So your mum was okay in the end then?' Alice asks.

'She was fine,' I say.

I gloss over the story of going back to the tower and I don't mention anything about us sleeping in the same bed.

It's the first time I've seen Alice since we moved Dad. We sit in her gran's kitchen, eating homemade flapjacks and drinking coffee.

Alice swirls single cream into her coffee. Like oil, it collects on the surface.

'Cream?' she asks, holding the tub over my mug.

'I'm fine with black,' I say.

When did she start putting cream in her coffee?

Alice's coffee turns caramel as she stirs. It looks good. Better than this bitter, black coffee that deep down I'm not convinced I really like. I wish I'd said yes to cream now.

'My muscles were totally aching afterwards,' says Alice. 'I was hobbling about like an old granny.'

'Me too.'

'I tried to pretend I was ill, but Gran wasn't buying it. She made me get up for school. I could barely keep my eyes open in Maths and fell asleep straight after dinner. I think Ray thought I was some kind of freak. I just said we'd been at a Halloween party.'

I imagine Ray wondering who I am. What I look like. Stalking me on Facebook like I stalk him. Jealous at the thought of me and Alice at a party together. It feels good and I help myself to another flapjack.

'Your gran didn't suspect anything?'

'Nah, she was totally clueless.'

'Where is she anyway?'

'Haddington.'

'No way. She still goes there.'

I put my hand over my eyes.

'Yup.'

'That's so gross. Did you not promise never to talk about that again?'

'You asked.'

It's in there before I can stop it. The image of Alice's gran, completely naked, everything hanging loose as she swims breaststroke. For some reason, the naked version of her is still wearing her gardening hat. I don't know why but my dick comes to life.

Alice pulls my hand away from my eyes. Her fingers on mine don't help, and I squirm in my seat.

She makes more coffee and I watch the granules swirl in the cafetière.

'What are you doing at the weekend?' I ask.

'We're staying at Simon's again. He and Mum are so loved up. It's gross, worse than Gran swimming naked.'

'That sucks.'

'I know. I've had to start hanging out with Ray just to get away from them.'

'I thought you hated him.'

She shrugs and pours more coffee into our mugs.

Ray.

That fucking name.

It keeps appearing in conversation. Ray did this. Ray said that. Why is she hanging out with him? Are they in his bedroom? In hers?

'What do you guys do?'

I want to know but I don't. Just the fact that he gets to spend time with her makes me jealous.

'Not much, mess about on his X-Box, watch movies.'

I take a drink of coffee so I don't have to reply. Act like I don't care what they do, when I really want to smack Ray over the head with his fucking X-Box.

I've never even met him, but I hate him. He gets to spend nights in the same house as her. To see her in her pyjamas, when she's just woken up, after she's showered.

'Did I tell you he has pet snakes?'

'Who?'

'Ray. He doesn't even keep them in his room but in this big tank out on the landing. I have to walk past them every time I go to the bathroom. And they move, but you never see them move. They freak me out. And there are dead mice in the freezer. We were making pizza for tea and there was a bag of frozen mice, right there, next to the garlic bread.'

'So, stay at your gran's instead. Say you don't want to stay there anymore.'

'Nah, that would just upset Mum. She's happy for once. And he's actually a pretty decent guy. I think Mum is seriously considering moving in with him permanently.'

'Do you want to live there?'

'I don't know. We might all move in together somewhere else. I heard her and Simon talking about it.'

Alice moving in with Ray. No need to come and stay with her gran anymore. No need to come and see me.

'I've been thinking about my dad a lot recently.' Alice says. 'You know, since Mum got serious with Simon and since your dad...'

'It's cool, you can talk about him.' I squash flapjack crumbs under my thumb.

'I want to look for him, my dad, I mean. Find out who he is.'

'What did your mum say about that?'

'I've not told her, and you can't say anything. She'd be really upset and think I was just doing it to mess things up between her and Simon. I know I've been a pain with some of her other boyfriends, but I genuinely do like Simon. And, like I said, Mum seems really happy. That's what's so weird about it all. I never really cared about my dad before, but now I have this sudden need to find out who he is.'

'Do you know anything about him? Your mum must talk about him.'

'Not really. I've got an old photo and his name's on my birth certificate but that's it. Ray said I should try Facebook.'

'Facebook?'

It hurts that she's told Ray about this before me and the word comes out more sarcastic than I mean it to.

'Yeah, he said he might have a profile on Facebook I could search for. You've got to be sixteen to do it the official way.'

'I suppose that might work. It's not that long till you're sixteen though.'

It's actually quite a good idea, but I don't want to admit that.

'It's still six months. Sometimes, if I'm on the bus or something, I'll look for men with, like, the same hair colour or the same eyes as me, and wonder. He and Mum were just a couple of years older than we are now when they had me.'

'I can't even imagine having a kid at this age.'

Like I've even kissed a girl, let alone got close to having babies with one. I wonder if Ray's had sex before? I bet he has.

'I might have brothers and sisters too that I don't know about.'

The thought of sharing her with Ray is bad enough, but having to share her with brothers and sisters too. I'm being a total dick.

I should be helping her, not thinking about how much this will affect me. I can't help it though.

'Do you think I could use your computer to search? Mum borrows mine sometimes, and I don't want her to find out.'

'Yeah, definitely.'

I start to feel better again. She's not asked Ray to use his computer. She's saved this part of the secret for me.

'Can we look now, while Gran's away? I've got the photo and stuff.'

'Yeah, okay.'

'Thanks, Sam, I knew I could ask you.'

'No problem.'

Fuck you, Ray.

Alice grabs her bag and we head through to mine. She wrinkles her nose as I shut the front door.

'Can you still smell it?'

'Just a wee bit. At least it's cosier in here now.'

'Yeah, the heating's back on.'

Alice glances at the bedroom door. Closed, even though he's not in there anymore.

He lingers in the house like a ghost. Invisible, but passing through us in the hallway, in the kitchen, as we lie in our beds.

We sit at the desk in my room and I open my laptop. For a moment our reflections stare back at us in the dark screen, before it blinks to life and illuminates Alice's face and hair.

As I log in, Alice pulls out a folder from the bookshelf.

'Letters from Alice,' she reads from the spine, then opens it at random.

'*Me again! I'm at Gran's now, I'm waving through the wall at you.* Oh my God, I can't believe I wrote that. And look at that picture, what is that even meant to be?'

She holds the folder at an angle, tries to show me one of her doodles.

'I can't believe you still have these.' She says.

'Don't you?'

'Yeah, somewhere. They're in a box under the bed, I think.'

I log into Facebook, try not to let on that I care.

She reads another letter.

'*For any future Historians who happen to be reading this letter, these are the facts about my day. I got up at 7:15am and had Crunchy Nut Cornflakes for breakfast.* This is so embarrassing. As if future historians even care about what I ate for breakfast and lunch, or what book I was reading. Put these away, Sam. Anyone could see them.'

'They're good to read back though. I'd completely forgotten that day we went swimming at Portobello Beach. Remember it was really hot but there was haar everywhere. You could hardly see anything in front of you.'

'Oh my God. Yeah. We got ourselves in such a panic because we lost sight of the beach. Then when we actually put our feet down we were only, what, up to our ankles or something? We thought we were going to die. I'd totally forgotten that. What losers!'

'Your gran was totally oblivious. Sitting in that café with her tea and cake and we'd had this near death experience.'

'I know. She just sat reading her book the whole time.'

I still remember the way we clung to each other as the water lapped around us. Too scared to try and stand up as we thought our heads would go under.

'Ray thinks it's weird that we write to each other.'

Ray, fucking Ray again.

'Ray's a dick. What does he know?'

I'd argue against anything he said, even if deep down I agreed with him.

'He's not that bad.'

'When did you tell him about our letters?'

'He saw my inbox and asked why I have so many emails from you. I said we used to write actual letters to each other as we thought future generations would read them and we'd save history or whatever.'

Used to. Thought. The past tense. Were they reading my emails and making fun of me?

I scroll down my Facebook feed and like a couple of status updates. Ones I'd usually ignore, but I want to make out like I have a life outside of Alice.

'It got me thinking,' she goes on. 'All those letters are a totally unreal representation of us. We were writing to these strangers in the future as well as each other.'

'So?' I reply. 'It was still us writing them.'

'Yeah, but even if you're writing a private diary, you're writing with some unknown reader in mind. It's completely subjective, you want them to take your side.'

'No, you don't.'

I agree with her but I don't admit it. When I write to her, I do try to make myself sound cooler, smarter, funnier. I don't want her to stop writing to me.

'That's not us.' I say. 'That's how other people use Facebook. They show off, make out like their lives are so exciting when they're just as dull as everyone else's.'

'It's kinda sad though, isn't it? That the human race is always acting, is never genuine. And we're part of that too. We're on Facebook aren't we?'

'Not like that though. We're genuine with each other.'

'Yeah,' she smiles at me.

'And Ray's still a dick.'

She laughs but I can tell she doesn't agree.

'Anyway…' I push the keyboard over to her side of the desk.

She reaches into her bag and brings out a photo and her phone.

'I went snooping in Mum's room when she was out and found my birth certificate.' She shows me the photo she's taken of it on her phone.

BIRTH Registered in the district of Edinburgh		Year 2003	Sex F
Forename(s) Alice Elizabeth	Surname(s) Wilson		
When 2003 April Tenth 1432 hours	Where Royal Infirmary Edinburgh		
Mother's forename(s) and surname(s) Lorna Margaret Wilson	Mother's maiden surname N/A		
Father's forename(s) and surname(s) Gareth Michael Hopes			
Mother's occupation Student	Father's occupation Student		

She types 'Gareth Hopes' into the search box at the top of the page and clicks the magnifying glass.

I get up and put on some Frightened Rabbit, then sit on my bed. I want to make it look like I'm respecting her privacy, even though I want to know everything about her.

'Now, I just need to see if any of these guys look like this guy?' She holds up the photo. 'Come and help me, don't sit way back there.'

The picture is cut from a photobooth strip. What happened to the other ones? Does Alice's mum have one hidden? Maybe Alice's dad still keeps one in his wallet?

Alice's mum is sticking her tongue out. Her hair is really short and she's wearing a denim jacket. Alice's dad is wearing a retro Adidas top and his hair's longer than Alice's mum's. He looks right at the camera, his arms round Alice's mum, a big grin on his face.

'They look really happy,' I say.

'I know. I really like this photo.'

'You look so much like your mum in this, or she looks so much like you.' I say.

'Everyone says that,' Alice nods.

I pick up her phone and look at the birth certificate.

Gareth Hopes, 05/08/1985, Student

1985.

I do the Maths in my head. Alice's dad is 33.

He was 18 when he had Alice. Just a few years older than I am now. Alice and I shouldn't really be the same age. We shouldn't really be friends.

'Do you think any of these look like him?' Alice asks.

'Not sure. Scroll again more slowly, so I can get a proper look,' I reply.

I don't admit that I've not been giving my full attention to the profiles she's brought up.

I wonder if I should tell her about how lucky we are to be friends, about how in some parallel universe she'd be younger than me. Maybe she'd be in primary school right now? Maybe she'd end up being best friends with my new little sister?

'Who knew there were so many Gareth Hopes.' I say.

'At least it's not John Smith,' she replies.

'Do you think he's still in Edinburgh? You could filter by that.' I suggest.

'That's better,' she replies.

'What about him?' She clicks on a photo, brings up that Gareth's timeline.

'No,' we both say at the same time as the photo is magnified in front of us.

We laugh as she clicks the back button.

'That one,' I point at the screen. 'He looks similar and it says he lives in Edinburgh.'

She clicks on another Gareth Hopes.

His profile picture is of a couple with a young baby. Alice clicks on the photo to magnify it.

Posted on the 16th June this year.

78 likes, 15 loves and three comments.

Jane Stanley – Beautiful family!! Xxx

Steve Mitchell – Youse are looking good in that one. Even Gaz, lol.

Suz Whyte – ☺ Congratulations, what lovely news! xx

'I think that's him,' I say.

His privacy settings are basic and I watch as Alice scrolls down the page. He lives in Edinburgh, works at Napier University. Got married in 2015. One daughter by the looks of things. 217 Facebook friends. He likes the Foo Fighters and *Game of Thrones* and supports Hearts. There are a few random status updates.

Twelve sleeps until holidays! Cant wait!

Jen and me are pleased too announce the birth of baby Holly. Born today at 7.35am. Mum and baby both doing well.

Gutted to here about David Bowie. Legend. RIP. ☹

We scroll through years at a time – photos of him in the pub with friends, on a beach with his wife, next to a holiday resort pool holding a pint, a few with the baby, a couple of him in a kilt on his wedding day.

The more we see, the more I'm sure it's the right Gareth.

'That's him, isn't it,' Alice's voice sounds weird and I realise she hasn't spoken since we clicked into his profile.

'Yeah.'

She clicks on his wife's name, brings up her profile.

Carla Hopes (Carla King)

The privacy settings are tighter though. There's a few of the same photos of her and Gareth and the baby, but nothing of much interest. Alice goes back to Gareth's profile.

'What now?' I ask.

'I don't know.'

She brings up a new tab, types in Napier University, then his name again.

There's a black and white photo of him. His job title – Computing Support Technician. An email address, a phone number. The sections headed 'About Me' and 'Activity' are blank.

'Should I email him, do you think? Or send him a friend request?' she asks.

'If he accepts then your mum might see it on her timeline. Plus you maybe shouldn't email him at work?'

'Yeah, I guess so.'

'You could send him a private message?'

Alice moves the cursor; hovers it over the link: *If you know Gareth, send him a message.*

She doesn't do anything. Just stares at the picture of her dad and his new family. Alice has a step-sister out there. Baby Holly. Her dad has a new family. One he hasn't abandoned.

'What would I say? He's never tried to contact me.'

'What do you want from this? I mean, why are you doing this?'

'What do you mean why? What sort of stupid question is that?'

'I mean, do you ultimately want to talk to him, meet up?'

'I don't know, do I?'

'I'm not having a go at you. You just have to decide. If you really want to contact him, your mum's probably going to find out.'

'What do you mean if I really want to. I'm not doing this for a laugh you know.' Alice closes down Facebook.

'That's not what I meant.'

'I've got to go.' She grabs her bag, rushes out of my room.

I hear the front door slam as she leaves.

Her photo lies on my desk, destined never to be a Facebook profile picture.

I open up Facebook again and click through into Gareth's profile. Alice's real dad lies on a pool lounger in swim shorts. Cuts his wedding cake with his wife. Holds a new-born baby in the hospital. I'm a total stranger but I can spy on these personal moments.

I see Alice in his face, around the eyes and mouth. It's definitely him. A bit older than Alice's photo, but not old, old.

Alice, the only child, suddenly has a younger sister and maybe an older brother in Ray. I'm jealous of them, of all of them. A guy I've never met, a baby, her real dad who abandoned her when she was a toddler. It's stupid to feel like this, but these parts of her life don't involve me.

I bring up Alice's profile next and scroll down her timeline.

Feeling proud of my new crochet hat!

Ahhh, I hate Chemistry. Who even needs to know this stuff anyway?

Courtney Barnett is my new favourite person. Love her album!

Ray Hewitt likes this.

Ray Hewitt likes this.

I hadn't noticed before how many likes and comments there are from him.

Ray likes this. Ray likes this.

Why is Maths so boring? That's what calculators were invented for!

 Ray Hewitt: Tell me about it, lol! See you later probably... ☺

Girl's night with Emma, reliving our childhood with old Twilight *movies!*

 Ray Hewitt: Loser! Next time your over we can watch something decent from my DVD *collection!*

Aggh, stupid bus stuck in football traffic on Gorgie Road. Sooooo annoying.

 Ray Hewitt: HHGH!! Fuck the Hibs!!

I click through onto his profile. There's nothing new from the last time I stalked him.

Ray Hewitt ran 5.78km with Runamondo

Ray Hewitt ran 9.43km with Runamondo

Ray Hewitt ran 7.89km with Runamondo

Okay, I get it. You like to go running.

I click through into his photos.

Ray at a house party. Ray with a group of guys.

Wait, there's Alice.

I click on the photo and enlarge it.

Alice, her mum, Ray and Ray's dad are sitting round a table at some restaurant. Nobody's tagged in it which must be why I've not seen it before. Alice is smiling; her arm round her mum.

Why does it bother me so much?

Doesn't she deserve that? The whole family thing?

Both our families changing. Hers growing and expanding. Mine...

Maybe they'll all move in together and I won't see her anymore. Or what if her gran dies? I never thought of that before. We'll drift apart. I'll just become a floating head scrolling up and down her Facebook timeline.

I click back to Alice's profile. I feel a sudden urge to post something on her page. Something public but cryptic. An in-joke. Something Ray will see and wonder about.

I don't usually send her messages on here. I don't need to. We both agree Facebook is 99% annoying but 100% unavoidable. Something we have to be part of if we want to keep up with what's going on or get invited anywhere.

My fingers hover over the comment box.

Hey you...

What should I say? What should I say?

Hey you, you left your photo here. I'll keep it for you. Let me know what you decide to do. S xx

I read it over. I've never in my life signed anything to her as 'S' before, but it seems more intimate than just Sam. Deep down I know I shouldn't post it but I don't care.

POST.

I bring up another tab and log into YouTube.

A zombie rips at a body which lies in an empty shopping centre.

A Zombie drags itself along the pavement.

My phone beeps.

It's a message from Alice.

What are you doing?

Messing about on YouTube

Is that supposed to be funny? I meant on Facebook!

I'm not on Facebook

You promised you wouldn't say anything.

I didn't say anything

Don't be a dick, Sam. You know what I mean. I trusted you.

What have I done?

I know of course, but I don't want to admit it.

I wait but she doesn't reply.

Alice, I'm sorry. I'll delete it.

I bring up her profile again but the comment has gone. She's deleted it herself.

Date: 13/09/2016 19:17
From:alice_gryffindor4@gmail.com
To: samredpath08@gmail.com
Subject: Helllllooooooooo!!!!!

Hi Sam!!!!

This is my first ever email to you, isn't that exciting!!! I know it kind of defeats the purpose of all our reasons for writing letters but it is soooo much easier this way. And we can still write actual letters to each other if we get the urge!

Even my gran uses email to keep in touch with the Friends! Time to join her in the 21st century!

Anyway I'm going to hit send now. Here comes my first email to you...

Love,

Alice

xx

Jude

I stand out on the front path, preparing myself for what I'm about to do. A carrier bag lies at my feet, full of everything that I need. Rubber gloves, cloths, lemon juice, bicarbonate of soda, vinegar, bin bags.

It's raining and I pull my hood down as I unlock the front door, can't help thinking of him up there in that tower. Soaking. Freezing. If he can feel that way anymore.

There's a carved pumpkin still sitting on the front step of Sadie's house. It's starting to soften and collapse. It sinks in on itself, the carved face squashed up like a gurner.

I let myself in and the house is silent. I've purposely waited until Sam was at school. Not because I want to keep more secrets from him but because I'm his mum and I need to protect him from this. I've already put him through so much; been such a burden, unable to do the simplest of tasks. When I was pregnant with Sam, I went swimming right up until I went into labour. I worked until just before my due date. I was sensible but I didn't act like the paranoid, crazy woman I am right now.

It's laughable really. Here I am, trying to shield my son from cleaning up the mess left by his monster father. When, in reality, the son has already taken care of the major problem.

I remember when my granny died and I went to see her body. As soon as I walked into that room, I regretted it. I kissed her cheek, wasn't expecting the cold, the tightness of her. All the warmth and squeeze gone, the best bits of her no longer there. But this. Jesus, how do you deal with this? He's not stiff and cold, he's oozing and rotting. Sam's seen so much, already far too much.

I feel like I'm preparing to go into battle; when all I'm about to do is clean my bedroom. That's all. It's a tiny, miniscule thing. A task done by people every day.

Hell, I should be embracing this, right? Channelling that nesting instinct that I hear so much about.

It's taken me a few days to get into the right frame of mind. To feel like I could really do this and do it properly. I need to be neutral and ruthless. There's no point spring cleaning or collecting things for charity if you're going to get sentimental about it. You need to fill those black bags. Dump that top you love but is full of holes. Those shoes that hurt your feet but cost you a fortune. That Dickens book you keep meaning to read but never get past the first page.

The bedroom door has been shut since the day Sam and I went to the tower. I don't know if Sam has even thought about the tidying and the clearing up that needs to be done. Maybe in his teenage-boy head that's it sorted for now. Or maybe I'm not giving him enough credit and he's like me. Avoiding it. Channelling our internal Scarlett O'Haras – time enough to think about things tomorrow.

I push the door open, face what awaits. It stinks in here. I thought that now he was gone, the smell might have subsided. Jesus, I don't know if I'll ever be able to get rid of the smell. I guess this is what people call the police about when they've not seen their neighbour for a few weeks. I can't even begin to describe what it's like either. The smell of death. Much, much worse than the worst smells you can imagine – farmers spraying the fields with manure, the food recycling if it's been left too long, a dog shit bin on a really hot day. I feel horrible, the way my brain springs these smells to mind, the way it connects them to Adam. As if I'm repulsed by him, something I'd try to wipe off the sole of my shoe. But it's all him. Fermenting and moist, up my nose, in my mouth, under my fingernails.

I reach into my wardrobe. The glass missing from the once-mirrored doors. All these clothes I've not been able to wear. Might still not be able to wear. They've all absorbed him. If I walk around in these clothes, the smell will follow. Trail behind me like a cloud of stink; my new perfume. Like when you're stuck behind a bin truck.

I reach into the back, pull an old silk scarf from a carrier bag. He brought this back from Paris for me. I wore it tied round my neck for weeks like I was some Hollywood classic. Once I tied him to the bed with it.

Now I wear it to cover my nose and mouth and breathe in the smell of ageing perfume, rather than the scent of ageing husband.

I head into the kitchen and boil the kettle then I pour the steaming water into a basin. The contents of my shopping bag are lined up on the counter. I stir in bicarbonate of soda. Vinegar. Lemon juice. Create my own concoction of smells. Like him they sink through my scarf, already moist from my breath. I should be using bleach, thick and heavy cleaning products, but I'm pregnant, so I don't. I slip on the rubber gloves, pick up the basin, some scouring sponges, a roll of black bags, and head back to the bedroom.

I don't know where to start. The whole room is such a mess. If I stop and think too much about it, it'll defeat me.

I start at the windows. I stand on a chair and unpick the pins holding up the sheet that Sam put there. It falls around me onto the carpet. The torn down curtains lie there too. I pick up the whole lot and stuff them into a black bag. I don't even consider whether or not they could be salvaged. Vanished back to life at 60° in the washing machine. I open the windows, push them wide, let the cold air rush in. It ruffles the bed, my hair, the scarf around my mouth. But it's clean and fresh. This room is like a vacuum, stagnant.

What's that theory? That we're all breathing in Caesar's last gasp? Am I breathing in Adam's too? I never really understood the science behind it.

Okay. What next? I look around, don't focus too much on anything in case I lose my resolve. It hurts too much to look at the detail. A part of me wants to savour this, but I can't let myself. I can't.

I guess the bed is the obvious place to go next. The place where he spent the most time. The place most soiled by him. There are multiple stains on the bedclothes.

Other, normal, widows get to lie in the bed, find comfort in the warmth and the smell. Lie on the stains of where they sweated, where they fucked. Not me. I strip the bed, everything goes in a black bag.

The mattress is stained too, he's seeped right through. Alongside the older, living stains of him. Of me too, I guess. Tea, coffee, cum, blood. That red wine I spilt the night we used this scarf. Our lives together illustrated by the grubby shapes we've left. Our own abstract, modern art exhibit.

The messes your body makes against your will; when you can't control it anymore.

The living stains exist and merge with these newer, dead stains. I kneel by the bed, plunge a scouring sponge into the basin. The water's so hot, I can feel my fingers smarting underneath the rubber gloves.

I scrub, scrub, scrub at the mattress. At the living and the dead stains. Congealed and sticky like jam. I put all my strength into it. Aware that I'm scrubbing away memories. Stains by rights I should get to keep, but can't.

The water in the basin turns brown immediately as I dip the sponge back into it. The colours of him, tertiary and sopping. I pour him down the kitchen sink, boil the kettle and start again.

Scrub, scrub, scrub, scrub.

There's dents and hollows in the mattress. From where he slept, where we slept. Head, shoulders, bum, feet. The weighty bits of us, the bits that anchor us.

I can't fit a mattress into a black bag so I scrub, scrub, scrub, scrub.

I don't stop.

Scrub, scrub, scrub, scrub.

If I stop, my head will drop. I'll let my cheek rest in the dent of him and I don't think I'll be able to lift it back out. So I don't stop and think, I just scrub and scrub and scrub. And I scrub the tears into the stains and clean everything away together.

Scrub, scrub, scrub, scrub.

After the bed, I start on the carpet. Follow the routes he made before we chained him up. His trails around the bedroom, looping and indirect like a snail, all leading to the main destination directly behind the bedroom door. Where he stood, listening to us, reaching out for us, desperately trying to break through to us.

Scrub, scrub, scrub, scrub.

As I go, I pick up the debris of his wandering, add it to the black bags. The alarm clock that used to balance on the corner of the headboard. The book he was reading. Clothes that hung over the back of a chair. Broken frames, a torn canvas of Sam that we had on the wall above our bed. Smashed glass from the cup of water on my bedside table.

I find his tooth. The one I was so angry at myself for losing. It goes in the black bag too. I have to be ruthless. The baby bumps against my thighs as I crawl around the floor.

The stain behind the door fades but won't disappear completely, no matter how hard I scrub. Like *The Canterville Ghost*. My shoulders and back ache as I lean into it. Sweat drips down my face and my hands tingle from the effort.

There are scratches on the back of the door.

Scrub, scrub, scrub, scrub.

I fill and refill the basin. Give up boiling the kettle every time, instead run the hot tap until it's steaming and gushing. Water slops over the side of the basin as I ferry it back and forward along the hallway, leaving puddles between kitchen and bedroom.

He's everywhere. Seeped into everything. I'm exhausted. I wipe the walls, stripping some of the paint that we put on when we first moved in. Him with the roller, me following with a paint-brush, touching up the finer details.

Scrub, scrub, scrub, sob, sob, sob.

Another basin of him washes down the kitchen sink, then another, then another. Bits of matter and gunk. Lumpy, fleshy bits that I ignore and hope won't block the pipes, like those 'fatbergs' they find in the London sewers. They eddy and swirl before sinking away, making a sucking noise in the drainpipe. Like hair in the shower, whiskers in the sink, toe nails in the bin. Human parts of us that drop off and we flush away.

Scrub, scrub, scrub, sob, sob, sob.

I do his wardrobe next then his chest of drawers. I grab handfuls of clothes without looking, don't allow the memories to get in the way. I don't even take the hangers off. Everything goes in. Boxers, socks, running kit, jeans, jumpers, shirts, ties. Then I take piles of my own clothes and stuff them in the washing machine. I use extra fabric softener to try and shift the smell.

I'm starting to slow. The initial oomph fading.

I spray perfume. Spritz it around the room, on the bed, on the carpet. The Shake 'n' Vac jingle pops into my head and I suppress laughter. I could dance around the room like some 50s fucking housewife. The perfume catches in my nose and I sneeze three times, lifting the scarf with each achoo.

I lift the baby monitor from where I'd set it up on one of the shelves. It's still switched on, so I turn it off. I dump it in the spare room, with the boxes of Sam's old baby stuff that Adam had looked out and we hadn't got round to going through yet. The cot waiting to be built. The mobiles waiting to be hung. All next on my to-do list.

I lug the bin bags to the back door. Stop and wipe my face with the scarf. My skin is all gritty, dried up tears and sweat.

I open the back door and drag the bags out to the bin, heft them up and stuff them in. There's too many of them and the lid of the bin doesn't shut properly. As I'm walking back towards the house, I hear the bedroom door slam shut. In my head I know it's just a through-draught because of the open back door, but it spooks me. My stomach tightens and releases, tightens and releases.

I could really do with a proper fucking drink right about now, but I guess decaf tea is my best option.

I need a shower too. I'm filthy, covered in muck and sweat and God knows what else. A bath would probably suit better, ease away the aches, but I can't stand the thought of lying in that soup. The bathwater the same colour as all those basins tipped away down the sink.

I'll have a drink, something to eat first. Summon the energy to face the shower.

My stomach is still heaving, tighten, release, tighten, release, tighten, release. I feel queasy.

I make myself a cheese sandwich, a glass of milk, sit at the breakfast bar.

What now? What do I tell people?

What about the will? Did we even make a will?

We never discussed this. Never discussed death. Certainly never discussed what to do when one of you becomes a walking monster.

My back aches and I push my hand against the bottom of my spine. The pain comes in waves and I press against the chair, arch my back to find some relief.

We thought we had more time.

The pain in my back is getting worse, so I stand and lean over the breakfast bar. Try to stretch it loose. Too much kneeling and squatting and scrub, scrub, scrubbing. Nobody can say I didn't put my back into it. Maybe a hot shower will help after all.

I'm walking out of the kitchen when it happens. I feel something slip inside me and then damp down the inside of my legs. In my pants, soaking into my jeans, dripping onto the lino.

Fuck. My waters have broken. I'm in labour.

Date: 13/09/2016 19:27
From:samredpath08@gmail.com
To: alice_gryffindor4@gmail.com
Subject: RE: Helllllooooooooo!!!!!

Hi Alice,

Thanks for the email. What is with that email address though? You are such a dork sometimes! And there must be 3 other losers with the same email address!

It's weird typing to you instead of writing but it's not so sore on the hands.

I can't believe your gran has an email address. I wonder what hot topics the Friends email each other about? How annoying Phoebe got towards the end of *Friends?* How lame the Barbados episodes were?

I guess this is quicker than letter writing too. I just have to hit send and whoooosh, my message is right with you. Unless you don't check your emails for ages of course! No having to check the post box (which is totally falling apart by the way) or having to be at your gran's house.

Okay, here goes. About to hit send. Whoooosh...

Sam

x

Sam

Are you home yet? Love you xx

Shit. I forgot I'd promised Mum I'd text her as soon as I got in.

That was a while ago now. When I got home I decided to try and sort out the spare room for her. I tried to build the cot but it was more complicated than I thought. It's half-done though. I hung the mobile above it and left a wee cuddly mouse that I bought in the hospital gift shop when I was getting change for the bus.

Yeah, sorry. I'm home safe. X

They're making Mum stay in. They kept going on about how it was for the best. She was an older mother, the baby had come early, and by the time they got the discharge papers ready it would be really late. I was surprised by the lack of protest from Mum about it.

Glad to hear it. Be safe tonight please. Keep in touch with me. I'll be up during the night anyway, no doubt! Xx

I will. Hope you're okay. X

Amy's sleeping right now, so I'm having some tea and toast. All feels very surreal. I love you xx

Love you too x

Make sure you have a proper dinner. Order pizza if you like? Xx

I'll be fine. X

I can't believe she's had a baby. That I've got a little sister.

My wee sister.

It feels weird to say that. I got to hold her in the hospital. I sat down, was too scared to stand, too scared to move in case I damaged her. She was like a doll, so tiny. But the warmth of her, the life of her. Her chest moving up and down, up and down, up and down. Her skin was so soft. It was like nothing I've ever felt before.

I check my phone. I also can't believe that Alice hasn't replied. I thought for sure that a text about the new baby would get some sort of response from her. She must be really mad. I read back the text I sent her earlier.

Hey, just to let you know Mum had the baby. She's called Amy. xx

It feels weird being in the house on my own. I don't think I've ever felt this lonely before. Dad should be here with me. It should be us boys together. Our last night before the girls catch up on us. As it is, I'm going to be out-numbered by girls.

I'm overcome by so much sadness that I burst out crying. It takes me by surprise. I don't know where it's all coming from. I haven't cried like this since I was a kid and all that stuff with Dad and the drugs happened.

I wait for it to stop, for me to get it under control but it just keeps coming. I lie face first on my bed, head in the pillow, and just cry and cry and cry. This is the worst I've ever felt.

This should have been a happy day. Dad and I should be out buying pink balloons and waiting to welcome Mum and Amy home.

Dad should be here.

Dad should be here.

Dad should be here.

Eventually, I force myself up off my bed and head through into the kitchen. I open the breadbin and take a slice of bread, scrunch it up into a ball and eat it. I do the same with a second slice as I look in the fridge. There's some of Dad's beer still in there. He was never a big drinker. Always too healthy. I lift a bottle and read the label. I've never been drunk before, but tonight seems a good night to try it.

I lift out the bottle and place it on the counter while I rummage in the cutlery drawer for a bottle opener.

I jump as there's a knock at the back door. I see the shape of a figure through the frosted glass and I put the bottle back in the fridge, it clinks against the others sitting there.

I unlock the door, my hand still tingling from the cold glass.

It's Alice's gran.

I don't know why I'm disappointed. Who did I think would be out there?

'Why didn't you tell me you were back?' She asks, as she comes into the kitchen.

She grips my arms and leans towards me. I think she's going to give me a hug but she just smiles, squeezes my arms, then lets go.

'Babies are an emotional time, aren't they?' She says.

I realise that my eyes must still be red from all that crying. I'm embarrassed that she knows I've been so upset. She might tell Alice. It feels like such a stupid thing to have done.

'I just got in a few minutes ago,' I lie.

'Why didn't you phone? I could have picked you up.'

'I got the 38, it's fine,' I shrug.

'Alice informs me she's called Amy,' she says.

So it's okay for her to tell her gran but she still can't be bothered replying to me.

Alice's gran puts the kettle on and dumps the canvas bag she's carrying onto the breakfast bar.

'I thought I'd bring you something for supper, seeing as you're home alone,' she says.

'You didn't have to.' I reply.

'Ach, it's nothing fancy. All lifted straight from the freezer.'

She pulls two Pyrex dishes from the bag.

'Now that's cottage pie and this one's apple crumble. You'll need to defrost them before you heat them up.' She glances around the kitchen. 'You've got a microwave haven't you? Yes, there you are. I'll do it for you now if you like?'

'No, that's okay. I can manage.'

'Well, at least let me make you a cup of tea so I can hear all about this baby,' she says.

'Okay,' I nod.

She doesn't ask where anything is, just opens cupboards and drawers until she finds what's she's looking for. As I watch her make the tea, it suddenly dawns on me. Home alone. She said home alone. Where does she think Dad is?

She places the two mugs of tea on the breakfast bar and we both stand. It's really awkward. I've never been on my own like this with her before. Usually Alice or Mum is with me, or it's just a quick hello in the garden.

'So, tell me about Amy.'

'Yeah. She's fine. Everything seems to be okay.'

'What weight was she?'

'Um, six stone something, I think.'

'Pounds you mean.'

'Yeah, yeah, something like that.'

'That's a good size considering she was early. And how's your Mum?'

'Tired, I think, but okay.'

This is it. The obvious place to ask about Dad. I brace myself for the question. Already deciding that I'll just say he's with Mum. It's easier than the web of lies we've built at the hospital. The midwives silently judging our family by his absence. Already deciding he's a shit dad, when it's not true. When it's not his fault.

Why isn't the father here?

The son has turned up but not the father.

I can feel the tears starting to force their way back and I take a drink of tea, look down at the breakfast bar. Just ask then, get it over with.

But she doesn't. She ignores the opening and breezes on past.

And now I can't stop thinking about him. Dad won't leave my head.

Dad, Dad, Dad, Dad, Dad, Dad.

And the more I think about him, the more I think I'm going to cry again. And the more I think about him, the more likely it is that she'll ask about him. I'm transmitting it, putting the subject out there for her to pick up on. The one thing I don't want to speak about. And it's weird. Why isn't she asking about him? What's wrong with her?

I'm not even really listening to what she's saying now. Yattering away about when she brought Alice's Mum home from the hospital, about how they kept you in longer back then, it was just expected that you'd stop working. Nothing like today.

Dad, Dad, Dad, Dad, Dad.

'Do you want a biscuit?' I ask, just to try and stop the flow of her voice. It's like she's casting a spell.

'No, no. I'm done now.'

I get the biscuit tin anyway, just to give myself something to do. I put it on the breakfast bar and help myself to a jammy dodger.

She pours the last of her tea down the sink, rinses her mug under the tap and leaves it on the draining board.

'And don't you fill up on biscuits,' she says, 'that pie will just take a few minutes in the microwave. Are you sure I can't heat it up for you?'

'No, it's okay,' I nod.

'Your mum's lucky to have you.' She turns and leans against the sink.

SAM

I smile, not really sure what to say.

She fumbles in a pocket, takes out a hankie and dabs her eyes. Jesus, I don't know where to look. It was bad enough before, but now she's crying.

'I'm sorry for being a daft old woman. Babies get me all sentimental and I was just remembering Alice's grandad. It doesn't matter how many years pass, you never stop missing them.'

I nod and pretend to study the food she's brought me. I don't want to look at her. I'm close to crying again too now and I can't cry in front of Alice's gran.

'Sometimes it's for the best. Alice's grandad was in a lot of pain towards the end. I couldn't bear to see that.'

How do I respond to this?

'Right, I'm going to love you and leave you now,' she says.

She walks towards the breakfast bar and for the second time tonight I think she's going to give me a hug. I brace myself for contact, but she just picks up her canvas bag.

'Oh, I almost forgot,' she looks in the bag, 'there's a letter in there too.'

A letter? Alice and I haven't written each other an actual letter in ages.

'You know, Alice doesn't need to come here after school anymore,' she says.

She's going to tell me off for the fight we've had.

'She's old enough to go home on her own, has been for a while. Now, I love having her and I like to flatter myself that her old gran is the reason she still comes, but... well... okay, I'll just leave the bag here; you can put the dishes in it when you're finished.'

She places the bag back down. What did she mean by all that? I try not to show how eager I am to read the letter. Just nod at her instead.

'Right, you take care. I'll be back round to see that baby sister of yours when she gets home, and I'll get everything back from you then, okay?'

'Yeah. See you, and thanks for the food,' I reply as she lets herself out the back door.

I lift the envelope out of the canvas bag. Now that Alice's gran has gone, I'm reluctant to open it. In case Alice is still mad at me. In case she's confessing to a relationship with Ray.

It doesn't feel very fat. Not like the old days when she would write pages and pages, doodles and scribbles and diagrams, with stickers and different coloured pens. The pages stuffed in a bulging envelope. Whatever it is she has to say, she's been succinct.

Fuck it. I rip open the envelope, pull out what's inside.

That's weird. I peer in the envelope, push my hand in to make sure I've not missed anything.

It's not a letter after all, but a cutting from what looks like *The Evening News*.

Strange Behaviour at Zoo

Visitors to Edinburgh Zoo have been reporting strange behaviour displayed by some of the animals.

One visitor claimed that the zebras, and other animals in the African Plains enclosure, were clearly agitated and in some distress.

'They were huddled together under the spectator viewing platform, and one zebra was so spooked, it kept running round in circles and pawing at the ground.'

'My five year old daughter was very upset by it and we had to take her home,' another visitor said.

Another stated that the Squirrel and Capuchin monkeys would not leave their inside enclosure, and were screeching and banging on the glass. The nearby Wallaby Outback, which allows visitors to walk inside the paddock alongside the wallabies, has been closed to the public and it is unclear when it will open again.

A spokesperson from the zoo declined to comment but the *Evening News* is aware that specialist vets and animal psychologists have been called in.

Zoologists are reportedly baffled by what has been witnessed, but have been trying to keep it a secret from the local public so as not to cause any alarm or face backlash from animal rights activists.

Occurrences such as these are rare, but have been known to happen at other zoos. They usually precede a natural disaster such as an earthquake or volcano, or during an eclipse.

I don't know what to make of it. There's not even a date or anything on it, and no note from Alice.

I text her.

Got your article. Don't know what you want me to do about it though.

I scrunch the cutting up into a ball and throw it across the room. I'm suddenly so angry, I want to throw things, smash something. I run my arms across the breakfast bar, sweep the bag, my empty mug, the biscuit tin onto the floor.

It's a bit of an anti-climax. I'm too much of a wuss to actually break Alice's gran's plates. My mug bounces without a crack. The lid pings off the biscuit tin and a couple of custard creams fall out. The bag lands with a thud on top of the lid.

There's something else in there.

I bend down and lift the bag, reach inside.

It's a set of keys. I pull them out onto the breakfast bar.

I recognise them right away.

Alice's gran's keys.

Her keys for the tower.

Fall From Grace by Adam Redpath

I understand when people say a two-year ban isn't long enough. I know other athletes, clean athletes, who have had injuries which have kept them out longer. Others who have had injuries which have ended their entire career. Where's the justice in that?

Once I had served my ban, there was no point trying to get back into competitive athletics. It was too difficult and I was too old by that stage. I was frozen out. I couldn't get races. I was ignored by my former team-mates. Booed by those who'd once called themselves fans.

It was impossible to make money from my sport anymore. I'd bled it dry and there was nothing left for me. I had to think of Jude and Sam, so decided to announce my retirement.

I was terrified because athletics was all I'd ever known, but it was also a relief to finally hang up my spikes. All that pressure, a lot of which I'd put on myself, was lifted. I began to remember what it was I loved about the sport, before the desire to win at all costs had consumed me.

I wanted to give something back, help at a grass roots level or get into coaching, but of course nobody wanted to be associated with me. I got some work as a personal trainer, but I also did what only someone in my position could do. I began visiting schools, youth clubs, sports teams, talking to kids, warning them against drugs and the route that I'd chosen. I hope I can make a difference that way and use whatever small influence I have to try and stop kids making the same mistakes I have; to try and keep the sport I love clean.

Jude

I defy the midwife, the one who said only to pull the curtain if I was feeding or trying to sleep. I'm not a twenty-year old first time mum. I don't want to share labour stories and have mealtimes at the communal table in the middle of the ward. I'm a mother of advanced maternal age after all, who's just been through a less than straightforward pregnancy and labour and who...

No, I can't let that thought through. The one about who should be...

No.

I pull the curtain round us. It doesn't quite fit; like a hospital gown, there's always an arse crack on show. Luckily I'm in a bed next to the wall, so I can hide myself on all sides. Our own little cubicle. Our bunker. Just me and Amy.

Why are hospital beds so uncomfortable? Even with the buttons you can press to make your head or legs go up and down. Even with the multitude of oversized pillows. The beds are always too high, too hard, with that starched sheet that's trying to do the job of a ten tog duvet.

Out in the ward one of the other mothers is pacing up and down, up and down, up and down, trying to sshhhhh her baby. The midwife whispers to her. I don't know why. Nobody actually sleeps in a ward like this.

Compared to out there, we are a zen garden. Amy lies in the plastic crib, see-through like a fish tank, swaddled in hospital blankets, although she's wrestled her tiny arms free. The pink knitted hat they gave her when she was born is still on her head, the faintest stain of blood soaked into the wool. Somehow she is asleep. The exhaustion of labour taking its toll on her, while having the opposite effect on me. It's left me wired and unable to close my eyes. Amy's chest moves up and down, up and down, up and down and she makes the occasional mew, like a kitten. I reach out to place my hand on her, feel that soft, soft skin again, but then stop myself. She's so peaceful. I don't want to disturb her.

I tuck my feet under the sheet to keep the chill off them. Maybe it's still the drugs coursing round me, but I don't feel like this is really happening. I don't feel like I'm really here. Already the labour pains are receding from memory and my body is filing away the memory of it. I can't even describe the way the contractions felt anymore. I guess that's why we continue to have babies. If only the pain of grief was so conveniently forgotten.

No, I can't think about that. How much I wanted him with me.

Another baby starts to cry from the far side of the ward. That new-born cry, completely different from any other cry. Amy stirs, her forehead crinkles, but she doesn't wake.

I remember that first night on the ward after having Sam. He wouldn't stop crying. He wouldn't sleep. I was exhausted but I kept pacing up and down, up and down, holding him in my arms. Everyone else seemed to be coping so much better than me. One woman was reading while her baby slept while another had gone for a shower.

The midwife came and drew the curtains round the bed, like I was some sort of nuisance that had to be hidden and spoken to in private. They brought in the breast-feeding expert as Sam wouldn't latch on properly. I didn't even realise that there was a proper way.

Adam had promised he would come back first thing in the morning and I couldn't wait for him to return and be an ally, for him to take me home. Everything would be alright once we were home. I couldn't wait to leave that ward behind.

Now, I just want to sit here. Sit here forever with Amy and not have to deal with anything outside. We're here and, in my head, Adam and Sam are at home. Girls and boys. I pretend that everything's okay. The rest has just been a weird, drug-induced dream. Labour does funny things to you. You become someone else.

And I can forget about the fact that I'm going to have to do this on my own. That I missed him so fucking much while I was in labour. His hand on mine, stroking my hair. Knowing me so well that with one look we could communicate a whole conversation.

Amy will be a Daddy's girl. I'll make sure of it. But, in order to do that, she can't ever get to meet him. I'll tell her how wonderful he was and how much he loved her and all the plans he had for her. She'll just have to trust me and believe what I tell her.

Amy opens her eyes and lets out a moan. I lean over and lift her out, cuddle her against me.

'Sshhh, it's okay, darling, it's okay.'

Her arms and legs automatically curl up, like one of those red fortune telling fish you get in cheap Christmas crackers. She's not had time yet to unfold herself from the nine months of being inside me. She's like Sam, a hot water bottle, warm and breathing and beating.

Alive. Everything about her alive.

She snuffles her mouth and nose towards my boob like a little piglet and I open my pyjama top, direct her head.

I want to cry but I can't. She pulls and sucks as my insides do the same thing.

Pull and suck, pull and suck, pull and suck.

The need to protect this tiny creature overwhelms.

Her fingers are closed in fists, her eyelids fluttering. Pull and suck, pull and suck, pull and suck.

The world behind those curtains doesn't exist.

We'll stay behind them. Just me and Amy. Forever. In this half-light, unconscious-conscious middle of the night stupor.

That scene from *Blue Planet*, with the mother walrus and her calf comes back to me. It haunted me for weeks after I watched it.

The way the mother cradled the calf underwater as she tried to find them an ice floe to rest on. Her flippers holding it like arms while it snuggled in to her chest. Then, later, they lay on top of the tiny iceberg, the calf's head resting on its mother's body as they floated. David Attenborough's voice telling me how close the bond is between mothers and their calves. How a son will eventually leave and start a family but a daughter stays with her mother for life.

Pull and suck, pull and suck, pull and suck.

Adam's not going to pop his head round the curtain, hold her in his arms, take her so I can go pee, brush my teeth, have a shower. He's not going to carry my bag or the car seat, he's not going to drive us home.

Pull and suck, pull and suck, pull and suck.

'Are you okay?' the midwife whispers as she peers round the curtain.

I nod. How dare she intrude on us?

'If you don't mind, I'll just check she's latched on properly.'

She leans over me, peering at Amy, lifts my pyjama top slightly.

'You're a pro,' she says. 'All good. I'll leave you to it. Buzz if you need anything.'

I nod again.

All good. All good. All good.

Her words are trapped behind the curtains with us, trying to find a way out but unable to.

All good.

What a strange phrase. I've never really thought about it before.

All is not good. All can never be good.

But all with Amy is good. And I can be thankful for that.

These last few weeks, it's like I've been in the womb myself. Floating but never getting anywhere and everything outside muffled.

Amy closes her eyes and her lips part, my nipple sliding out from her mouth as she falls asleep. I hold her to me and cover myself up.

Inside my stomach is still pulling and sucking, pulling and sucking, pulling and sucking. But I think it always will. Whenever I think of Adam, it will always tug and pull and suck at the core of me.

But I have this little sleeping baby to look after now. And I have Sam. And I know that Adam would tell me that our children were more important than anything else.

And so I will sit here for now. But, in the morning, I will open the curtains and I will try to carry on without him.

Pull and suck, pull and suck, pull and suck.

Pull and suck, pull and suck, pull and suck.

Pull and suck, pull and suck, pull and suck.

Fall from Grace by Adam Redpath

I stand in front of the blocks, can just make out the tinny sound of the microphone as the stadium announcer introduces me.

'In lane four, representing Great Britain and Northern Ireland, Adam Redpath.'

The noise is overwhelming and the stadium announcer's voice is swallowed by the crowd. I allow myself to enjoy it for just a moment, take on board the cheers, the applause. I give a wave to acknowledge it and then I shut it out again.

I look down the track, ignore what's going on around me, ignore the other athletes, ignore the shouts of my name. I don't care about anyone else now. When I visualise the race, I visualise only me.

Me.

My race.

I know exactly how I'm going to execute it. I have my race plan and I will stick to it. The track doesn't matter, the weather doesn't matter, my competitors don't matter. I can only control myself.

I will go out hard and fast. Drive out of the blocks and through into the first bend. Once I hit the back straight, I will settle into my run, maintain my rhythm, use the momentum from that first bend and stay strong. Coming into the top bend, I have to stay relaxed and focussed, keep the legs turning over. With 150m to go, I will kick for home. Find that extra burst, that reserve of energy that will take me over the line. I am relaxed, I am strong. I am a winner.

Me.

My race.

The starting judge calls for quiet and there's a collective sshhhhh around the stadium, as the crowd goes quiet and the camera flashes stop.

I jump up and down on the spot, shake my arms and legs, allow myself one more beat before I get into position.

This is it.

Me.

My race.

I kneel on the track, adjust my feet in the blocks, my hands on the start line. Then I'm still.

On your marks.

Get set.

Go.

Sam

I don't sleep, don't even try to, even though I probably should. *You need to get a good night's sleep.* That's what people say, don't they? Before an exam, or a big race. But that's usually the night that your body has other ideas and the sleep doesn't come.

I wonder if Dad felt nervous before he used to run? He never gave much away, not to me anyway. I was a lot younger then, I guess. Maybe he opened up to Mum more about the nerves, the sleepless nights, the anxiety.

But no, I can't think about Dad. Not now. Not until it's over.

Zombie, zombie, zombie.

It has to be today. Before Mum brings Amy home.

I look at the photo of Mum and Amy on my phone. The one I took in the delivery room at the hospital earlier. Mum is lying on the bed holding Amy and Amy's eyes are closed. She's wearing a pink, woollen hat, a streak of dried blood on the side of it.

This is why I'm doing it.

I've made up my mind.

Zombie, zombie, zombie.

I get my school bag and empty everything out onto my bedroom floor. Pencil case, notebooks, textbooks, PE kit.

Then I wander the house, filling it with everything I think I'll need.

Most of it comes from the kitchen.

Bread knife.

Steak knife.

Who knows what knife.

I pull the bottle opener out of the cutlery drawer too. Fizz open one of the beers from the fridge. I hold it to my mouth, then swig a mouthful. I gag as I swallow it down. It's fucking gross. I don't care though. I take another swig and carry it with me as I throw more stuff in the bag.

Screwdriver.

Head torch.

Bottle of water.

I zip the bag shut and leave it at the front door. The keys to the tower lying on top.

Ready to go as soon as it starts to get light out.

I head back into my room and turn on my computer, log into YouTube.

Zombies with grey and purple faces are shot in the head. Blood spills from the wounds.

Zombies on the horizon, coming over the hill. One by one the gunshots sound and they crumple.

A crowd of zombies mown down by someone driving a truck.

As I watch I listen to the theme from 28 *Days Later* on repeat: 'In the House – In a Heartbeat'

'In the House – In a Heartbeat'

I lay out clothes on my bed. Lots of layers again. I'll put them on before I leave. My uniform.

I bring up the photo of Mum and Amy on my phone. Mum's hand looks so big the way it cradles Amy's body.

I feel a bit light-headed. Wonder if it's the beer. I've never been drunk before and I'm not sure what it feels like. It's starting to go warm, tastes even worse. I head into the kitchen, pour the dregs down the sink, and open another one from the fridge.

It's fizzy and bitter and feels like it's too big for my mouth. I swallow it down before I have to spit it out.

A man pins a zombie to the ground by its neck, then pushes a knife into its forehead.

A zombie is grabbed by the shoulders, its head repeatedly smashed off a rock.

'In the House – In a Heartbeat'

It's simple really. One stab to the head to take out the brain.

And it won't hurt him, it will help him. I'm putting him out of his misery. Because he's a…

It's a…

Zombie, zombie, zombie.

A machete scalps the top of a zombie's head like a boiled egg.

A crossbow arrow is pushed into a zombie's ear.

'In the House – In a Heartbeat'

One stab to the head to take out the brain.

And don't let him bite me.

Only two things to remember.

Take out the brain. Don't let him bite me.

Take out the brain. Don't let him bite me.

I get up and stumble into the door frame. I take everything out of my bag to check it, then put it all back in again. I'm careful not to cut myself on the knives.

A screwdriver in the eye socket of a zombie.

A shard of glass plunged into the top of a zombie's head.

'In the House – In a Heartbeat'

I look out my bedroom window but I can't see shit. There's no point going to do this in the dark.

I take a drink from the beer but this one's warm now too. I pour it down the kitchen sink, help myself to another.

The food from Alice's gran is still sitting there on the breakfast bar. I stick one of the dishes into the microwave.

I check my phone again. Still no message from Alice. I flick to the photo of Mum and Amy. The exhaustion on Mum's face, the tiny squashed up nose of Amy.

A zombie doused in petrol is set alight.

A man hits a zombie over the head with an over-sized wrench.

'In the House – In a Heartbeat'

Take out the brain. Don't let him bite me.

Take out the brain. Don't let him bite me.

I go through my bag again. Take everything out. Lay it on the carpet.

Knife.

Knife.

Knife.

Knife.

Keys.

Water.

Torch.

Screw driver.

Put everything back in the bag.

I look at the photo again. Amy's head cradled in Mum's elbow crease. The dried blood on her knitted hat.

What's that noise? Oh yeah, the microwave. I head back into the kitchen. Fuck, the dish is burning. I drop it onto the floor and it smashes, hot apple crumble spatters onto the floor at my feet and I jump back.

Fuck sake.

It's too hot to clean up properly so I leave it where it is for now.

Two girls on a funfair ride going up and down, up and down. A zombie grabs onto the ride as it shoots up once more and is catapulted off into the sky.

A man holds a shot gun and blasts approaching zombies. The force of each shot sends them spinning and ricocheting into each other.

'In the House – In a Heartbeat'

I retrieve the newspaper article that Alice sent, from where it's scrunched up in the bin.

strange behaviour being displayed by some of the animals

so spooked, it kept running round in circles and pawing

screeching and banging

natural disaster such as an earthquake or volcano

I should write a reply to her. I've not written an actual letter to her for ages.

I get one of my notebooks from the floor, rip out a page, then get a pen from my pencil case.

Dear Alice,

My hands are wobbly. I think I'm drunk. I lift the beer bottle to my mouth, but I'm starting to feel sick now. I empty the rest of it down the kitchen sink and make myself coffee instead. What the fuck's that? Oh yeah, the crumble. It's cooled now, I try a bit of it. It tastes pretty good. I eat some of it off the floor then realise how gross that is, so scoop up the remains and dump it in the bin. I cut myself on Sadie's dish and that goes in the bin as well. We'll have to get her a new one to replace it. I pick up the cafetière and take it with me back to my room, spilling some of the coffee as I go.

A zombie's head is sliced open by the rotating blades on a helicopter.

A crashing helicopter smashes through a horde of zombies. Limbs and heads fly off in a cloud of red.

'In the House – In a Heartbeat'

Oh yeah, I was meant to be writing a letter to Alice.

Dear Alice,

I go back to the kitchen and get a pile of custard creams and two bags of salt and vinegar crisps. Check the bag again before I head back to my room.

Keys. Water. Torch. Knife.

Where are the biscuits?

I wander back along the hallway. Realise I've packed them in the bag by mistake.

A girl holds the pads of a defibrillator on either side of a zombie's head, there's a fizz as the zombie's hair starts to burn before the insides of its brain are mulched out of its eye sockets.

A zombie stumbles into an electric fence. He convulses as the current takes hold, sparks shooting round him before his head goes on fire.

'In the House – In a Heartbeat'

I look out the window again; still dark.

A chainsaw slices through a zombie's head.

I pick up the paper and pen and start to write.

Dear Alice,

I realise I've written that three times now, but this is an important letter. I have two rules to follow.

~~Take out the bite, don't let him~~

Take out the brain, don't let ~~him bite~~ it bite me

Take out the brain. Don't let it bite me.

Thanks for your letter about the weird zebras and the banging monkeys. I'm sorry we had a fight. I was being a dick. ~~You're just I think I~~

SAM

If I don't come back, I want you to know that I love you. I hope I will come back though. If I do, you'll probably never read this as I'll go and get it back out of the post-box. If I don't come back though, then I just wanted you to know.

This paper is from my Geometry book, that's why it's squared and not lined.

I read over what I've written. Wonder if I should write a letter to Mum and Amy now too. Just in case?

An old lady pulls a cord which releases a piano. It falls onto an approaching zombie.

A flare gun is fired at a zombie which sets the zombie's head on fire, a man lights his cigarette from the flames.

'In the House – In a Heartbeat'

I knock over my mug and spill coffee everywhere. Shit. I feel it burn my thighs under my jeans. I wipe at it with one of the t-shirts lying amongst my uniform then pour myself another mug. I dunk a custard cream into it and eat it whole. Then another. Then another.

Sorry about the coffee stains, I spilt my coffee while I was writing this and I can't be bothered writing it all out again. There might be some blood on this too, I cut my finger on your gran's food.

Anyway, I think that's all I wanted to say.

~~Than~~ Thanks for being such a good friend.

Oh, if I don't come back, can you tell Mum and Amy that I'm sorry and I loved them too.

I look at the photo of them again from the hospital. Mum's hair un-brushed, the wrinkles round her eyes as she smiles for the camera. Amy's tiny nose and lips.

Sam

xxxx

P.S. I think your gran knows.

I fold the letter and look around my room for an envelope. I can't find one though, so I rip another page from the notebook, fold it round the letter and fasten it with some Sellotape. I write her name in the centre and underline it.

<u>ALICE</u>

I head out into the garden. The security light comes on and I freeze like a cartoon burglar caught in a spotlight. I wait until the light times out and then I feel my way along the hedge, stumbling as I go. The post-box is around here somewhere. Eventually I find it. The rotting wood crumbles beneath my fingers and I hear a crack as I stuff the letter inside. The motion sensor light flicks back on as I head into the kitchen and lock the back door. I look out the window into the illuminated garden, the swing is moving forwards and backwards, forwards and backwards in the breeze, then the light goes out again and the garden disappears into darkness.

The beer bottles are lying in the sink, so I pick them up and put them in my rucksack. If Mum sees them she'll go mental. I'd better take them with me and dump them somewhere on the way.

I've finished the biscuits so start on the crisps now. The coffee is starting to go cold but I finish that off too.

I toy with the idea of making that other dish that Alice's gran brought over but I can't be bothered with the hassle after what happened to the crumble.

A man holds a lawnmower out in front of him as he walks towards a group of zombies. The blades slice and dice as blood and lumps of meat splatter around him.

A group of zombies are led towards a junkyard compactor. One by one they fall in, the spinning saw slicing them up as they disappear, meaty remains sliding out on a conveyer belt.

'In the House – In a Heartbeat'
Zombie is stabbed in the head.

Zombie is stabbed in the head.

Zombie is stabbed in the head.

'In the House – In a Heartbeat'

I look out the window, it's starting to get light. Maybe I fell asleep?

I pull on clothes, starting with the tightest fitting and moving onto the more baggy ones. I swing my arms and legs around after each layer. I still need to be able to move too.

I pull on normal socks then football socks, tug them over my jeans. I can barely lace my trainers, my feet are so bulked up.

One last check of my bag. And then another glance at the photo of Mum and Amy. I kiss my fingertip and tap each one of them in turn before I put my phone away. As I swing my bag on my back, the beer bottles clatter against each other and I suddenly wonder if I should have wrapped the knives up in something.

Too late for that now. I need to get going.

The bag is tight on my shoulders over all the layers and I loosen off the straps then get my bike.

It's freezing so I pull a couple of hoods over my head and tuck my hands inside the sleeves of the many jumpers I'm wearing. As I start to cycle, the bottles clash against each other so I stop at the first bin I see and dump them.

I'm sweating and I feel like I could puke, so I slow the pace down as I cycle along the pavement towards Corstorphine hill. The red light from the mast at the top of the hill guides me like a beacon. I fixate on it and end up crashing my bike into a parked car at the side of the road. I get back on. Keep going.

It's getting lighter. Like in a film, the streetlights turn off in succession as I cycle past. There should be music playing over the top of this.

'In the House – In a Heartbeat'
Take out the brain. Don't let it bite me.

Take out the brain. Don't let it bite me.

I'm at the bottom of the hill before I know it. I stash my bike behind the wall and start to climb. The mud below my feet has frozen solid with the cold. Hard and bumpy underfoot. Instead of meandering up the pathways, I edge my way up the boundary wall instead, feel the cold bricks under my hand as I struggle upwards. My fingers brush against something sticky, a brown slug weaving its trail, then a patch of damp moss. There's graffiti scrawled in pink spray paint.

Flat Earth

My nose is dripping and my cheeks burn from the cold while, underneath my clothes, sweat drips down the inside of my thighs and between my toes.

I'm out of breath and I suddenly puke without warning. It projectiles out of me, spatters the ground at my feet and my trainers. I can feel my hair prickle against my scalp and I lean against the wall. Beer and coffee and custard creams and apple crumble and salt and vinegar crisps. I puke again and again until I'm retching but there's nothing more to come.

Take out the brain. Don't let it bite me.

My breathing's so loud. I hold my breath. All I can hear are the creak of the branches, the brush of the leaves. There's nobody else around. Just me. Me and the monster in the tower.

I can't hold my breath for long and it rushes out of me, loud and erratic as I suck in the air.

I take the bottle of water out of my bag and swill some around in my mouth before spitting it out. Take another drink, swallow it this time. Then I keep climbing. My rucksack bouncing up and down on my back. The knives and screwdriver and water bottle clattering against each other.

Take out the brain. Don't let it bite me.

I wish I could take out my own brain. Just for half an hour. Just until this is all over.

Am I starting to change my mind…?

No, it's just because I'm here now. This is becoming more and more real, and I'm scared. I don't mind admitting that. I'm scared. But that's okay. I can use that fear.

Take out the brain. Don't let it bite me.

I'm knackered, panting and out of breath, so I stop at the Rest and Be Thankful. I lean against the information board and look out across Edinburgh at the sunrise. It's beautiful. Colour everywhere. The pink and orange of the sky, the red and gold of the trees. The green of the golf course spreading away beneath me. The greys and silvers of the flats and houses, of the castle. The beauty of it makes me feel so low. My insides are sore. And not because I puked my guts up. They're sore the way that a piece of music can make you sore. The way a happy memory can make you sore. It's not a pain that can be fixed and you never know when it's going to hit, but when it does, you feel like it might kill you.

'*When we got near to the place called Rest-and-be-Thankful, and looked down on Corstorphine bogs and over to the city and the castle on the hill, we both stopped, for we both knew, without a word said, that we had come to where our ways parted.*'

Kidnapped *by Robert Louis Stevenson.*

I suddenly remember that thing Dad always used to say instead of good luck.

Keep the heid.

Keep the heid.

Shit, shit. I need to keep going. I shouldn't have stopped. I shouldn't have stopped.

Take out the brain. Don't let it bite me.

Take out the brain. Don't let it bite me.

Take out the brain. Don't let it bite me.

I repeat the words over and over and over. Walk in time to them.

Take out the brain. Don't let it bite me.

Take out the brain. Don't let it bite me.

Take out the brain. Don't let it bite me.

Repeat. Repeat. Repeat. All the way to the bottom of the tower.

I look up. Sniff the air. Can I smell him? Hear him? Or am I just imagining it?

What if he's not there anymore? Maybe one of the Friends decided to use the tower off-season and accidentally set him free? Maybe that Friend is now just a body inside or, even worse, has become what Dad is?

I try the door. It's still locked. I peer in the window. It's dark inside but nothing seems disturbed or out of place. The picnic chairs and the broom still lean against the wall where they were the last time.

Or maybe Dad, I mean it, worked himself up into a frenzy and threw himself off the tower. I circle it, checking the ground.

What if it's already over? Decomposed. Gone. The rain and the wind and the sun and the four seasons in one day, crazy Scottish weather, have done their thing and he's just a skeleton, picked clean.

There's only one way to find out. I take the keys out, try to line them up with the keyhole but I can't keep my hands steady.

Come on, Sam. Come on.

Keep the heid.

I stop for a moment, compose myself; unlock the door and step inside. My hands are shaking and the keys jangle uncontrollably. Everything I do feels so loud. He must be able to hear me down here.

Take out the brain. Don't let it bite me.
Take out the brain. Don't let it bite me.

I climb the stairs, gripping the bannister. My knees are wobbly, it gets worse the higher I go. The echo of my footsteps vibrates all around me, ricocheting up and down the tower like a pinball. I try to be quiet. Take it slowly.

I stop. Why am I creeping? If this is going to be a fair fight, he should know I'm coming.

I run up the rest of the stairs. Smack my hands off the bannister, stamp my feet as I go, and make as much noise as possible. Pump myself up.

'I'm here! I'm here! I'm here! Take out the brain. Don't let it bite me. Take out the brain. Don't let it bite me! Keep the heid! Keep the heid! Keep the heid!'

I'm soaked with sweat by the time I get to the top. I want to take a jumper off, roll up my sleeves, but I need to keep the layers on. I take a drink of water, hope it's enough to stop me from passing out.

I bang on the door. Scream as loud as I can. No actual words, I just scream.

Then I hear him. Scraping, moaning. The smell starts to creep under the door and through the keyhole. He's there. Right there, on the other side.

Take out the brain. Don't let it bite me.

Take out the brain. Don't let it bite me.

The snap of his teeth.

His teeth. Regular human teeth. I've seen them brushed, seen them chew food, seen deep inside his mouth when he's laughed with me. His fillings, that one false tooth.

I bite down on the back of my hand, harder and harder until it's too painful to keep going. It hurts like fuck and I'm nowhere near spilling any blood. I bite again, my teeth leaving white indentations on the back of my hand. A map of my mouth.

I'm scared of the sort of pain he can inflict. The sort of pain I can't even imagine.

Take out the brain. Don't let it bite me. Take out the brain. Don't let it bite me.

I open my rucksack, and take out one of the knives and the screwdriver. A weapon for each hand. Then I put the bag back on over my chest this time, like a breast plate from a suit of armour. Leave it unzipped. Easy access. Just in case.

That's the bit they always go for.

The juicy bits. Guts and organs. All those videos on YouTube I watched of zombies leaning over dead bodies. Ripping out intestines with their teeth, heads burrowed into the belly. It's just nature. It's what lions and tigers and bears do. They eat out the juicy insides. The bones are all that's left, the hollow frame as the ribcage juts from the ground. Blood staining the face and mouth. Bits of me stuck between his teeth.

I bob up and down like a boxer, swing my arms, shake my head from side to side.

Take out the brain. Don't let it bite me.

Take out the brain. Don't let it bite me.

I'm about to unbolt the door when a thought jumps into my head. What do I do after? With the… with it? In all the films and TV I've watched, the humans kill and move on. I can't do that.

I shake my head again, shake away the thought. That's for after. Let's get the hard bit out of the way, then we can think about what happens next.

One thing at a time.

Okay. Okay. I can do this. I'm ready. I'm ready.

Take out the brain. Don't let it bite me.

Take out the brain. Don't let it bite me.

Right, come on. The sooner you do this, the sooner it's over.

Take out the brain. Don't let it bite me.

Take out the brain. Don't let it bite me.

Keep the heid.

I pull back the bolt, take a step backwards and then shove all my weight against the door. I drop the screwdriver and I hear it clatter backwards down the stairs but, it's okay, I still have the knife. The daylight blinds me for a moment and I stop and blink. Shapes flickering in front of my eyes.

It stumbles backwards, groaning, trying to regain its balance. I must have hit it with the door. It's almost funny, how clumsy and ungainly it is.

For a moment everything stops and we just face each other.

It's changed. Constantly changing.

Deteriorating.

Rotting.

What's left of the skin is black and there's mushrooms growing from it. Frost sparkles on the exposed bones. It's almost bald; the remaining hair hangs lank, like an old man with a comb over. The smell is flowery, musty and sweet.

It makes it easier for me. There's less of the him I know in there.

Take out the brain. Don't let it bite me.

Take out the brain. Don't let it bite me.

A new plan starts to form. Leave it here, lock the door, until it disappears completely. Till it's just a skeleton for the seagulls and the crows.

The hesitation is my downfall.

It doesn't stop. It doesn't hesitate. It doesn't think.

It has one desire and it comes for me.

It's quicker than I expect and, in my panic, I drop the knife. I bend to get it but the rucksack and all the layers impede me and it's coming towards me. I tug at the bag which slips from my shoulders, slides down my arms and onto the ground. Then it's there. Right there.

We both fall and it's on top of me. Clutching and grabbing at me. Head burrowing closer and closer and closer. I give up trying to reach my bag and just focus on trying to hold it off. I can see its jawbone, the actual white of it, see it working. The mechanism as it snap, snap, snaps at me.

I need both hands, all my strength, to keep it at bay. It's on top of me. My fingers sink into it. It's soft and warm and bits fall onto me, oozing and dripping and crumbling. The smell fills me, makes me light-headed. The overpowering sweetness.

Sweat drips, stings my eyes and I blink. I try to kick it off me, but I can't do it. With each blink it's closer, like ones of those flick books.

A footballer kicking a ball, foot, knee, head, foot, knee, head, foot, knee, head.

A stickman jumping up and down, up and down, up and down.

A hand waving, side to side, side to side, side to side.

I realise that I'm the one groaning now. Shouting. Screaming at it to get off me. Get the fuck away from me.

But I can't. It's not working. My arms are getting weaker, I can't hold it. I'm too hot, too many layers. Black dots flash, my head fuzzy. I can barely see it anymore for the shapes between us. My brain goes that messy way, like when you're dropping off to sleep. I'm losing it. I'm losing it.

I shout. No words again, just noise. I scream with frustration, with adrenaline, with fear. Its face doesn't change; the bread white jawbone snaps closer and closer and closer.

'Sam, Sam, wake up, Sam.'

Everything's out of focus at first, but then my eyes start to adjust, like the lens of a telescope. Far away then close.

Someone's leaning over me.

Dad?

I jerk away, try to fight them off.

'Sam. It's okay. It's me.'

Alice kneels beside me. Blue sky behind her head.

'Sam, I thought you, I thought...'

Her voice breaks and she sniffs, wipes her eyes.

I try to get up but I can't move. She reaches under my shoulders and lifts. Her hair tickles against my mouth and nose. My knees buckle underneath the weight of me as she helps prop me up against the wall.

The wall of the tower. I'm at the top of the tower. The tower.

Fuck. As I sit up, everything starts to shift and reel again.

'No, no, Sam, don't you dare. Lean your head forward.'

'Fuck,' I hear her say.

Alice rummages about in my bag. She leaving me again, being sucked backwards along a tunnel.

I see her mouth moving but I don't hear her anymore.

She draws her hand out of my bag and sucks the blood off her finger. She tips the bag, lets the contents fall out around her. Picks up the bottle of water and pours some of it over my head. The cold shocks me, brings everything into focus. She hands me the bottle and I drink.

I hear the snap of teeth, see the jawbone. I can still smell it. Where is it? I try to stand but my legs aren't working and I slump against the wall.

'Where is it? Alice, where is it?'

She doesn't answer.

'We need to find it,' I say.

'What were you thinking, coming here on your own?'

I try to stand again.

'Stay where you are,' she pushes a hand against my chest.

'No, we have to find it.'

I look down at myself, my jacket's ripped, covered in stains, and I can see the t-shirts underneath.

'Did he bite you?' Alice asks.

'I don't know,' I reply, as I finger the torn clothing.

'Can't you feel it?'

'I'm sore all over. I can't tell.'

She reaches towards me, pushes her hand into the rips in my jacket, and I can feel her fingers stroke bare skin. She looks at me but doesn't say anything. I know without her telling me. These are teeth marks, he's chewed on me.

'Am I?'

'I don't know,' she looks at her hand, 'this is my blood, I think. I don't know.'

I struggle up from where I'm slumped. Dizzy and disorientated, I start to pull off my clothes. Stripping off, layer after layer, jumpers and t-shirts and underarmour. Shoes, trousers, socks, everything. Until I'm standing there in only my boxers.

I spin in front of Alice, while she runs her fingers over me. Checking every part of me. Warm and tickling. I can feel her; every line she traces on my bare skin. The map she draws as she studies me.

'I think you're okay.' She pulls me towards her, wraps her arms around me. I squeeze her, bury my head in her neck. It's only when I look over her shoulder that I see.

I see it.

I see him.

Dad.

I let go of Alice, push her aside.

'I'm sorry, Sam, I had to. He was going to...'

I take a step towards him but she pulls me back.

'Don't look. You need to get dressed. It's freezing.'

I pull my arm away from her.

He's not moving. The first time he's been completely still since it all happened.

He's on his side, curled up and facing away from me.

'I'm sorry,' Alice is still talking. 'It was all I had. I was up half the night finishing that baby blanket. Then I thought I'd leave it at your back door. That's when I found your letter. The post-box was broken, I went to pick it up and I found your letter. I'm sorry. I had to get him off you.'

'It's okay,' I say, my teeth chattering.

Alice pulls a t-shirt over my head, then a jumper, guides my arms through the sleeves. Then she lifts my legs, pulls a pair of jeans on me; dressing me like a baby.

I step towards him and she follows me. Takes my hand as we stand there, looking down at him.

The winter sun glints off the metallic crochet needle that protrudes from his head.

Fall From Grace by Adam Redpath

I want to thank my wife and son for their love and support, and for their loyalty, despite everything I put them through. I couldn't have made it through the difficult times without them. I am sorry for all the pain and hurt I caused you. Jude and Sam, I love you both, this book is dedicated to you.

Acknowledgements

Thanks go to –

Gavin, Jennie, Eilidh, Rachael and Lauren at Luath Press, plus Emily, Kaera, Abigail and Harriet for all their help and hard work. Emily and Jennie, thank you so much for all your editing advice.

The Friends of Corstorphine Hill for volunteering their time to look after the Corstorphine Hill area in Edinburgh and helping to keep the tower open for visitors.

My dear friend Alice and her mum Angela. It was always them versus the world but I was lucky enough to be allowed to join them sometimes. I miss you.

Fiona Sharkey for teaching me how to crochet!

My family (and extended family) for their constant love and support. Special mention to Eils for introducing me to the curious process of anti-doping, and for reading the first draft to fact check for me.

Allan, Corrie and Alasdair, for all the love, joy and nonsense. You are my world.

Trackman
Catriona Child
ISBN 9781908373434 PBK £9.99

Trackman Trackman Trackman
Trackman Trackman Trackman
Trackman

Davie was about to leave the MP3
player lying on the pavement when
something stopped him. A voice in
his head. You'll regret it if you leave
it. You'll only come back for it later.

Can a song change your life? Can a
song bring people, places and
moments in time alive again? Davie
Watts is the Trackman. He knows
what song to play to you and he
knows exactly when you need to hear it. Davie seeks out strangers in
need and helps them using the power of music.

*In her debut novel, Catriona Child has all the makings of a cult hit...
She handles the tension between the fantastical premise and the raw
and sensitive matter of a dead schoolboy tastefully, and the book's
sense of place makes it a delight for lovers of Edinburgh.* THE HERALD

Also published by **LUATH PRESS**

Swim Until You Can't See Land
Catriona Child
ISBN 9781912147021 PBK £8.99

Swim Until You Can't See Land charts the relationship between two women born sixty years apart, whose chance encounter marks a watershed for the younger woman.

In her early twenties, Hannah Wright is forced to give up a promising career as a professional swimmer, and is adjusting with difficulty to her narrowed horizons. She is in danger of becoming embittered, haunted by a lost future.

Mariele may now be frail and old, but as her exploits during WW2 unfold, she is revealed as a woman of extraordinary spirit, unbroken by capture and interrogation as an agent in occupied France. Hannah's delight in the medium of water and the rhythms of swimming are set in dramatic counterpoint to Mariele's of torture by water, an ordeal that puts her in touch with her core strength – something Hannah starts to discover in herself.

One of the brightest prospects among a thriving breed of fresh Scottish writing talent. EDINBURGH EVENING NEWS

Luath Press Limited

committed to publishing well written books worth reading

LUATH PRESS takes its name from Robert Burns, whose little collie Luath (*Gael.*, swift or nimble) tripped up Jean Armour at a wedding and gave him the chance to speak to the woman who was to be his wife and the abiding love of his life. Burns called one of the 'Twa Dogs' Luath after Cuchullin's hunting dog in Ossian's *Fingal*. Luath Press was established in 1981 in the heart of Burns country, and is now based a few steps up the road from Burns' first lodgings on Edinburgh's Royal Mile. Luath offers you distinctive writing with a hint of unexpected pleasures.

Most bookshops in the UK, the US, Canada, Australia, New Zealand and parts of Europe, either carry our books in stock or can order them for you. To order direct from us, please send a £sterling cheque, postal order, international money order or your credit card details (number, address of cardholder and expiry date) to us at the address below. Please add post and packing as follows: UK – £1.00 per delivery address; overseas surface mail – £2.50 per delivery address; overseas airmail – £3.50 for the first book to each delivery address, plus £1.00 for each additional book by airmail to the same address. If your order is a gift, we will happily enclose your card or message at no extra charge.

Luath Press Limited
543/2 Castlehill
The Royal Mile
Edinburgh EH1 2ND
Scotland
Telephone: +44 (0)131 225 4326 (24 hours)
Email: sales@luath.co.uk
Website: www.luath.co.uk

Ro Rest
clay Ru